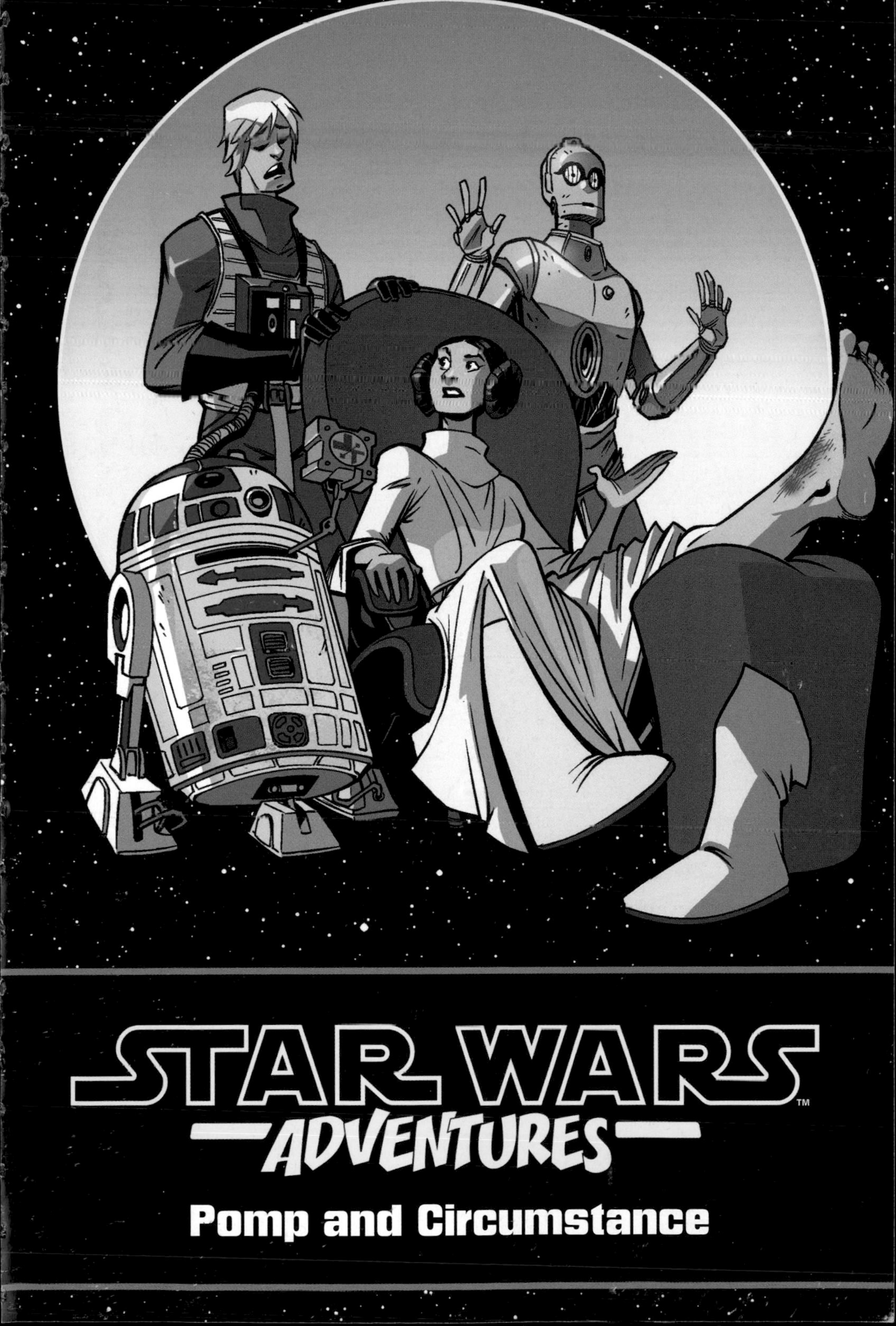

STAR WARS™ ADVENTURES

Pomp and Circumstance

Facebook: **facebook.com/idwpublishing**
Twitter: **@idwpublishing**
YouTube: **youtube.com/idwpublishing**
Tumblr: **tumblr.idwpublishing.com**
Instagram: **instagram.com/idwpublishing**

ISBN: 978-1-68405-569-2   22 21 20 19   1 2 3 4

COVER ARTIST
JON SOMMARIVA

LETTERER
TOM B. LONG

SERIES ASSISTANT EDITOR
ELIZABETH BREI

SERIES EDITORS
BOBBY CURNOW
& DENTON J. TIPTON

COLLECTION EDITORS
JUSTIN EISINGER
& ALONZO SIMON

COLLECTION DESIGNER
CLYDE GRAPA

Originally published in STAR WARS ADVENTURES ANNUAL
2018 and in STAR WARS ADVENTURES issues #14–17.

Chris Ryall, President, Publisher, & CCO
John Barber, Editor-In-Chief
Cara Morrison, Chief Financial Officer
Matt Ruzicka, Chief Accounting Officer
David Hedgecock, Associate Publisher
Jerry Bennington, VP of New Product Development
Lorelei Bunjes, VP of Digital Services
Justin Eisinger, Editorial Director, Graphic Novels & Collections
Eric Moss, Senior Director, Licensing and Business Development

Ted Adams and Robbie Robbins, IDW Founders

Lucasfilm Credits:
Robert Simpson, Senior Editor
Michael Siglain, Creative Director
Pablo Hidalgo, Matt Martin, and
Emily Shkoukani, Story Group

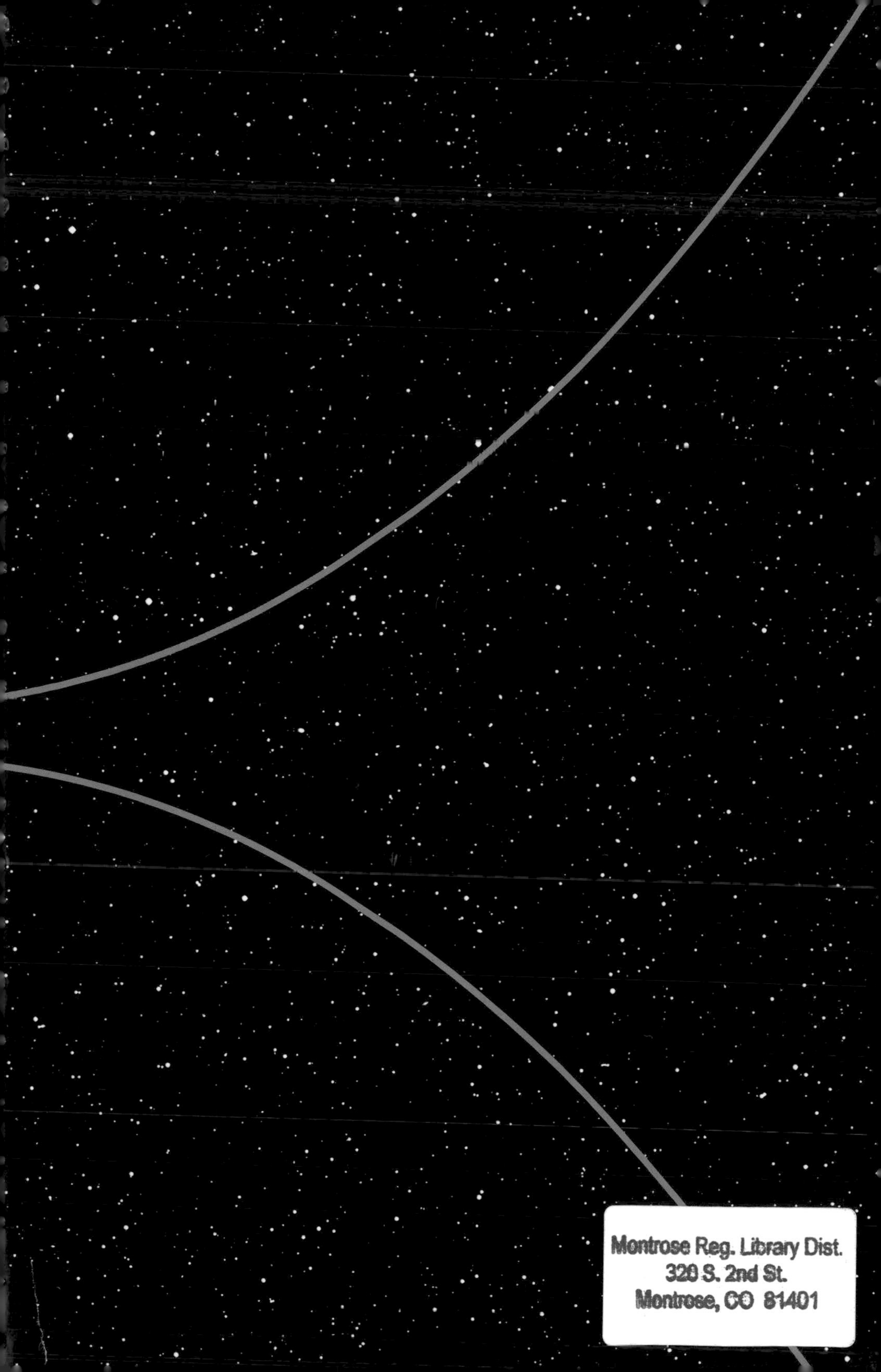

STAR WARS ADVENTURES

Mind Your Manners

WRITER
JOHN JACKSON MILLER
ARTIST
JON SOMMARIVA
COLORIST
MATT HERMS

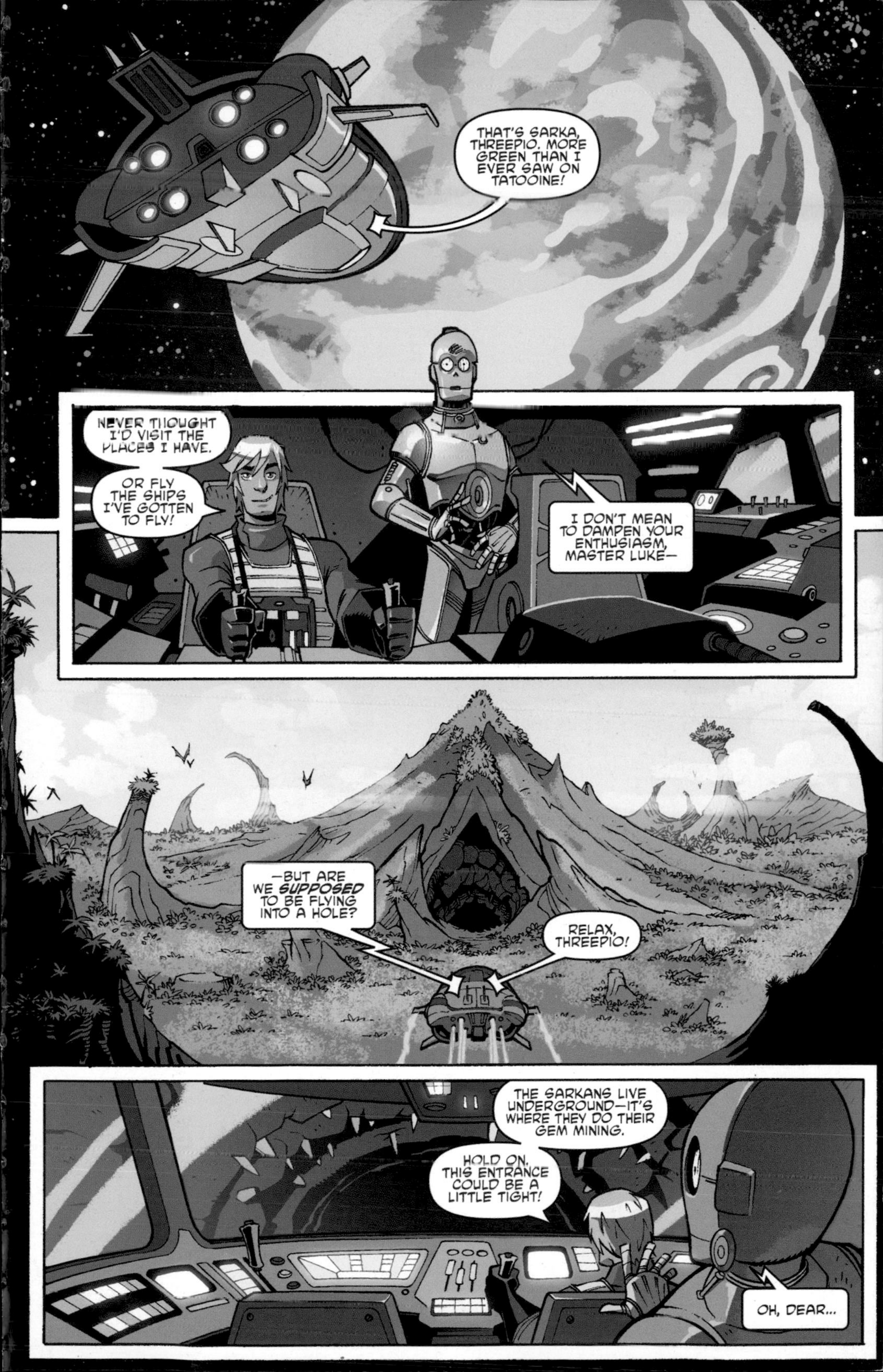
THAT'S SARKA, THREEPIO. MORE GREEN THAN I EVER SAW ON TATOOINE!
NEVER THOUGHT I'D VISIT THE PLACES I HAVE.
OR FLY THE SHIPS I'VE GOTTEN TO FLY!
I DON'T MEAN TO DAMPEN YOUR ENTHUSIASM, MASTER LUKE—
—BUT ARE WE SUPPOSED TO BE FLYING INTO A HOLE?
RELAX, THREEPIO!
THE SARKANS LIVE UNDERGROUND—IT'S WHERE THEY DO THEIR GEM MINING.
HOLD ON. THIS ENTRANCE COULD BE A LITTLE TIGHT!
OH, DEAR...

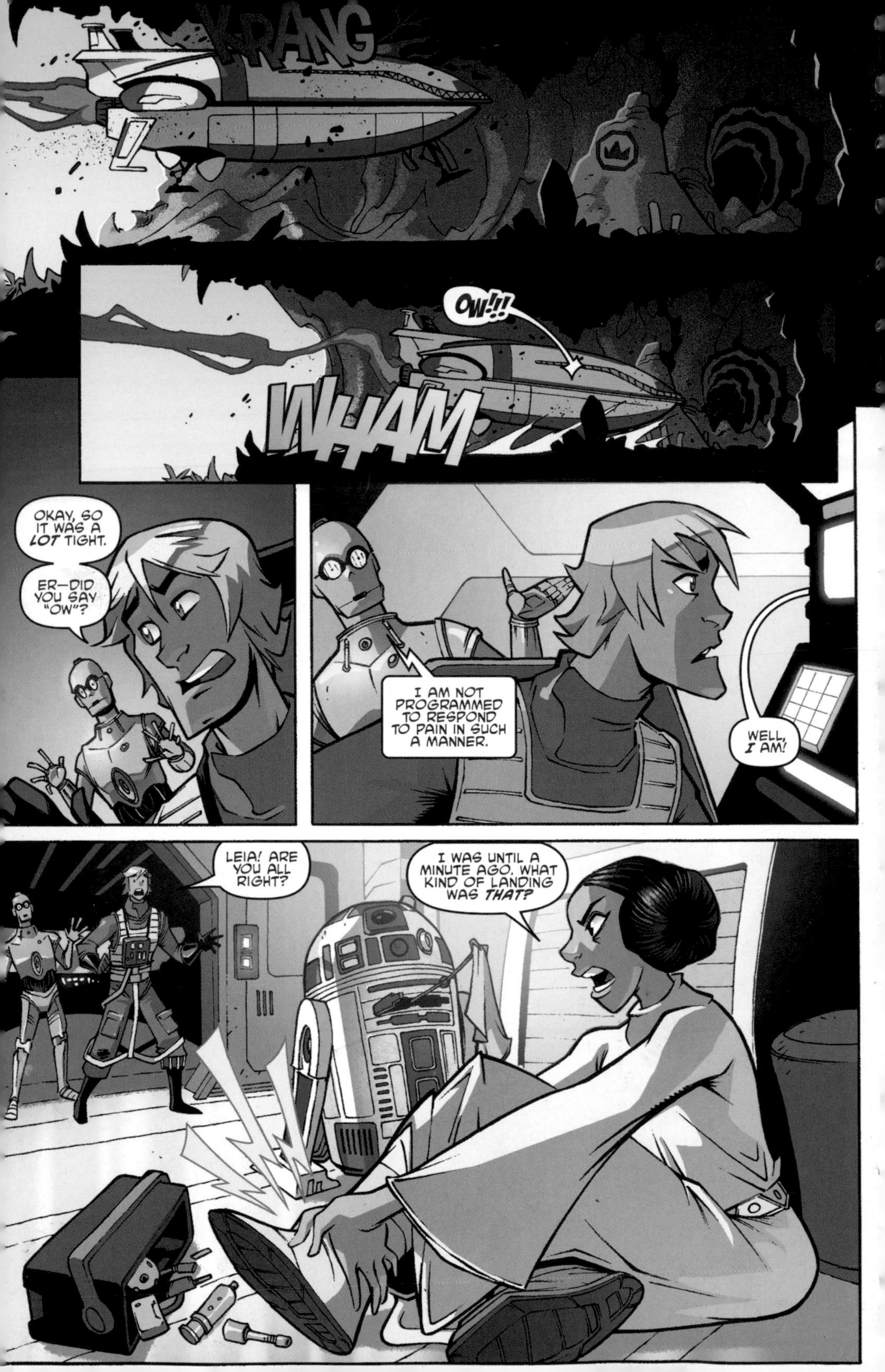
K-RANG
OW!!!
WHAM
OKAY, SO IT WAS A LOT TIGHT.
ER—DID YOU SAY "OW"?
I AM NOT PROGRAMMED TO RESPOND TO PAIN IN SUCH A MANNER.
WELL, I AM!
LEIA! ARE YOU ALL RIGHT?
I WAS UNTIL A MINUTE AGO. WHAT KIND OF LANDING WAS THAT?

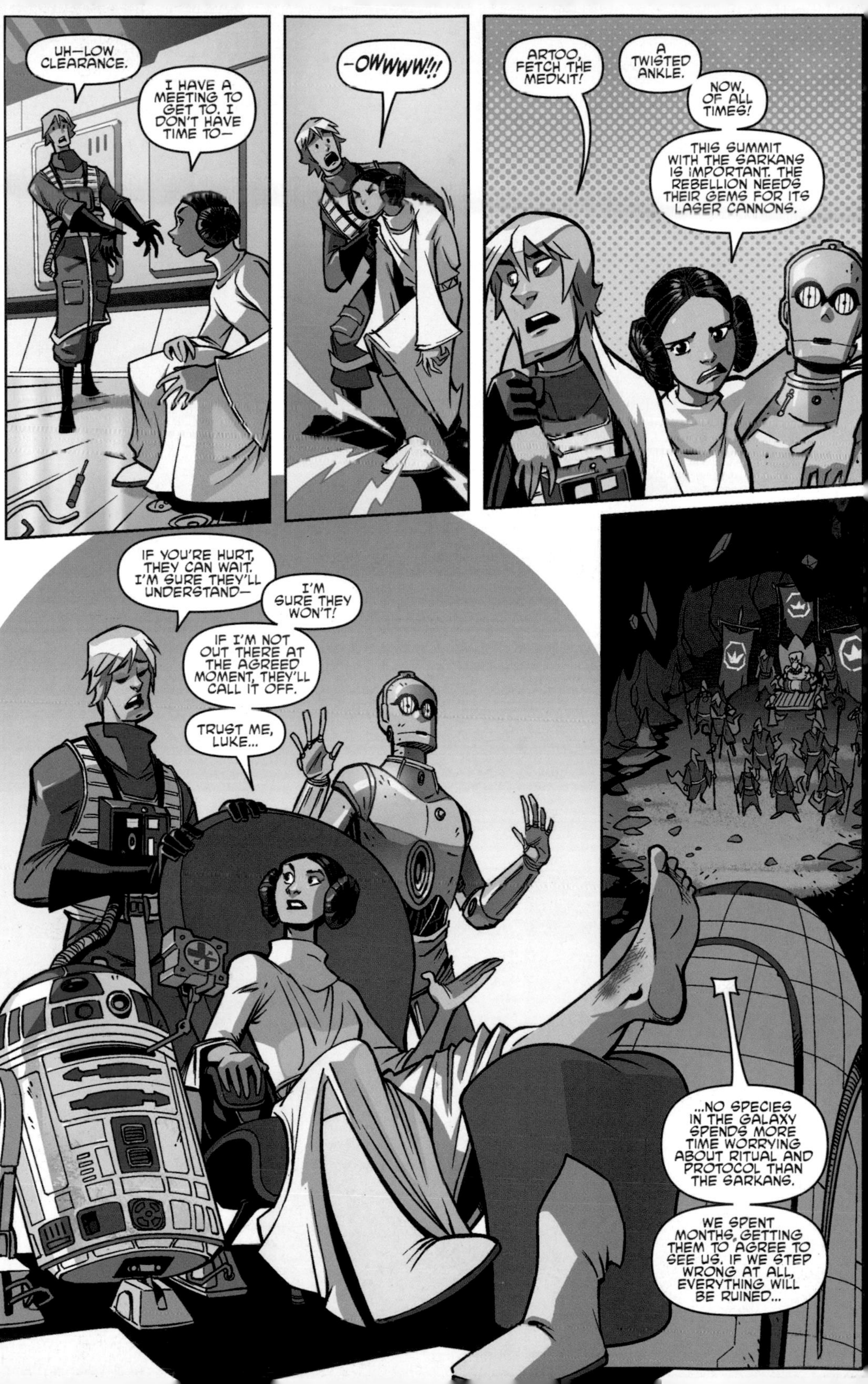

UH—LOW CLEARANCE.
I HAVE A MEETING TO GET TO. I DON'T HAVE TIME TO—
-OWWWW!!!
ARTOO, FETCH THE MEDKIT!
A TWISTED ANKLE.
NOW, OF ALL TIMES!
THIS SUMMIT WITH THE SARKANS IS IMPORTANT. THE REBELLION NEEDS THEIR GEMS FOR ITS LASER CANNONS.
IF YOU'RE HURT, THEY CAN WAIT. I'M SURE THEY'LL UNDERSTAND—
I'M SURE THEY WON'T!
IF I'M NOT OUT THERE AT THE AGREED MOMENT, THEY'LL CALL IT OFF.
TRUST ME, LUKE...
...NO SPECIES IN THE GALAXY SPENDS MORE TIME WORRYING ABOUT RITUAL AND PROTOCOL THAN THE SARKANS.
WE SPENT MONTHS GETTING THEM TO AGREE TO SEE US. IF WE STEP WRONG AT ALL, EVERYTHING WILL BE RUINED...

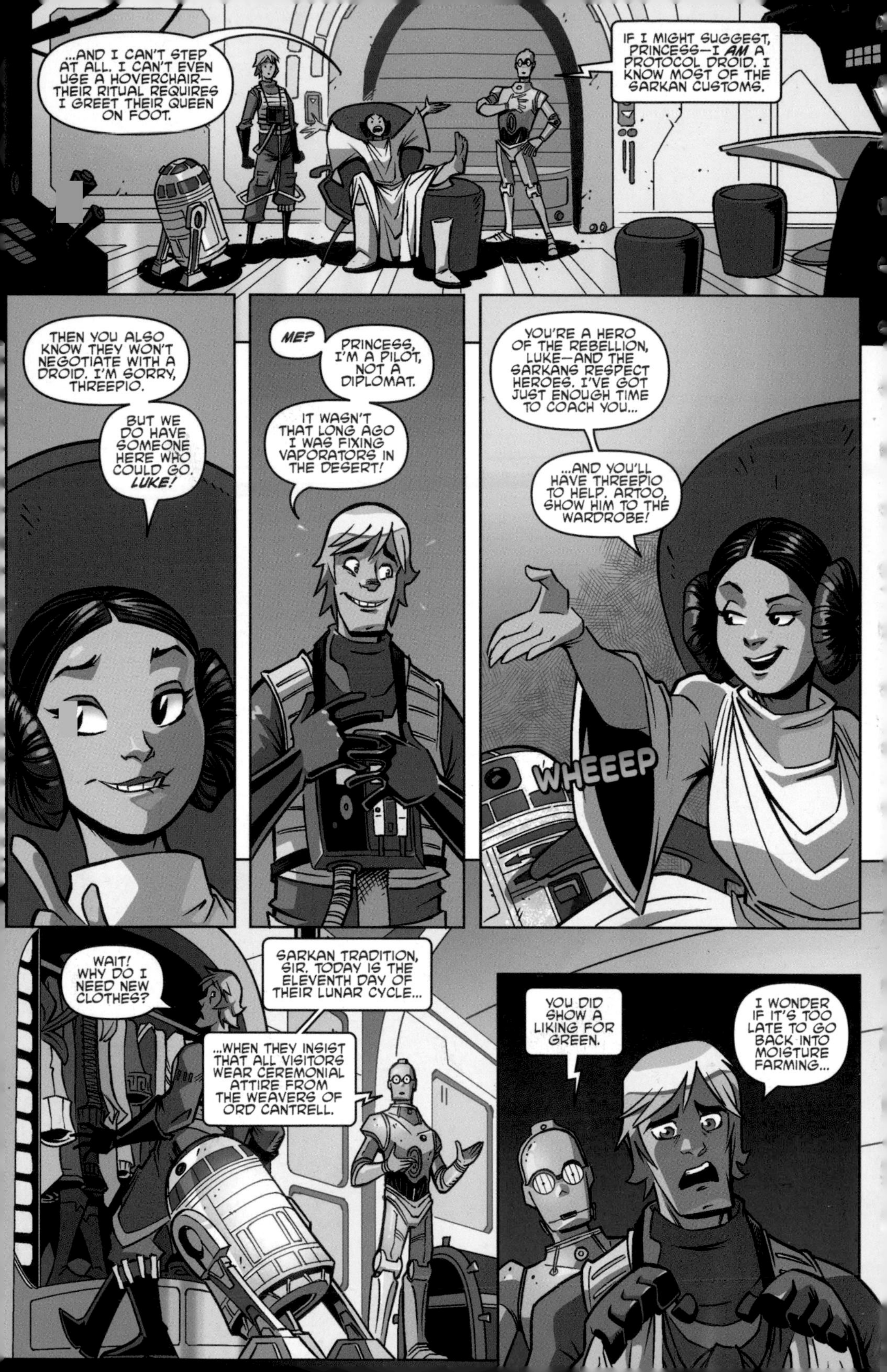
...AND I CAN'T STEP AT ALL. I CAN'T EVEN USE A HOVERCHAIR—THEIR RITUAL REQUIRES I GREET THEIR QUEEN ON FOOT.
IF I MIGHT SUGGEST, PRINCESS—I AM A PROTOCOL DROID. I KNOW MOST OF THE SARKAN CUSTOMS.
THEN YOU ALSO KNOW THEY WON'T NEGOTIATE WITH A DROID. I'M SORRY, THREEPIO.
BUT WE DO HAVE SOMEONE HERE WHO COULD GO. LUKE!
ME?
PRINCESS, I'M A PILOT, NOT A DIPLOMAT.
IT WASN'T THAT LONG AGO I WAS FIXING VAPORATORS IN THE DESERT!
YOU'RE A HERO OF THE REBELLION, LUKE—AND THE SARKANS RESPECT HEROES. I'VE GOT JUST ENOUGH TIME TO COACH YOU...
...AND YOU'LL HAVE THREEPIO TO HELP. ARTOO, SHOW HIM TO THE WARDROBE!
WHEEEP
WAIT! WHY DO I NEED NEW CLOTHES?
SARKAN TRADITION, SIR. TODAY IS THE ELEVENTH DAY OF THEIR LUNAR CYCLE...
...WHEN THEY INSIST THAT ALL VISITORS WEAR CEREMONIAL ATTIRE FROM THE WEAVERS OF ORD CANTRELL.
YOU DID SHOW A LIKING FOR GREEN.
I WONDER IF IT'S TOO LATE TO GO BACK INTO MOISTURE FARMING...

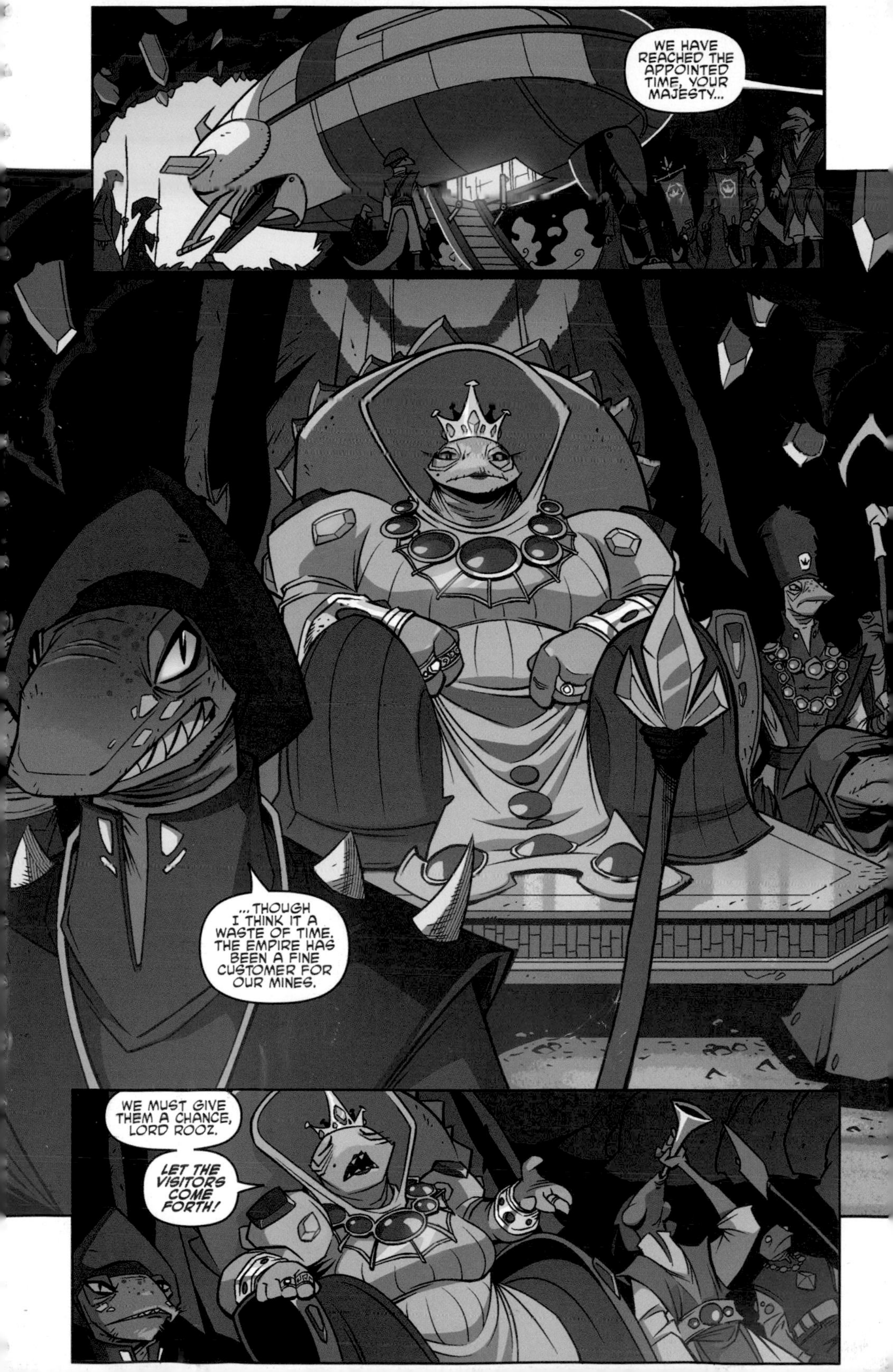
WE HAVE REACHED THE APPOINTED TIME, YOUR MAJESTY...
...THOUGH I THINK IT A WASTE OF TIME. THE EMPIRE HAS BEEN A FINE CUSTOMER FOR OUR MINES.
WE MUST GIVE THEM A CHANCE, LORD ROOZ.
LET THE VISITORS COME FORTH!

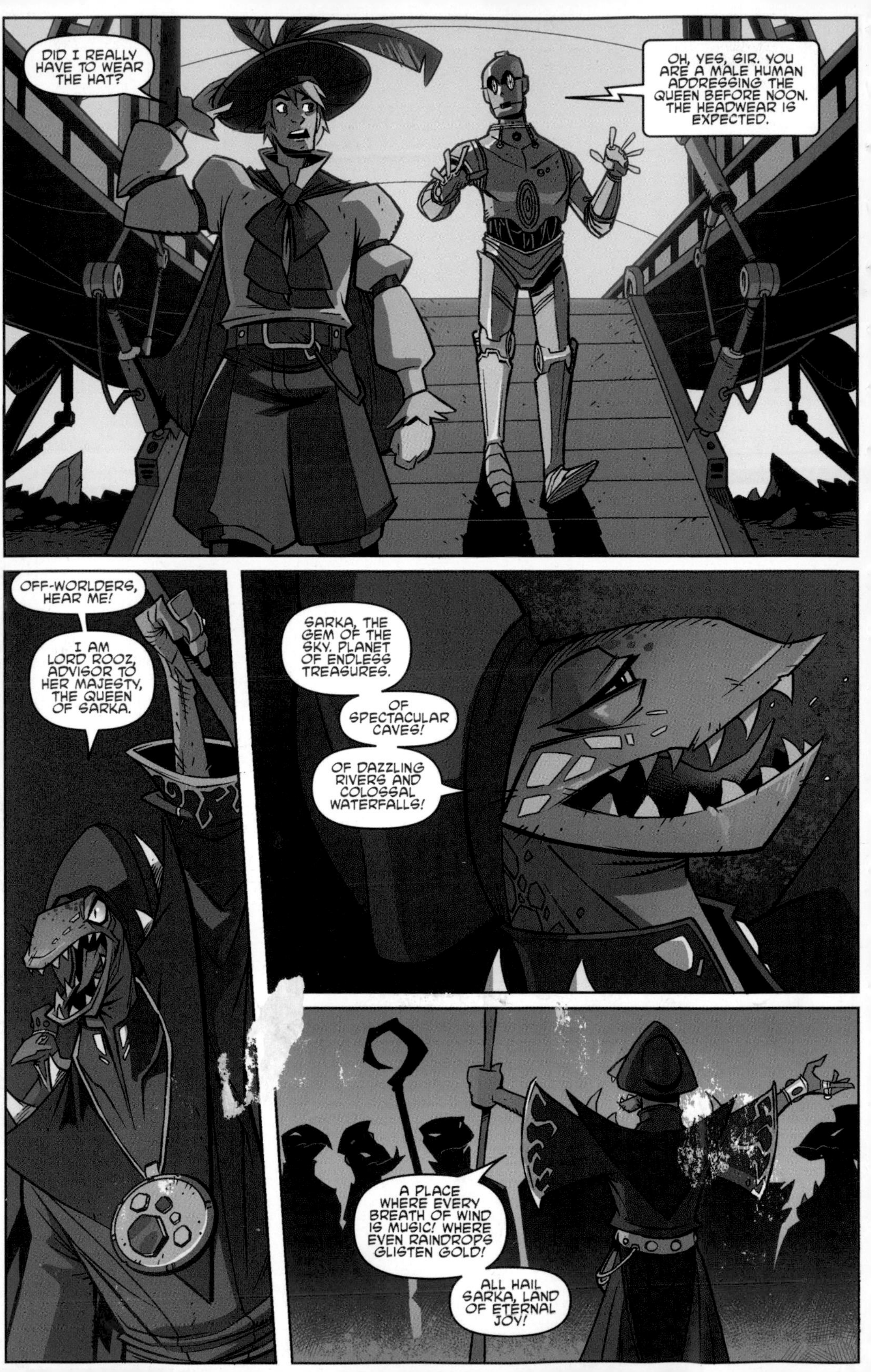
DID I REALLY HAVE TO WEAR THE HAT?
OH, YES, SIR. YOU ARE A MALE HUMAN ADDRESSING THE QUEEN BEFORE NOON. THE HEADWEAR IS EXPECTED.
OFF-WORLDERS, HEAR ME!
I AM LORD ROOZ, ADVISOR TO HER MAJESTY, THE QUEEN OF SARKA.
SARKA, THE GEM OF THE SKY. PLANET OF ENDLESS TREASURES.
OF SPECTACULAR CAVES!
OF DAZZLING RIVERS AND COLOSSAL WATERFALLS!
A PLACE WHERE EVERY BREATH OF WIND IS MUSIC! WHERE EVEN RAINDROPS GLISTEN GOLD!
ALL HAIL SARKA, LAND OF ETERNAL JOY!

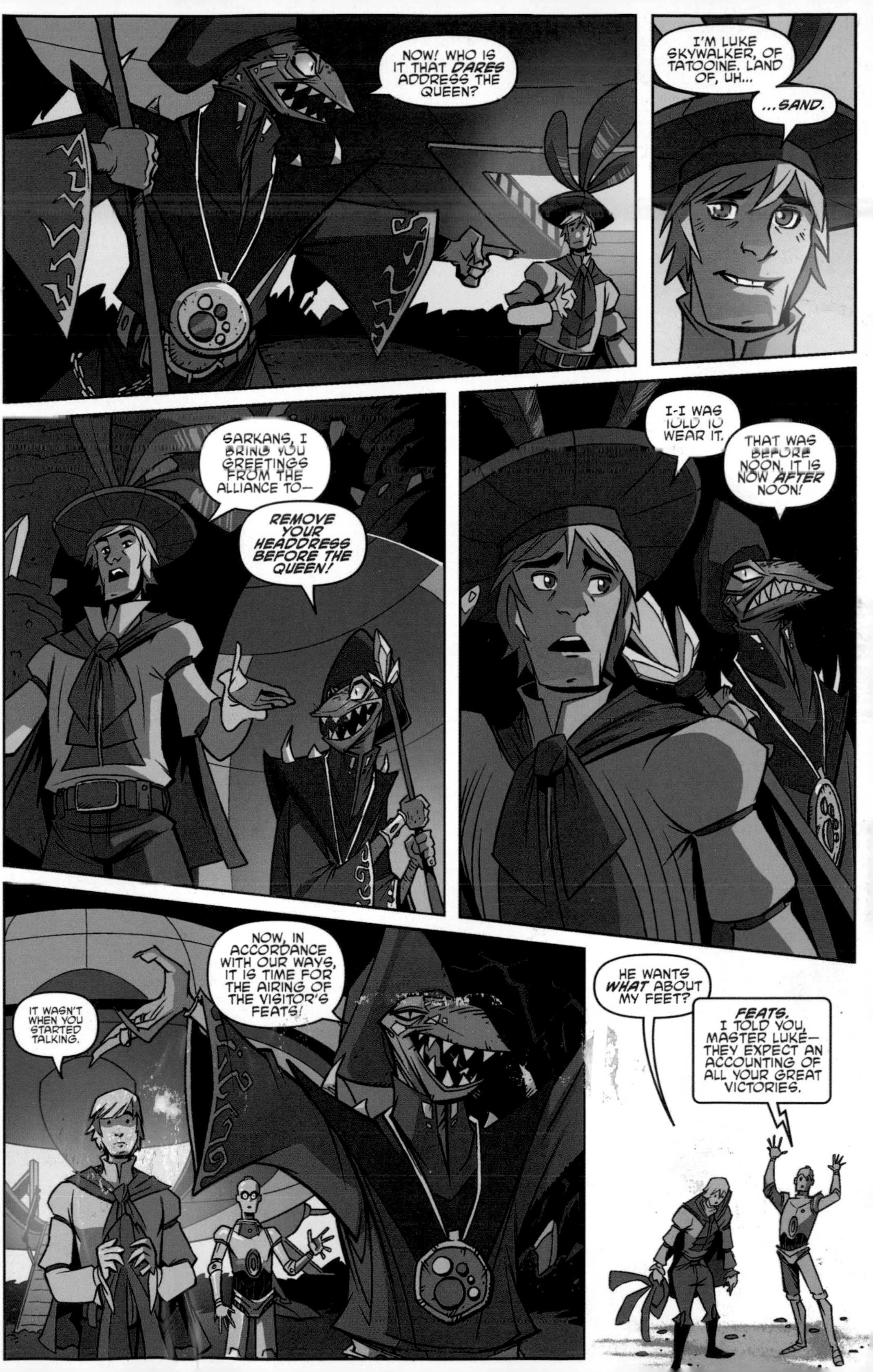
NOW! WHO IS IT THAT *DARES* ADDRESS THE QUEEN?
I'M LUKE SKYWALKER, OF TATOOINE. LAND OF, UH...
...*SAND.*
SARKANS, I BRING YOU GREETINGS FROM THE ALLIANCE TO—
REMOVE YOUR HEADDRESS BEFORE THE QUEEN!
I-I WAS TOLD TO WEAR IT.
THAT WAS BEFORE NOON. IT IS NOW *AFTER* NOON!
IT WASN'T WHEN YOU STARTED TALKING.
NOW, IN ACCORDANCE WITH OUR WAYS, IT IS TIME FOR THE AIRING OF THE VISITOR'S FEATS!
HE WANTS *WHAT* ABOUT MY FEET?
FEATS. I TOLD YOU, MASTER LUKE— THEY EXPECT AN ACCOUNTING OF ALL YOUR GREAT VICTORIES.

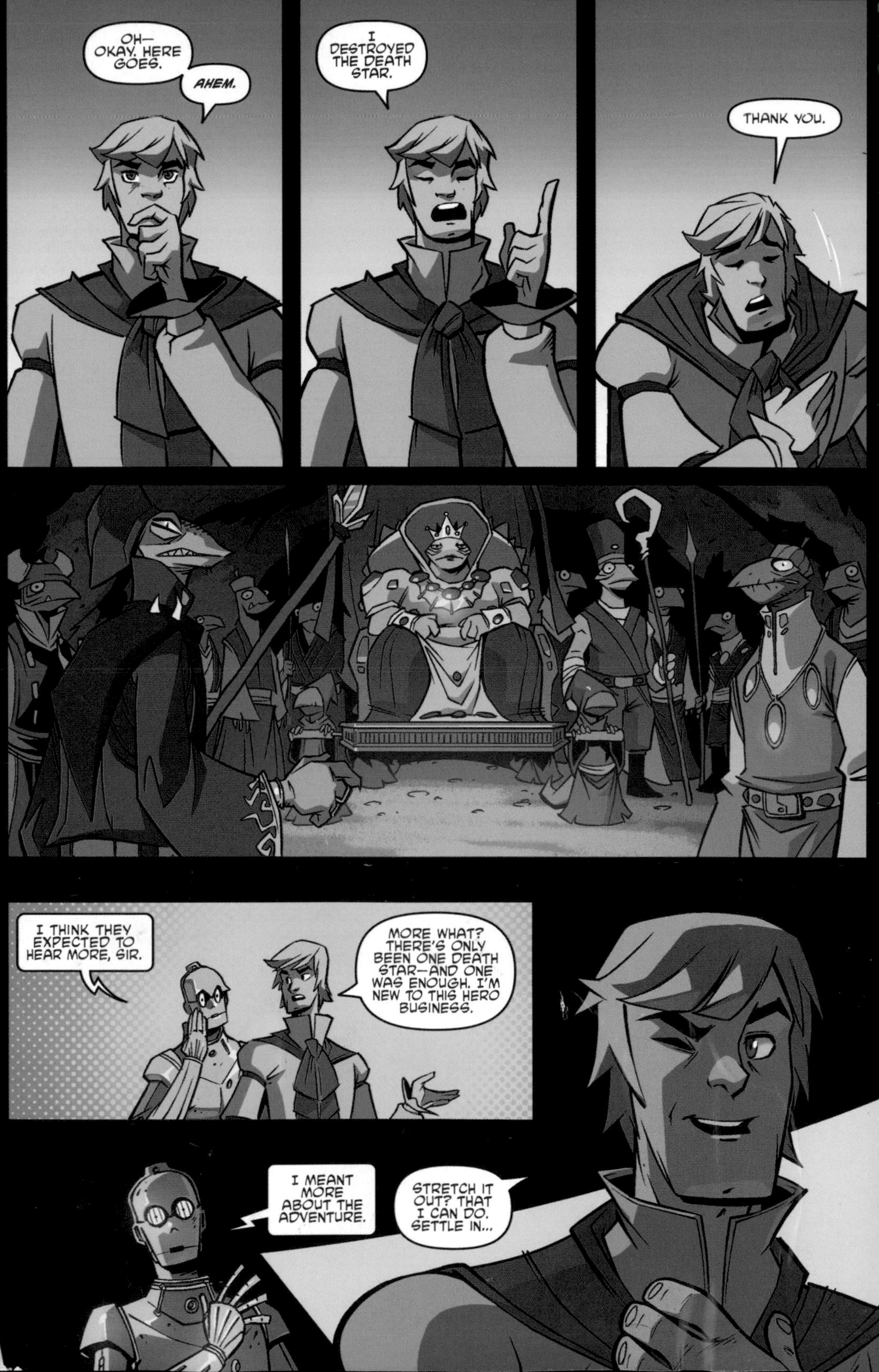
OH— OKAY. HERE GOES.
AHEM.
I DESTROYED THE DEATH STAR.
THANK YOU.
I THINK THEY EXPECTED TO HEAR MORE, SIR.
MORE WHAT? THERE'S ONLY BEEN ONE DEATH STAR—AND ONE WAS ENOUGH. I'M NEW TO THIS HERO BUSINESS.
I MEANT MORE ABOUT THE ADVENTURE.
STRETCH IT OUT? THAT I CAN DO. SETTLE IN...

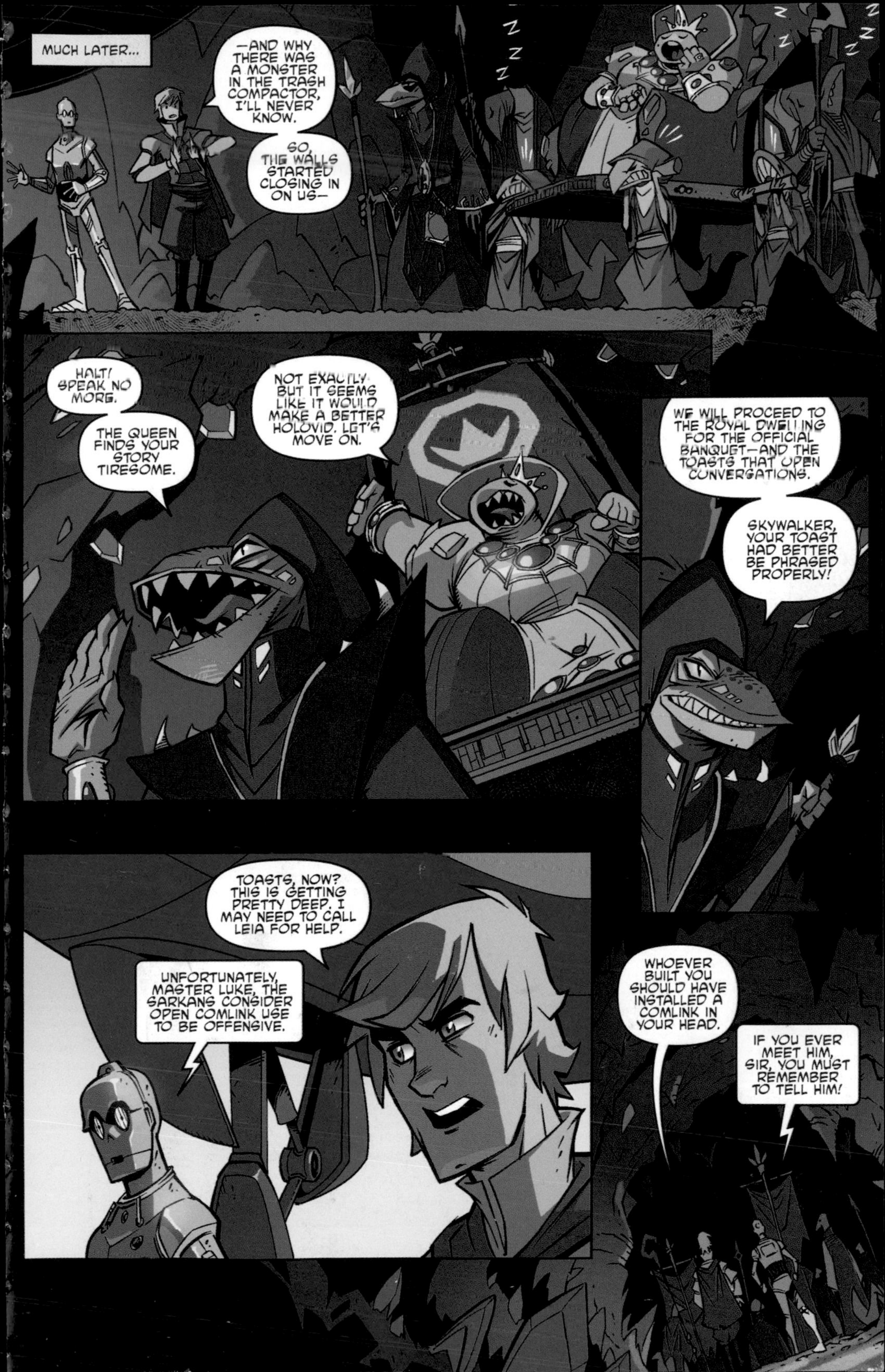
MUCH LATER...
—AND WHY THERE WAS A MONSTER IN THE TRASH COMPACTOR, I'LL NEVER KNOW.
SO, THE WALLS STARTED CLOSING IN ON US—
Z Z Z
HALT! SPEAK NO MORE.
THE QUEEN FINDS YOUR STORY TIRESOME.
NOT EXACTLY. BUT IT SEEMS LIKE IT WOULD MAKE A BETTER HOLOVID. LET'S MOVE ON.
WE WILL PROCEED TO THE ROYAL DWELLING FOR THE OFFICIAL BANQUET—AND THE TOASTS THAT OPEN CONVERSATIONS.
SKYWALKER, YOUR TOAST HAD BETTER BE PHRASED PROPERLY!
TOASTS, NOW? THIS IS GETTING PRETTY DEEP. I MAY NEED TO CALL LEIA FOR HELP.
UNFORTUNATELY, MASTER LUKE, THE SARKANS CONSIDER OPEN COMLINK USE TO BE OFFENSIVE.
WHOEVER BUILT YOU SHOULD HAVE INSTALLED A COMLINK IN YOUR HEAD.
IF YOU EVER MEET HIM, SIR, YOU MUST REMEMBER TO TELL HIM!

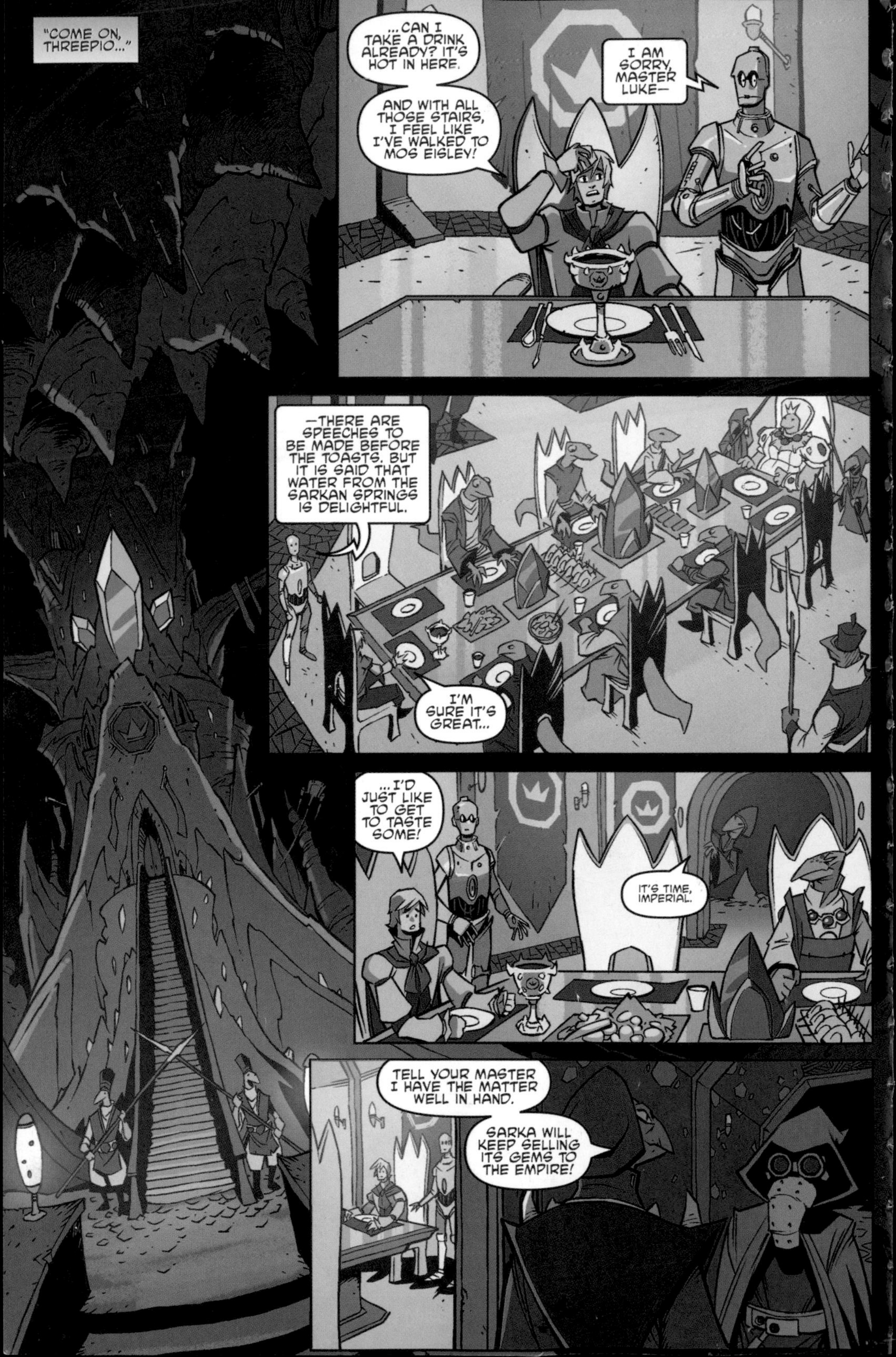
"COME ON, THREEPIO..."
...CAN I TAKE A DRINK ALREADY? IT'S HOT IN HERE.
AND WITH ALL THOSE STAIRS, I FEEL LIKE I'VE WALKED TO MOS EISLEY!
I AM SORRY, MASTER LUKE—
—THERE ARE SPEECHES TO BE MADE BEFORE THE TOASTS. BUT IT IS SAID THAT WATER FROM THE SARKAN SPRINGS IS DELIGHTFUL.
I'M SURE IT'S GREAT...
...I'D JUST LIKE TO GET TO TASTE SOME!
IT'S TIME, IMPERIAL.
TELL YOUR MASTER I HAVE THE MATTER WELL IN HAND.
SARKA WILL KEEP SELLING ITS GEMS TO THE EMPIRE!

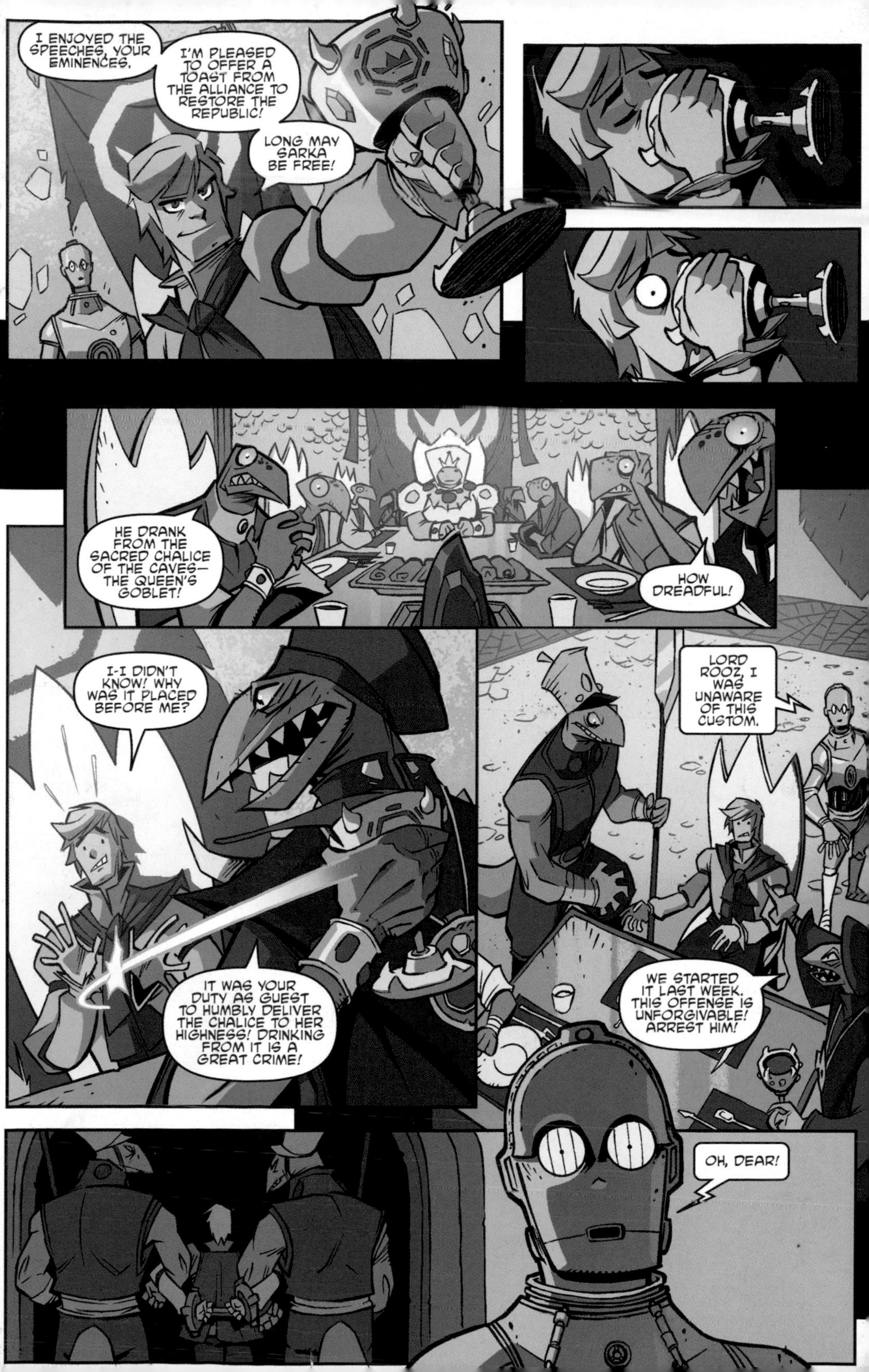
I ENJOYED THE SPEECHES, YOUR EMINENCES.
I'M PLEASED TO OFFER A TOAST FROM THE ALLIANCE TO RESTORE THE REPUBLIC!
LONG MAY SARKA BE FREE!
HE DRANK FROM THE SACRED CHALICE OF THE CAVES— THE QUEEN'S GOBLET!
HOW DREADFUL!
I-I DIDN'T KNOW! WHY WAS IT PLACED BEFORE ME?
IT WAS YOUR DUTY AS GUEST TO HUMBLY DELIVER THE CHALICE TO HER HIGHNESS! DRINKING FROM IT IS A GREAT CRIME!
LORD ROOZ, I WAS UNAWARE OF THIS CUSTOM.
WE STARTED IT LAST WEEK. THIS OFFENSE IS UNFORGIVABLE! ARREST HIM!
OH, DEAR!

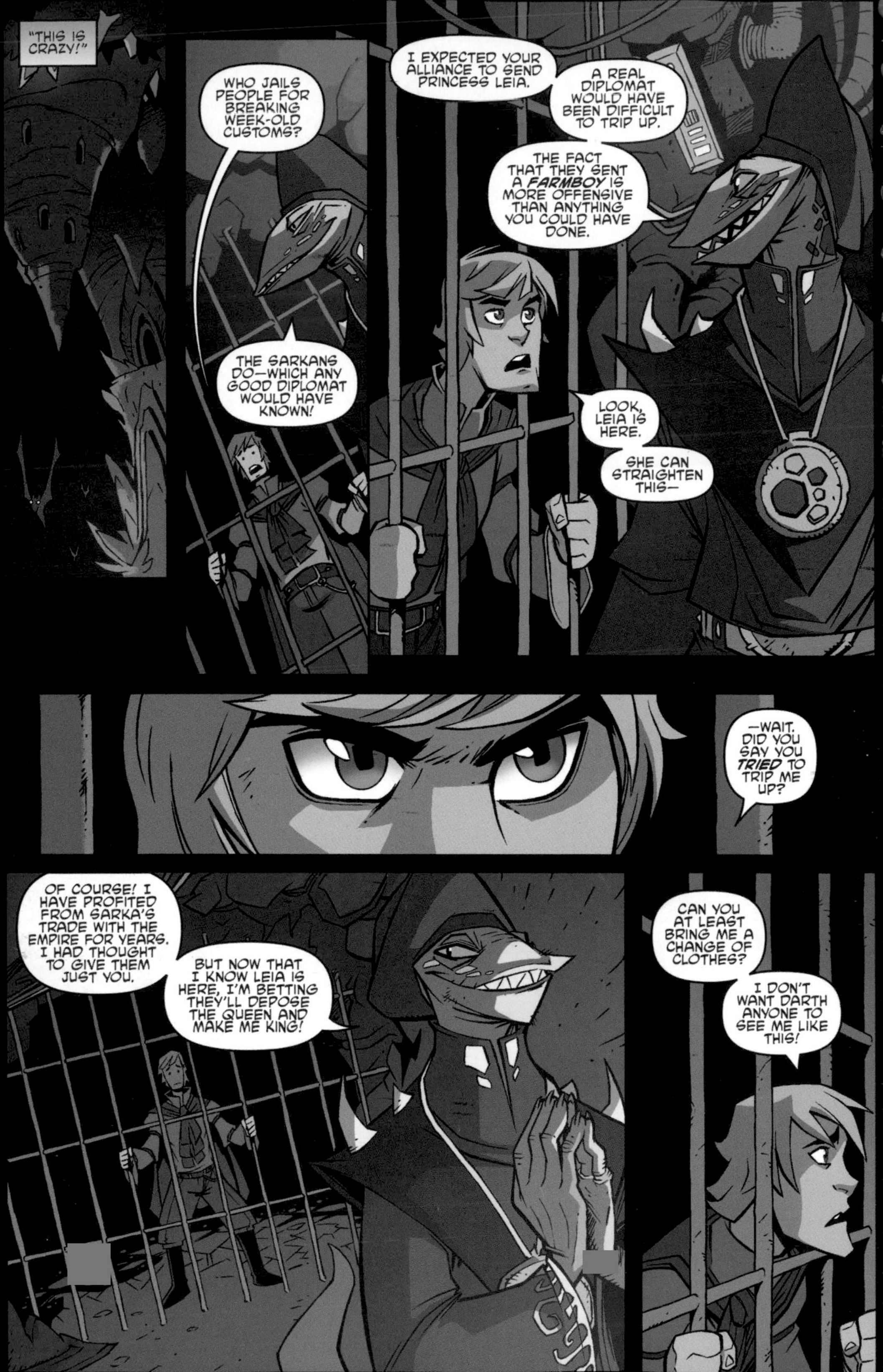
"THIS IS CRAZY!"
WHO JAILS PEOPLE FOR BREAKING WEEK-OLD CUSTOMS?
THE SARKANS DO—WHICH ANY GOOD DIPLOMAT WOULD HAVE KNOWN!
I EXPECTED YOUR ALLIANCE TO SEND PRINCESS LEIA.
A REAL DIPLOMAT WOULD HAVE BEEN DIFFICULT TO TRIP UP.
THE FACT THAT THEY SENT A FARMBOY IS MORE OFFENSIVE THAN ANYTHING YOU COULD HAVE DONE.
LOOK, LEIA IS HERE.
SHE CAN STRAIGHTEN THIS—
—WAIT. DID YOU SAY YOU TRIED TO TRIP ME UP?
OF COURSE! I HAVE PROFITED FROM SARKA'S TRADE WITH THE EMPIRE FOR YEARS. I HAD THOUGHT TO GIVE THEM JUST YOU.
BUT NOW THAT I KNOW LEIA IS HERE, I'M BETTING THEY'LL DEPOSE THE QUEEN AND MAKE ME KING!
CAN YOU AT LEAST BRING ME A CHANGE OF CLOTHES?
I DON'T WANT DARTH ANYONE TO SEE ME LIKE THIS!

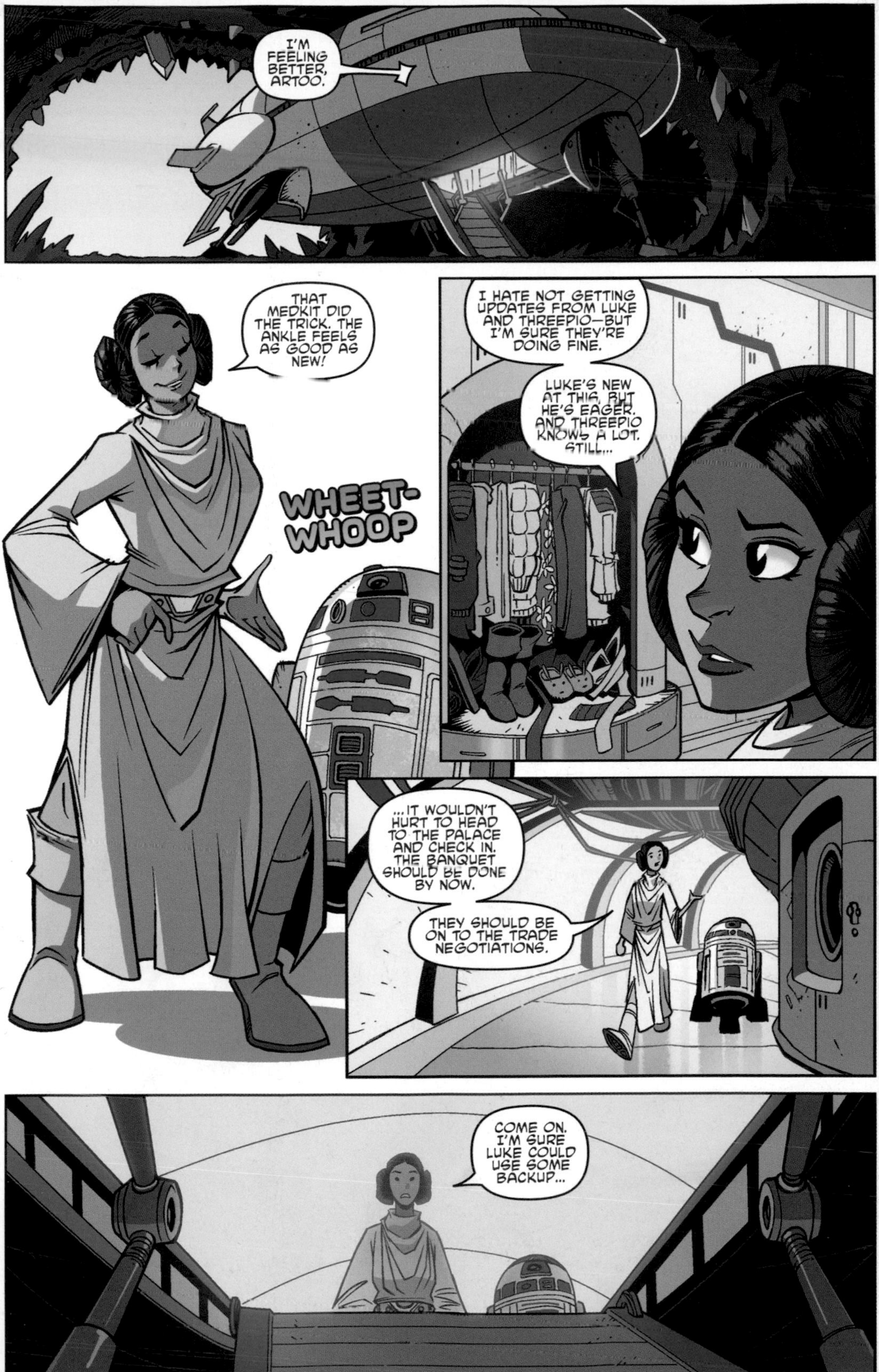
I'M FEELING BETTER, ARTOO.
THAT MEDKIT DID THE TRICK. THE ANKLE FEELS AS GOOD AS NEW!
WHEET-WHOOP
I HATE NOT GETTING UPDATES FROM LUKE AND THREEPIO—BUT I'M SURE THEY'RE DOING FINE.
LUKE'S NEW AT THIS, BUT HE'S EAGER. AND THREEPIO KNOWS A LOT. STILL...
...IT WOULDN'T HURT TO HEAD TO THE PALACE AND CHECK IN. THE BANQUET SHOULD BE DONE BY NOW.
THEY SHOULD BE ON TO THE TRADE NEGOTIATIONS.
COME ON. I'M SURE LUKE COULD USE SOME BACKUP...

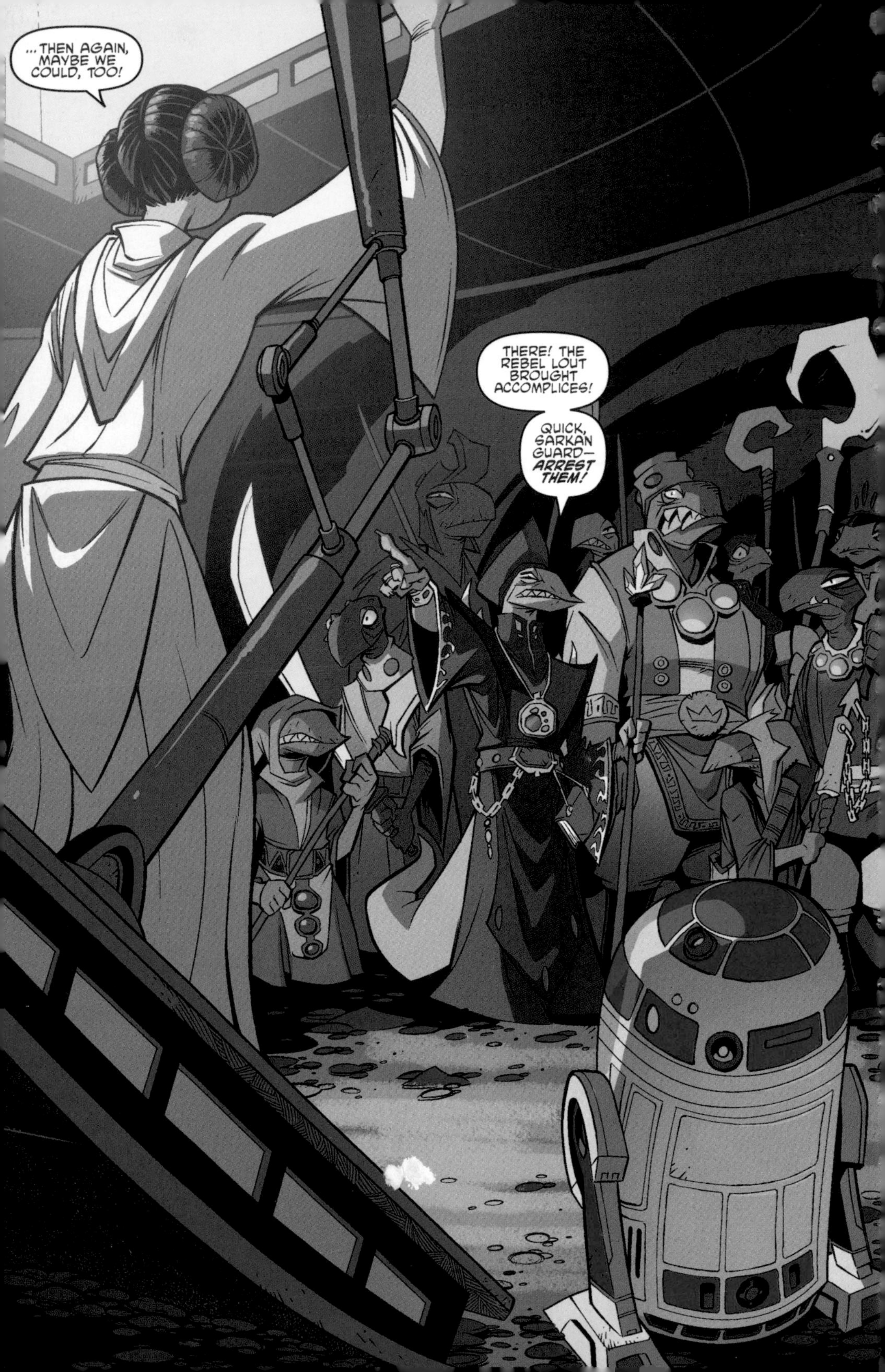
...THEN AGAIN, MAYBE WE COULD, TOO!
THERE! THE REBEL LOUT BROUGHT ACCOMPLICES!
QUICK, SARKAN GUARD— ARREST THEM!

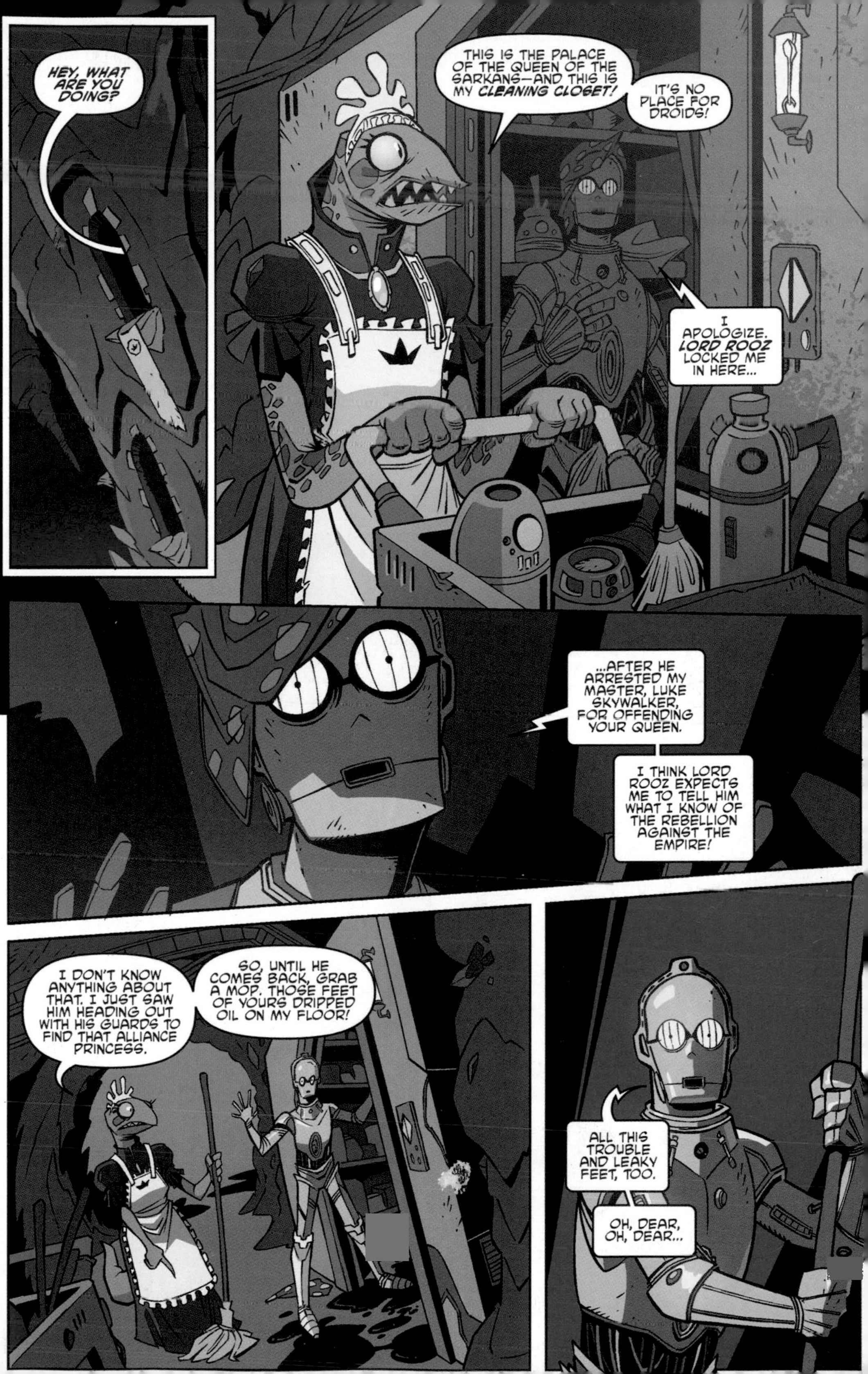
HEY, WHAT ARE YOU DOING?
THIS IS THE PALACE OF THE QUEEN OF THE SARKANS—AND THIS IS MY CLEANING CLOSET!
IT'S NO PLACE FOR DROIDS!
I APOLOGIZE. LORD ROOZ LOCKED ME IN HERE...
...AFTER HE ARRESTED MY MASTER, LUKE SKYWALKER, FOR OFFENDING YOUR QUEEN.
I THINK LORD ROOZ EXPECTS ME TO TELL HIM WHAT I KNOW OF THE REBELLION AGAINST THE EMPIRE!
I DON'T KNOW ANYTHING ABOUT THAT. I JUST SAW HIM HEADING OUT WITH HIS GUARDS TO FIND THAT ALLIANCE PRINCESS.
SO, UNTIL HE COMES BACK, GRAB A MOP. THOSE FEET OF YOURS DRIPPED OIL ON MY FLOOR!
ALL THIS TROUBLE AND LEAKY FEET, TOO.
OH, DEAR, OH, DEAR...

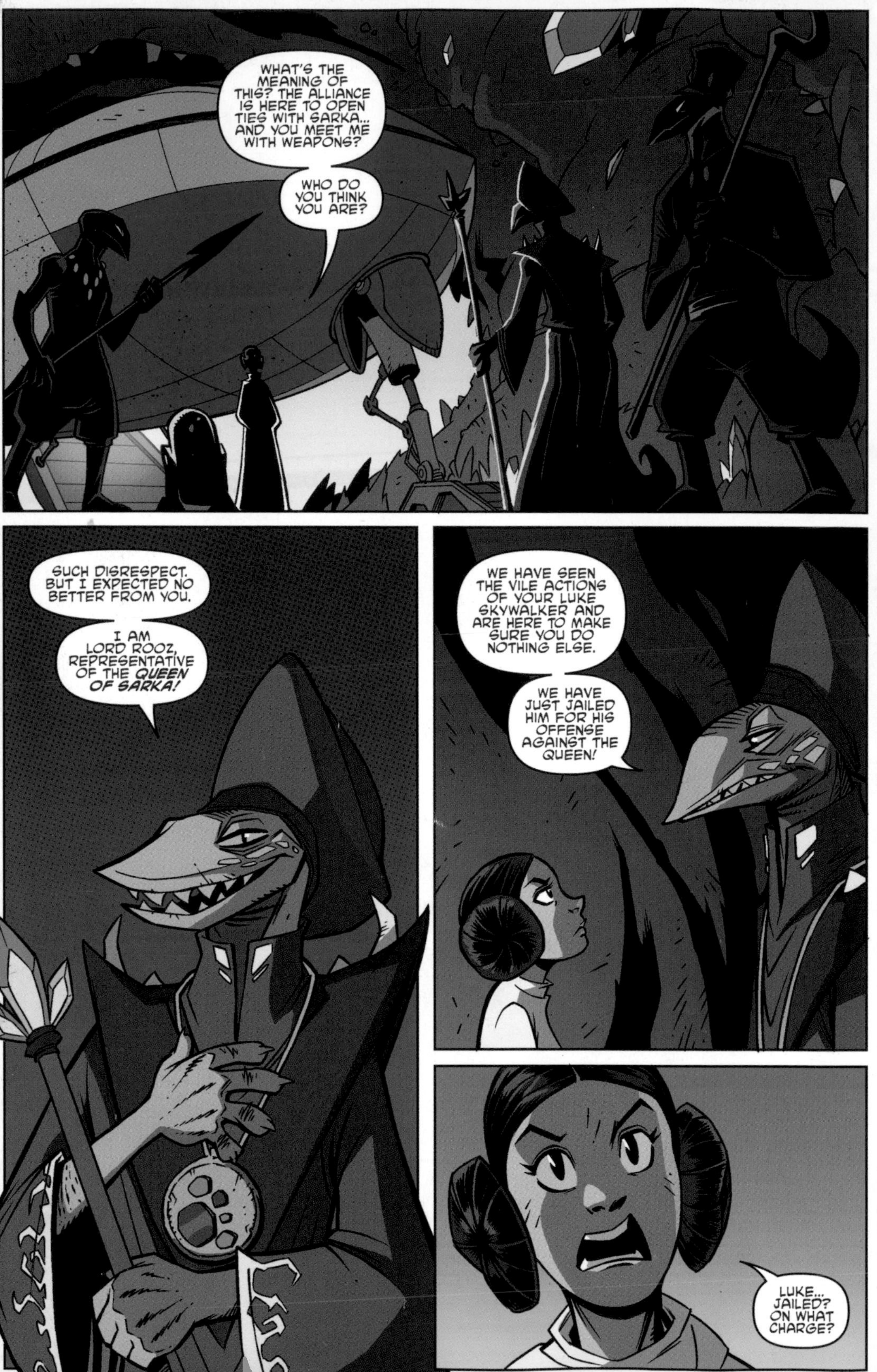
WHAT'S THE MEANING OF THIS? THE ALLIANCE IS HERE TO OPEN TIES WITH SARKA... AND YOU MEET ME WITH WEAPONS?
WHO DO YOU THINK YOU ARE?
SUCH DISRESPECT. BUT I EXPECTED NO BETTER FROM YOU.
I AM LORD ROOZ, REPRESENTATIVE OF THE *QUEEN OF SARKA!*
WE HAVE SEEN THE VILE ACTIONS OF YOUR LUKE SKYWALKER AND ARE HERE TO MAKE SURE YOU DO NOTHING ELSE.
WE HAVE JUST JAILED HIM FOR HIS OFFENSE AGAINST THE QUEEN!
LUKE... JAILED? ON WHAT CHARGE?

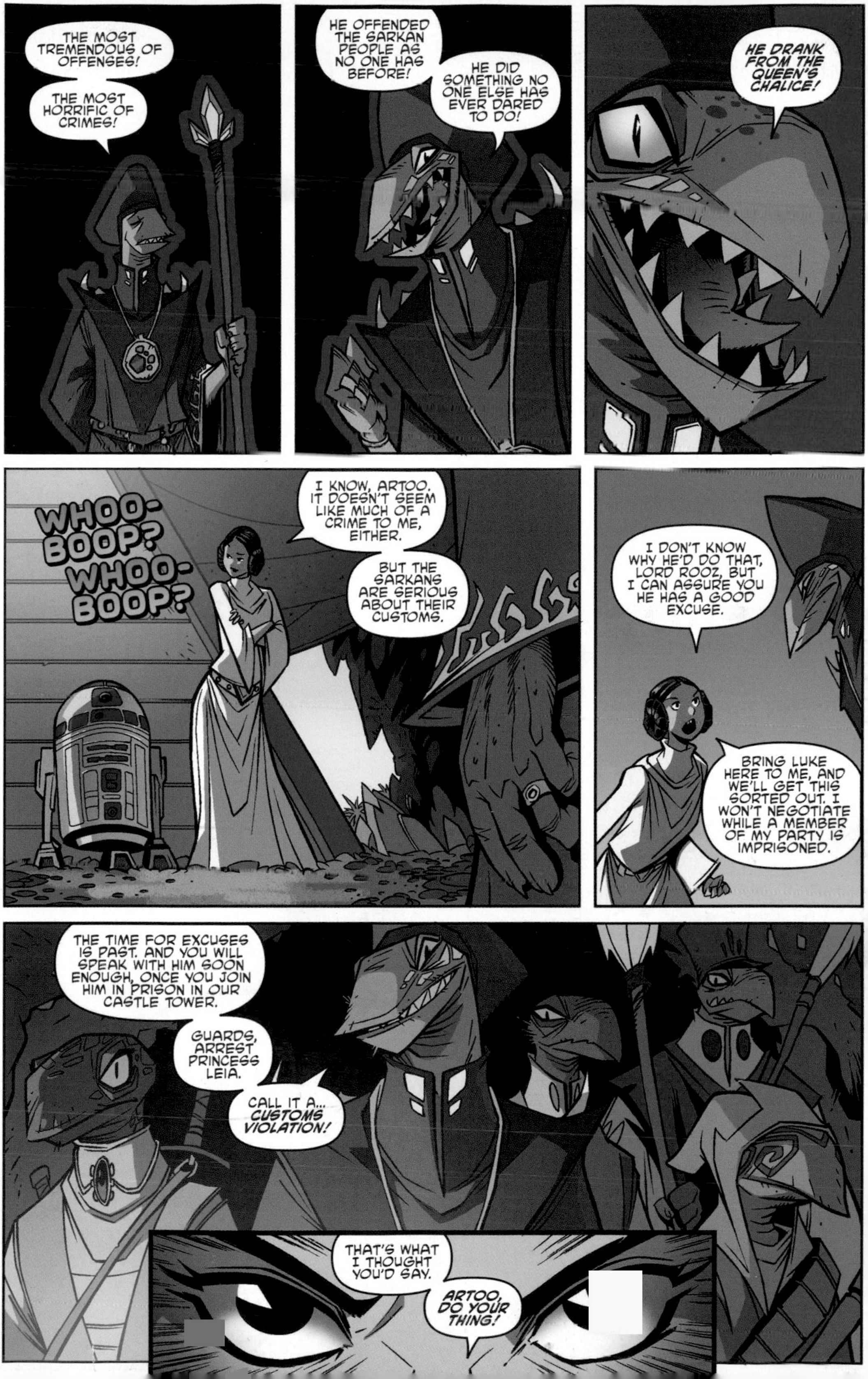
THE MOST TREMENDOUS OF OFFENSES!
THE MOST HORRIFIC OF CRIMES!
HE OFFENDED THE SARKAN PEOPLE AS NO ONE HAS BEFORE!
HE DID SOMETHING NO ONE ELSE HAS EVER DARED TO DO!
HE DRANK FROM THE QUEEN'S CHALICE!
WHOO-BOOP? WHOO-BOOP?
I KNOW, ARTOO. IT DOESN'T SEEM LIKE MUCH OF A CRIME TO ME, EITHER.
BUT THE SARKANS ARE SERIOUS ABOUT THEIR CUSTOMS.
I DON'T KNOW WHY HE'D DO THAT, LORD ROOZ, BUT I CAN ASSURE YOU HE HAS A GOOD EXCUSE.
BRING LUKE HERE TO ME, AND WE'LL GET THIS SORTED OUT. I WON'T NEGOTIATE WHILE A MEMBER OF MY PARTY IS IMPRISONED.
THE TIME FOR EXCUSES IS PAST. AND YOU WILL SPEAK WITH HIM SOON ENOUGH, ONCE YOU JOIN HIM IN PRISON IN OUR CASTLE TOWER.
GUARDS, ARREST PRINCESS LEIA.
CALL IT A... CUSTOMS VIOLATION!
THAT'S WHAT I THOUGHT YOU'D SAY.
ARTOO, DO YOUR THING!

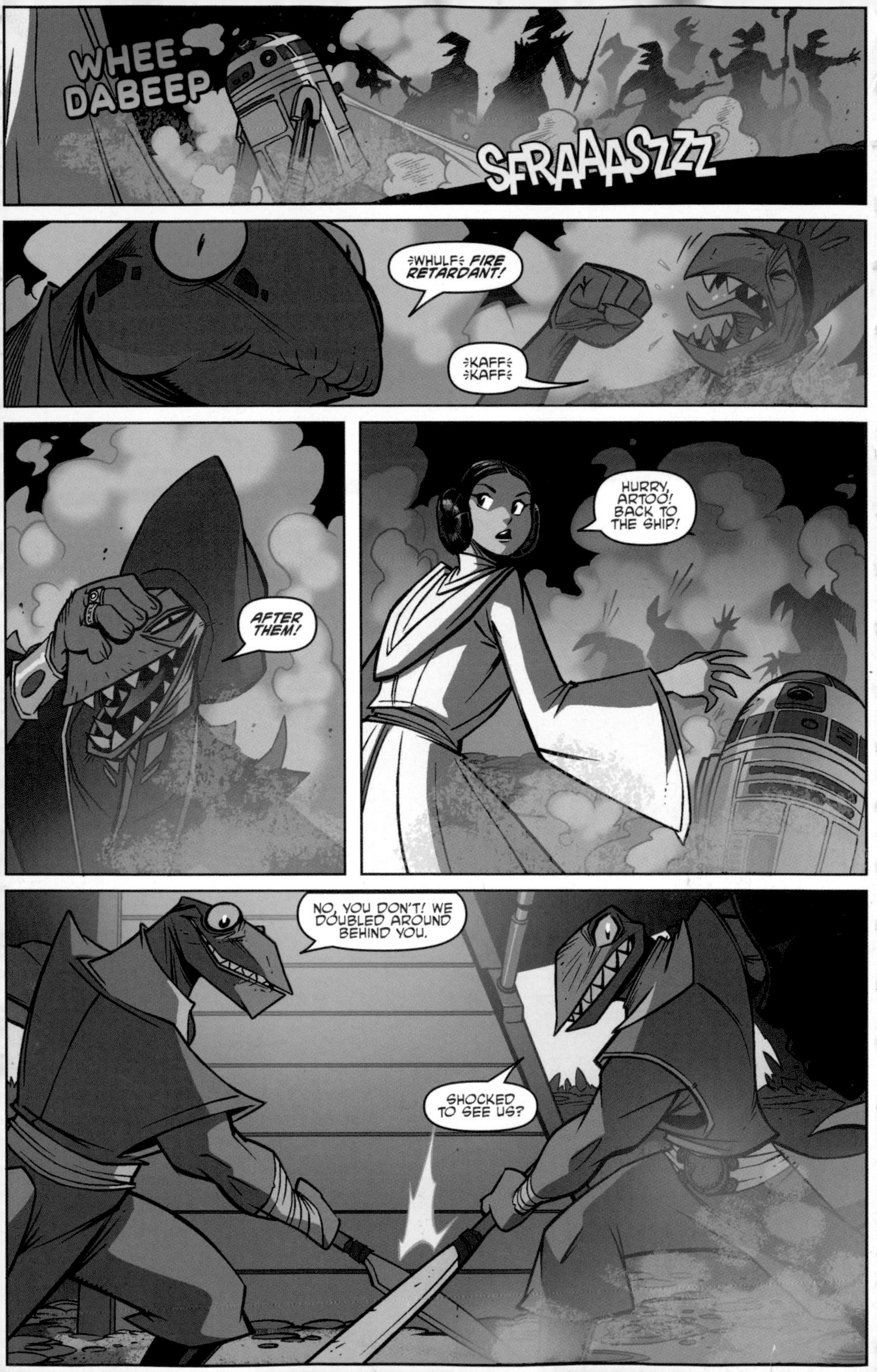
WHEE-DABEEP
SFRAAASZZZ
WHULF FIRE RETARDANT!
KAFF KAFF
AFTER THEM!
HURRY, ARTOO! BACK TO THE SHIP!
NO, YOU DON'T! WE DOUBLED AROUND BEHIND YOU.
SHOCKED TO SEE US?

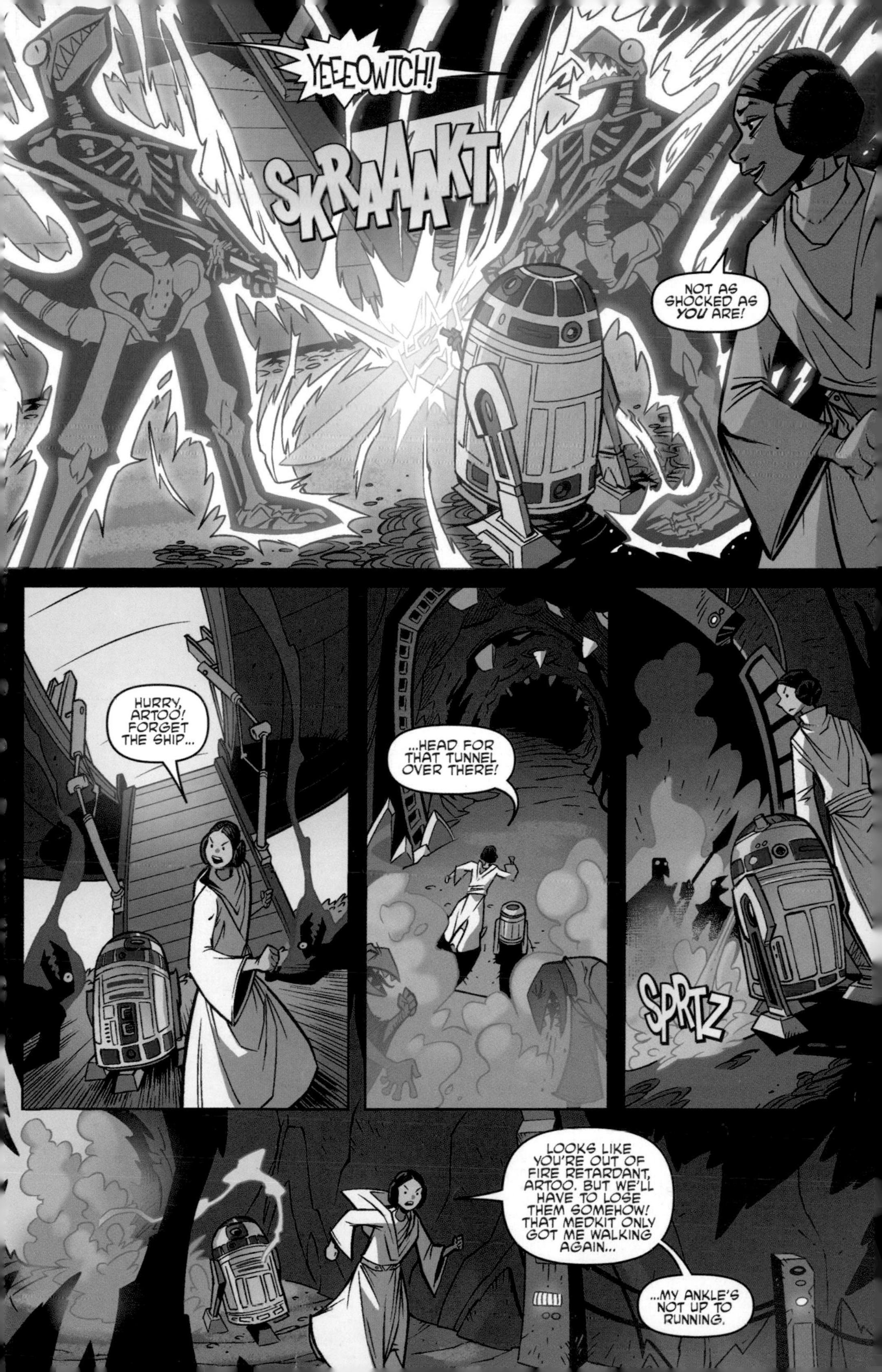
YEEEOWTCH!
SKRAAAKT
NOT AS SHOCKED AS YOU ARE!
HURRY, ARTOO! FORGET THE SHIP...
...HEAD FOR THAT TUNNEL OVER THERE!
SPRTZ
LOOKS LIKE YOU'RE OUT OF FIRE RETARDANT, ARTOO. BUT WE'LL HAVE TO LOSE THEM SOMEHOW! THAT MEDKIT ONLY GOT ME WALKING AGAIN...
...MY ANKLE'S NOT UP TO RUNNING.

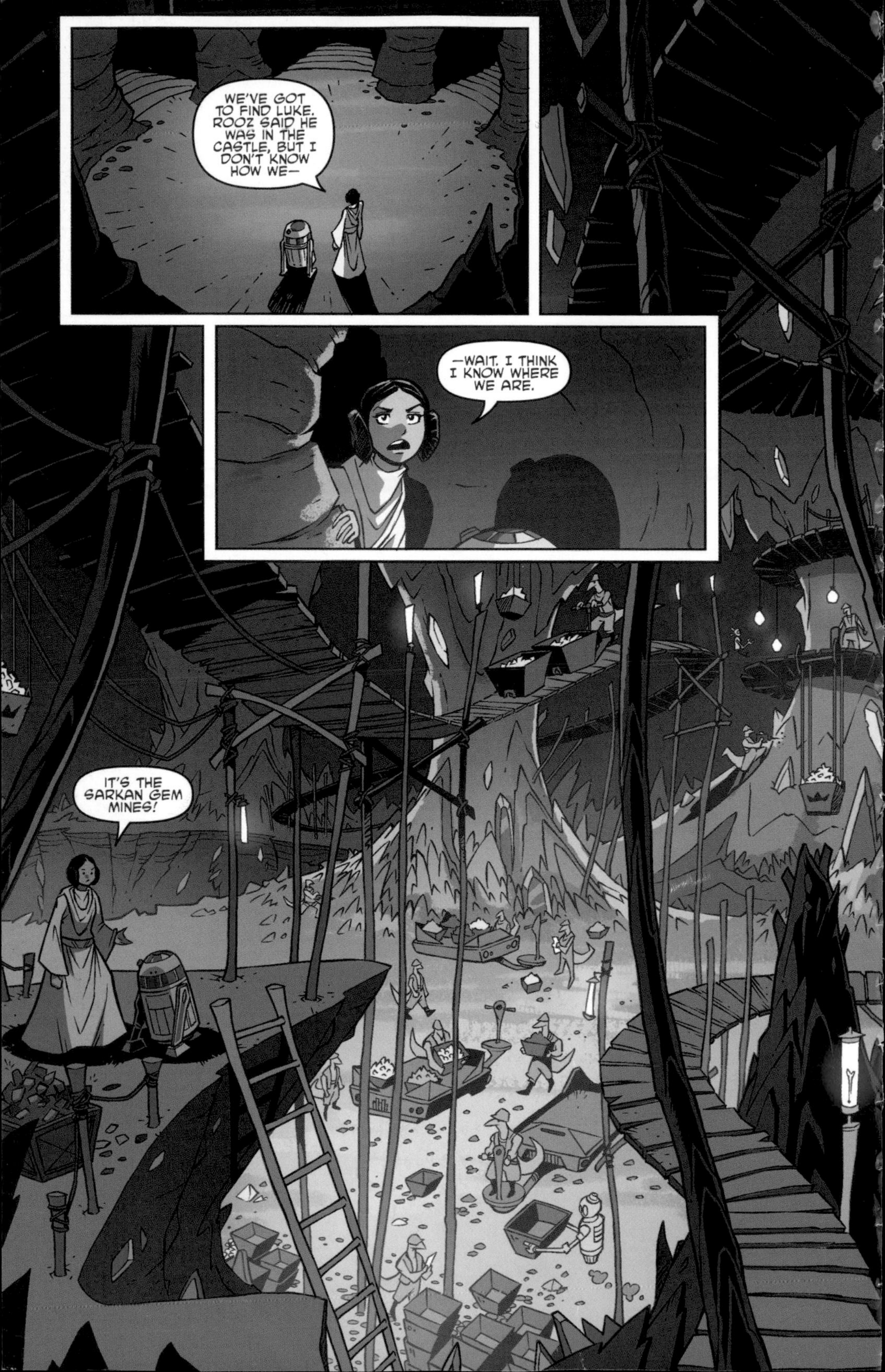
WE'VE GOT TO FIND LUKE. ROOZ SAID HE WAS IN THE CASTLE, BUT I DON'T KNOW HOW WE—
—WAIT. I THINK I KNOW WHERE WE ARE.
IT'S THE SARKAN GEM MINES!

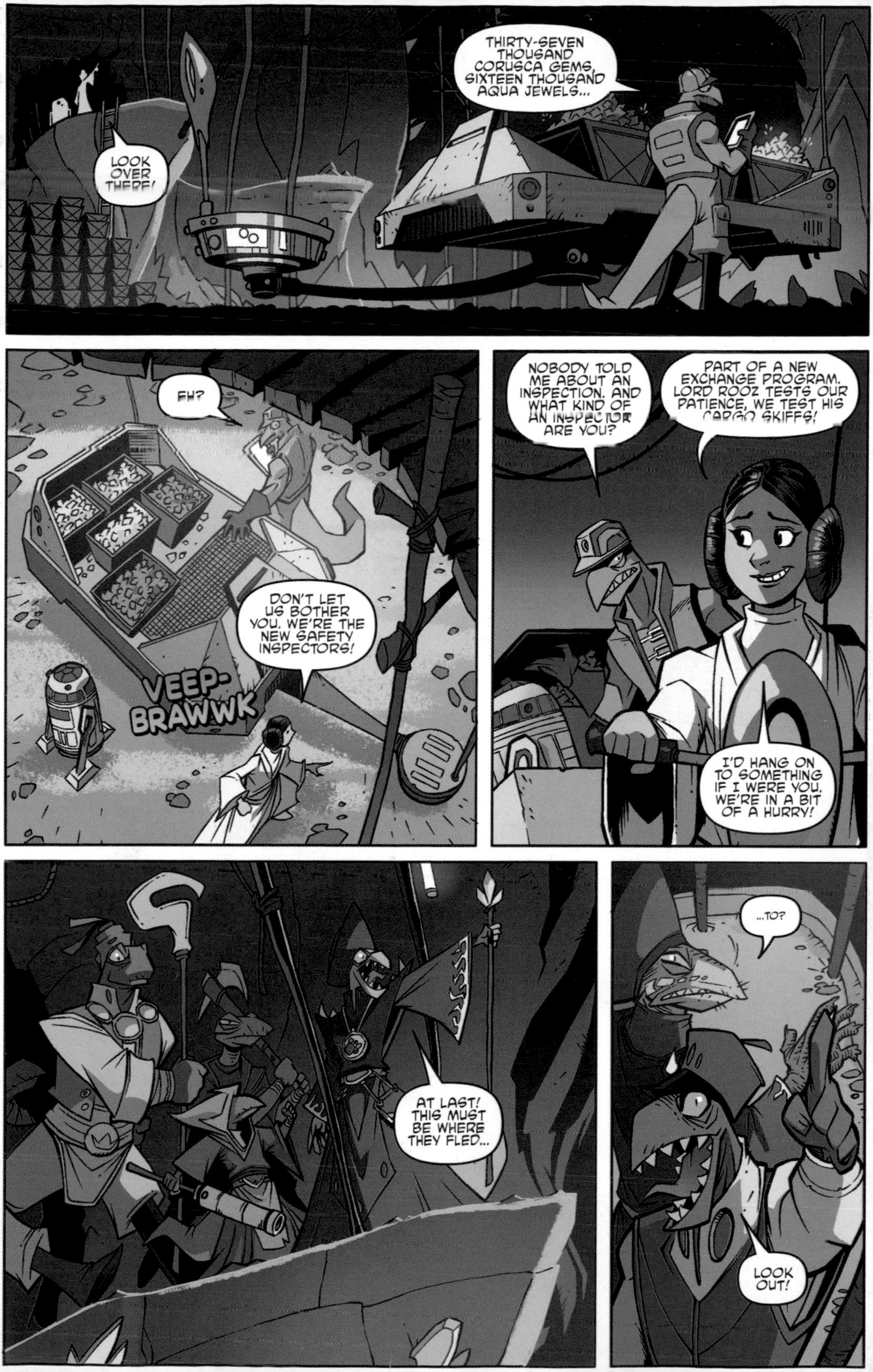
THIRTY-SEVEN THOUSAND CORUSCA GEMS, SIXTEEN THOUSAND AQUA JEWELS...
LOOK OVER THERE!
EH?
DON'T LET US BOTHER YOU. WE'RE THE NEW SAFETY INSPECTORS!
VEEP-BRAWWK
NOBODY TOLD ME ABOUT AN INSPECTION. AND WHAT KIND OF AN INSPECTOR ARE YOU?
PART OF A NEW EXCHANGE PROGRAM. LORD ROOZ TESTS OUR PATIENCE, WE TEST HIS CARGO SKIFFS!
I'D HANG ON TO SOMETHING IF I WERE YOU. WE'RE IN A BIT OF A HURRY!
AT LAST! THIS MUST BE WHERE THEY FLED...
...TO?
LOOK OUT!

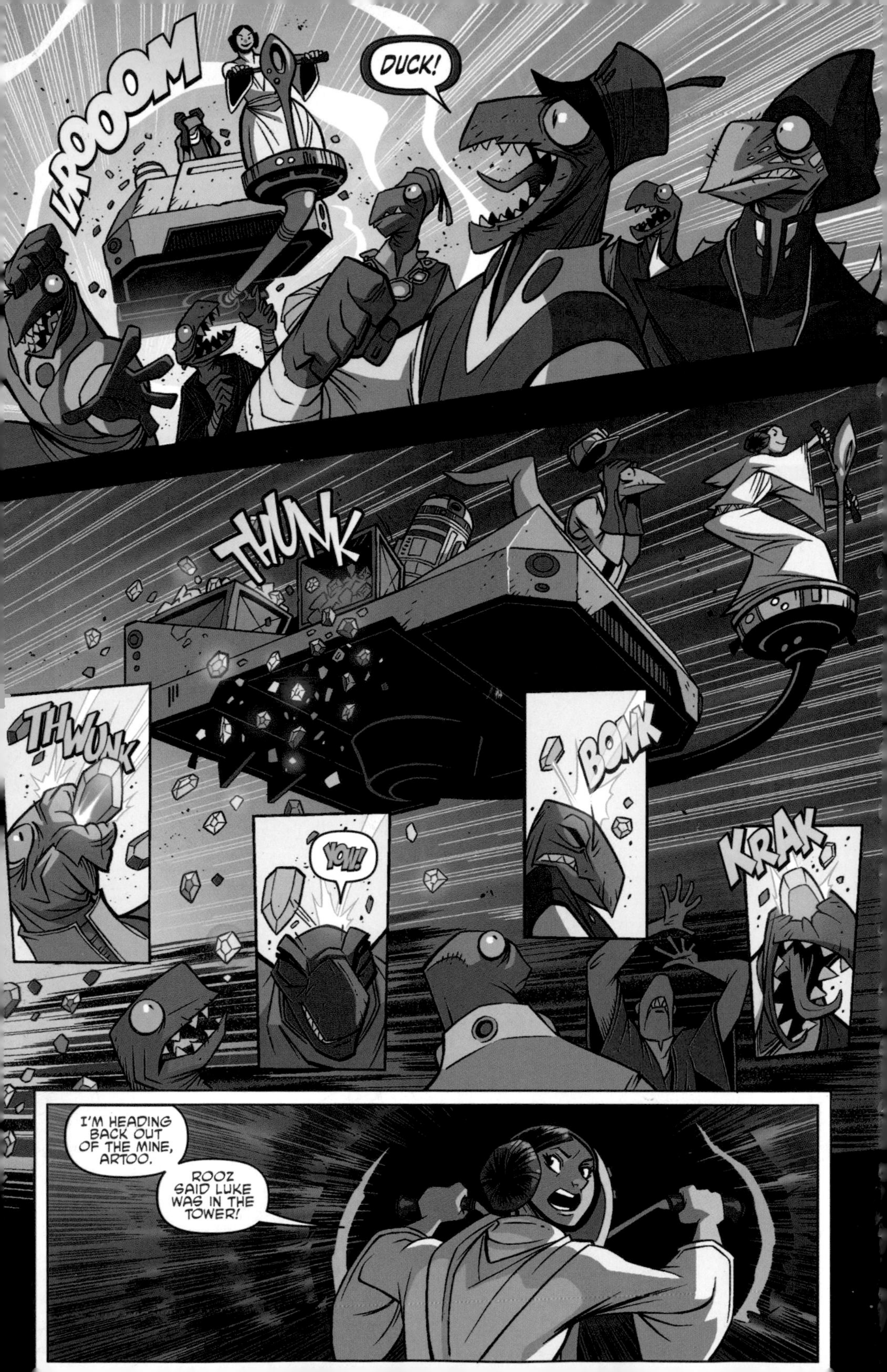
VROOOM
DUCK!
THUNK
THWUNK
YOW!
BONK
KRAK
I'M HEADING BACK OUT OF THE MINE, ARTOO.
ROOZ SAID LUKE WAS IN THE TOWER!

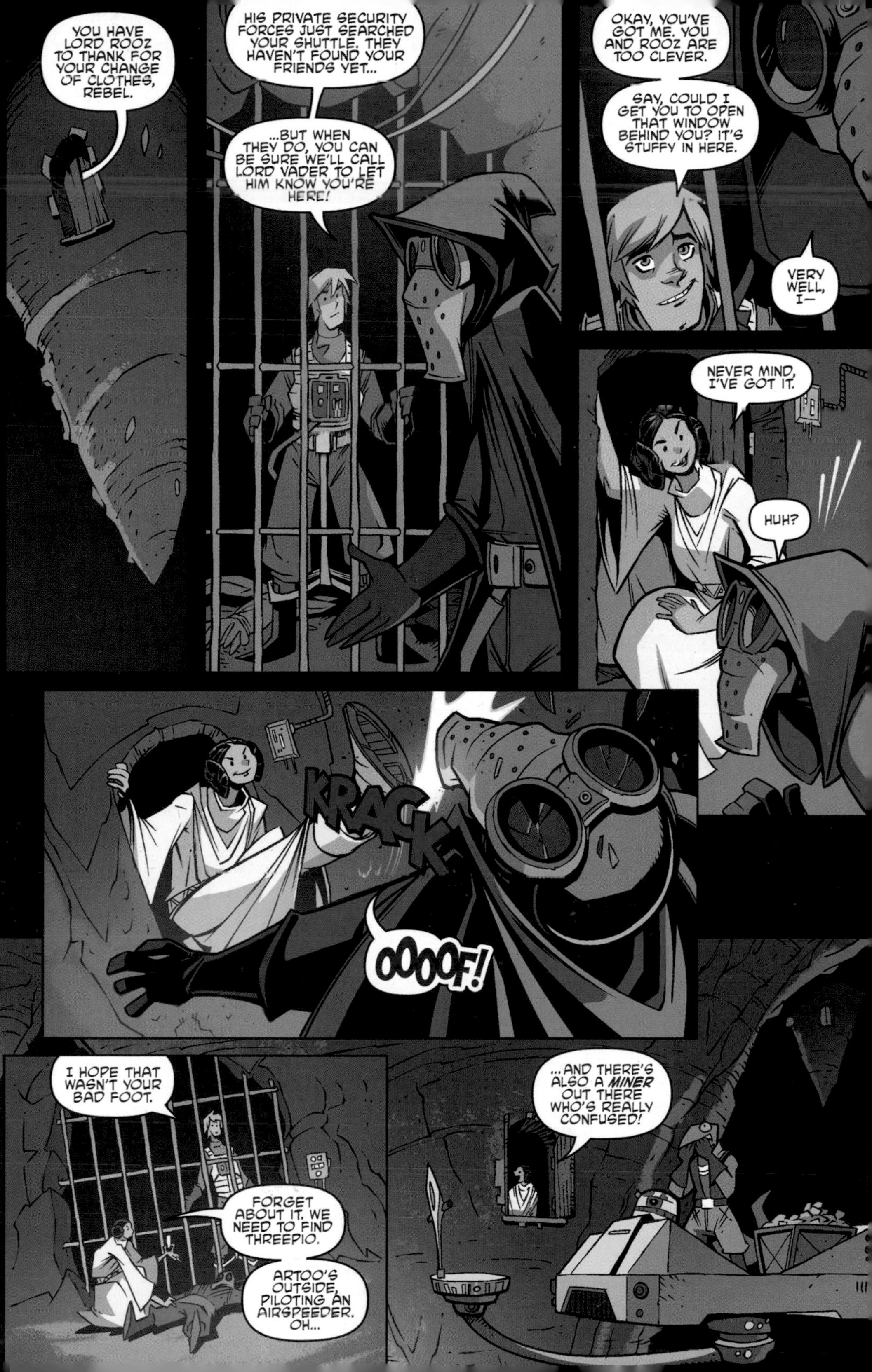
YOU HAVE LORD ROOZ TO THANK FOR YOUR CHANGE OF CLOTHES, REBEL.
HIS PRIVATE SECURITY FORCES JUST SEARCHED YOUR SHUTTLE. THEY HAVEN'T FOUND YOUR FRIENDS YET...
...BUT WHEN THEY DO, YOU CAN BE SURE WE'LL CALL LORD VADER TO LET HIM KNOW YOU'RE HERE!
OKAY, YOU'VE GOT ME. YOU AND ROOZ ARE TOO CLEVER.
SAY, COULD I GET YOU TO OPEN THAT WINDOW BEHIND YOU? IT'S STUFFY IN HERE.
VERY WELL, I—
NEVER MIND, I'VE GOT IT.
HUH?
KRACK
OOOOF!
I HOPE THAT WASN'T YOUR BAD FOOT.
FORGET ABOUT IT. WE NEED TO FIND THREEPIO.
ARTOO'S OUTSIDE, PILOTING AN AIRSPEEDER. OH...
...AND THERE'S ALSO A *MINER* OUT THERE WHO'S REALLY CONFUSED!

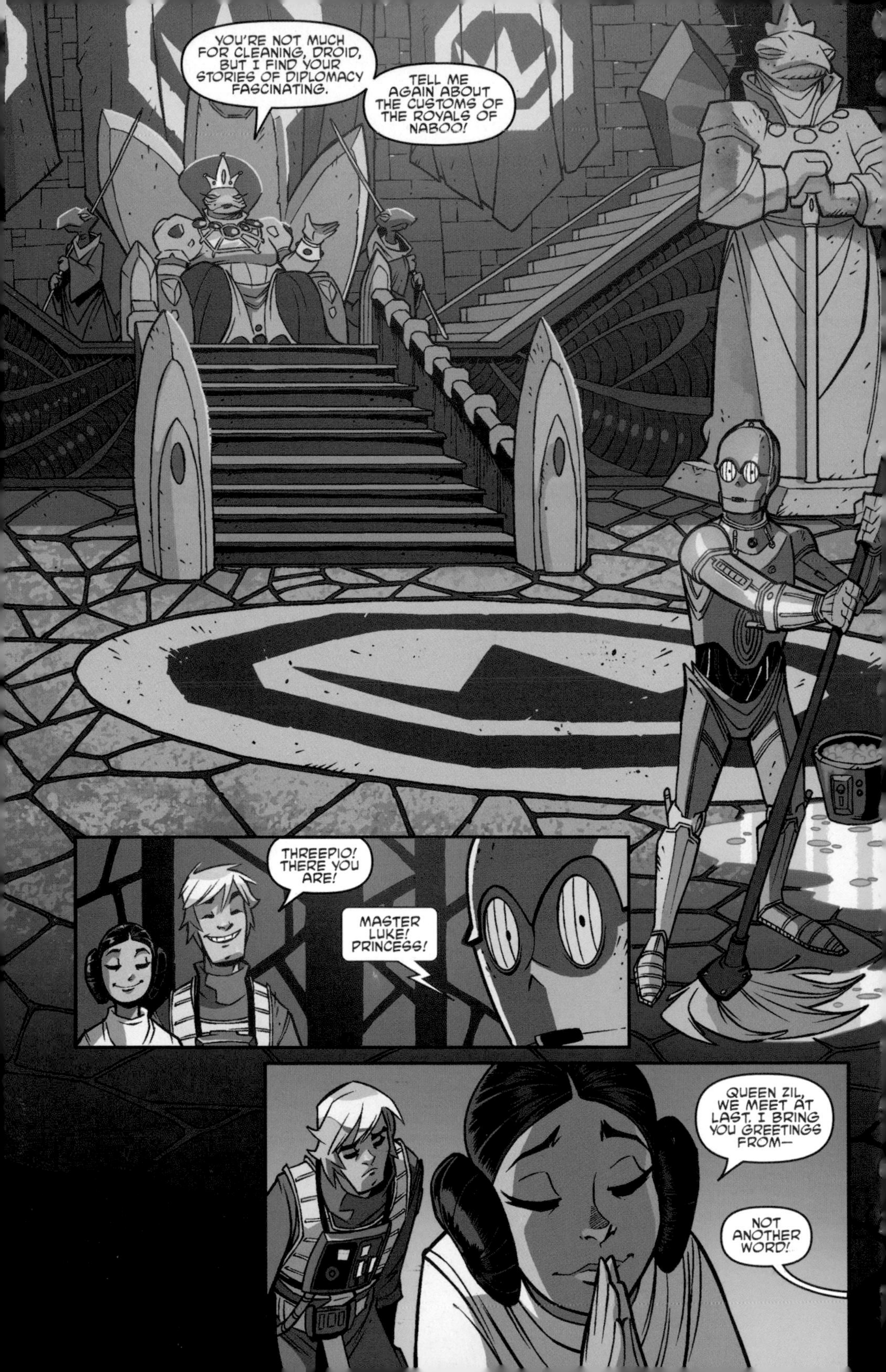
YOU'RE NOT MUCH FOR CLEANING, DROID, BUT I FIND YOUR STORIES OF DIPLOMACY FASCINATING.
TELL ME AGAIN ABOUT THE CUSTOMS OF THE ROYALS OF NABOO!
THREEPIO! THERE YOU ARE!
MASTER LUKE! PRINCESS!
QUEEN ZIL, WE MEET AT LAST. I BRING YOU GREETINGS FROM—
NOT ANOTHER WORD!

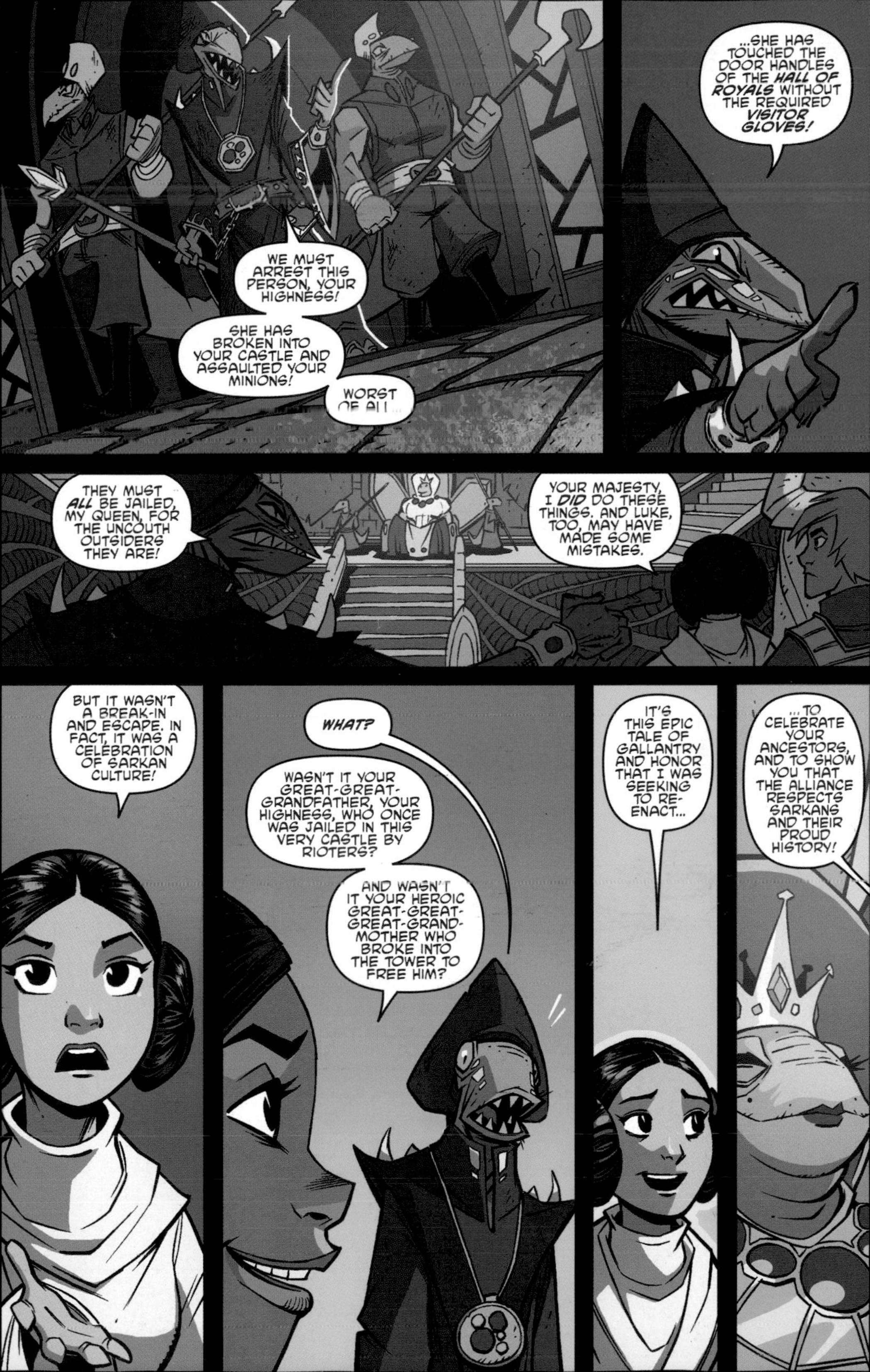
WE MUST ARREST THIS PERSON, YOUR HIGHNESS!
SHE HAS BROKEN INTO YOUR CASTLE AND ASSAULTED YOUR MINIONS!
WORST OF ALL...
...SHE HAS TOUCHED THE DOOR HANDLES OF THE HALL OF ROYALS WITHOUT THE REQUIRED VISITOR GLOVES!
THEY MUST ALL BE JAILED, MY QUEEN, FOR THE UNCOUTH OUTSIDERS THEY ARE!
YOUR MAJESTY, I DID DO THESE THINGS. AND LUKE, TOO, MAY HAVE MADE SOME MISTAKES.
BUT IT WASN'T A BREAK-IN AND ESCAPE. IN FACT, IT WAS A CELEBRATION OF SARKAN CULTURE!
WHAT?
WASN'T IT YOUR GREAT-GREAT-GRANDFATHER, YOUR HIGHNESS, WHO ONCE WAS JAILED IN THIS VERY CASTLE BY RIOTERS?
AND WASN'T IT YOUR HEROIC GREAT-GREAT-GREAT-GRAND-MOTHER WHO BROKE INTO THE TOWER TO FREE HIM?
IT'S THIS EPIC TALE OF GALLANTRY AND HONOR THAT I WAS SEEKING TO RE-ENACT...
...TO CELEBRATE YOUR ANCESTORS, AND TO SHOW YOU THAT THE ALLIANCE RESPECTS SARKANS AND THEIR PROUD HISTORY!

WHAT NONSENSE! YOU EXPECT US TO BELIEVE THIS CLAPTRAP?

ARE YOU CALLING MY ANCESTORS' EXPLOITS NONSENSE, LORD ROOZ?

I—OF COURSE NOT, YOUR HIGHNESS. SHE IS JUST AFRAID I WILL—

WILL WHAT? CALL THE EMPIRE? THAT WAS WHAT YOU WERE PLANNING ON DOING, WASN'T IT?

THE EMPIRE? I NEVER AUTHORIZED THAT.

I AGREED TO LET THE ALLIANCE VISIT. TURNING THEM OVER TO THE EMPIRE WOULD BE TERRIBLE MANNERS!

PARDON ME, YOUR HIGHNESS...

...BUT IN MY BRIEF TIME CLEANING, I HAVE THOUGHT A LOT ABOUT FLOORS.

IT REMINDED ME THAT IN YOUR CULTURE, NO SARKAN MAY STAND ON THE ROYAL SEAL. IT IS THE GREATEST OFFENSE OF ALL!

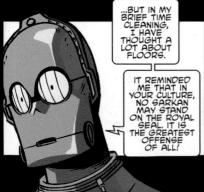

WHAT OF IT?

LOOK DOWN.

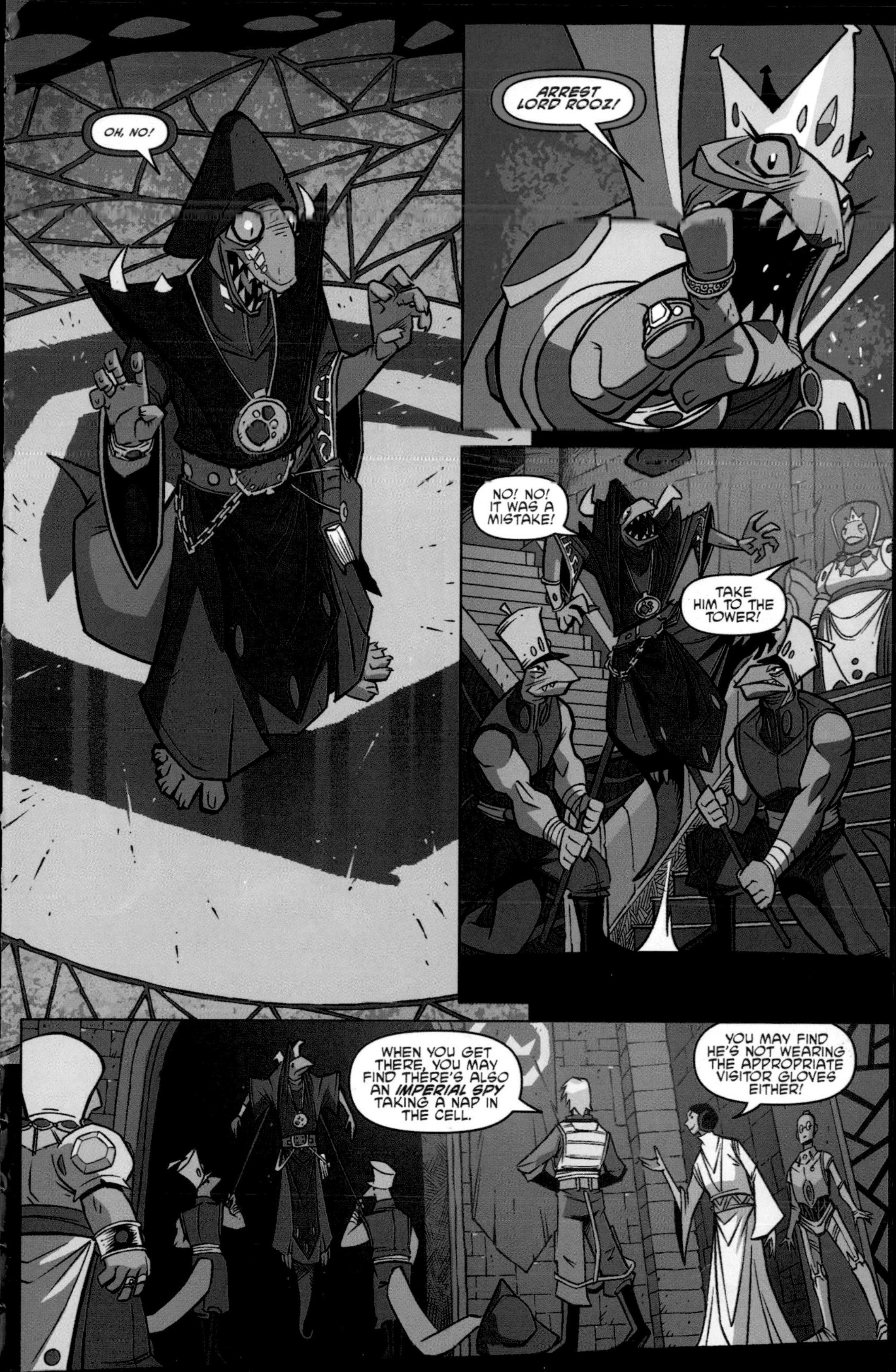
OH, NO!
ARREST LORD ROOZ!
NO! NO! IT WAS A MISTAKE!
TAKE HIM TO THE TOWER!
WHEN YOU GET THERE, YOU MAY FIND THERE'S ALSO AN IMPERIAL SPY TAKING A NAP IN THE CELL.
YOU MAY FIND HE'S NOT WEARING THE APPROPRIATE VISITOR GLOVES EITHER!

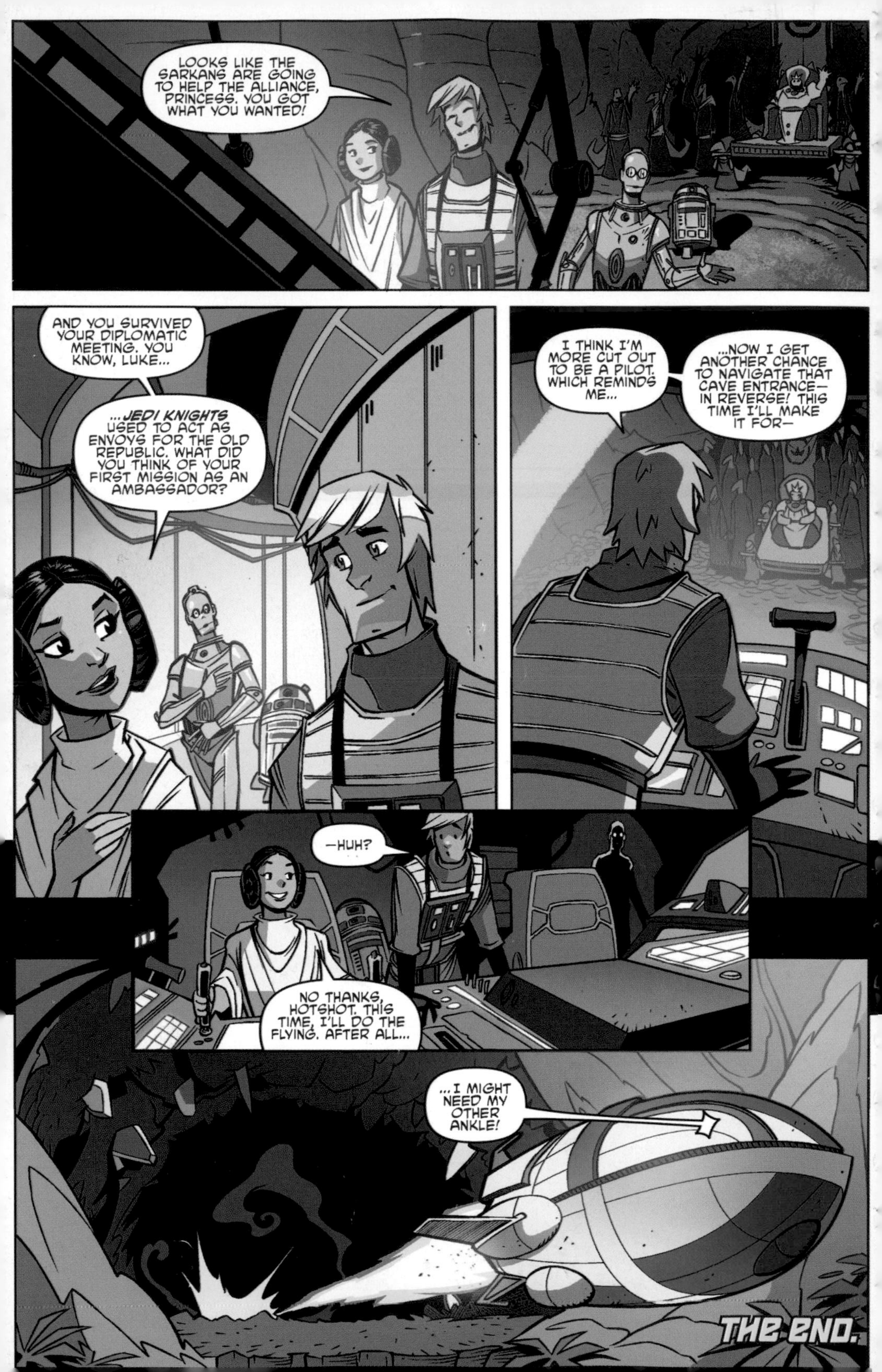
LOOKS LIKE THE SARKANS ARE GOING TO HELP THE ALLIANCE, PRINCESS. YOU GOT WHAT YOU WANTED!
AND YOU SURVIVED YOUR DIPLOMATIC MEETING. YOU KNOW, LUKE...
...JEDI KNIGHTS USED TO ACT AS ENVOYS FOR THE OLD REPUBLIC. WHAT DID YOU THINK OF YOUR FIRST MISSION AS AN AMBASSADOR?
I THINK I'M MORE CUT OUT TO BE A PILOT. WHICH REMINDS ME...
...NOW I GET ANOTHER CHANCE TO NAVIGATE THAT CAVE ENTRANCE— IN REVERSE! THIS TIME I'LL MAKE IT FOR—
—HUH?
NO THANKS, HOTSHOT. THIS TIME, I'LL DO THE FLYING. AFTER ALL...
...I MIGHT NEED MY OTHER ANKLE!
THE END.

STAR WARS
ADVENTURES

Chewie's Day Off

WRITER
JOHN BARBER

ARTIST
MAURICET

COLORIST
CHARLIE KIRCHOFF

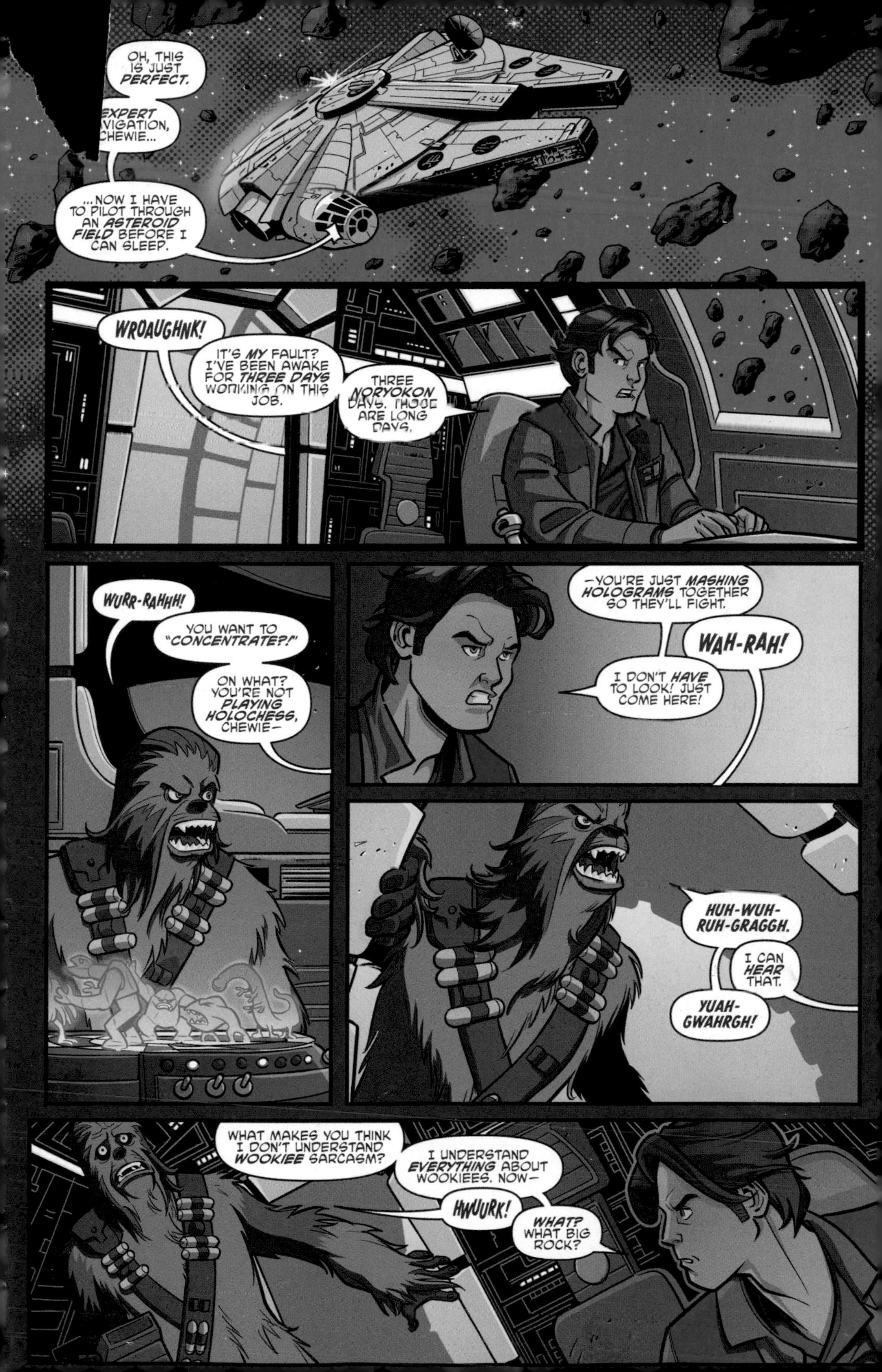
OH, THIS IS JUST PERFECT.
EXPERT AVIGATION, CHEWIE...
...NOW I HAVE TO PILOT THROUGH AN ASTEROID FIELD BEFORE I CAN SLEEP.
WROAUGHNK!
IT'S MY FAULT? I'VE BEEN AWAKE FOR THREE DAYS WORKING ON THIS JOB.
THREE NORYOKON DAYS. THOSE ARE LONG DAYS.
WURR-RAHHH!
YOU WANT TO "CONCENTRATE?!"
ON WHAT? YOU'RE NOT PLAYING HOLOCHESS, CHEWIE—
—YOU'RE JUST MASHING HOLOGRAMS TOGETHER SO THEY'LL FIGHT.
WAH-RAH!
I DON'T HAVE TO LOOK! JUST COME HERE!
HUH-WUH-RUH-GRAGGH.
I CAN HEAR THAT.
YUAH-GWAHRGH!
WHAT MAKES YOU THINK I DON'T UNDERSTAND WOOKIEE SARCASM?
I UNDERSTAND EVERYTHING ABOUT WOOKIEES. NOW—
HWUURK!
WHAT? WHAT BIG ROCK?

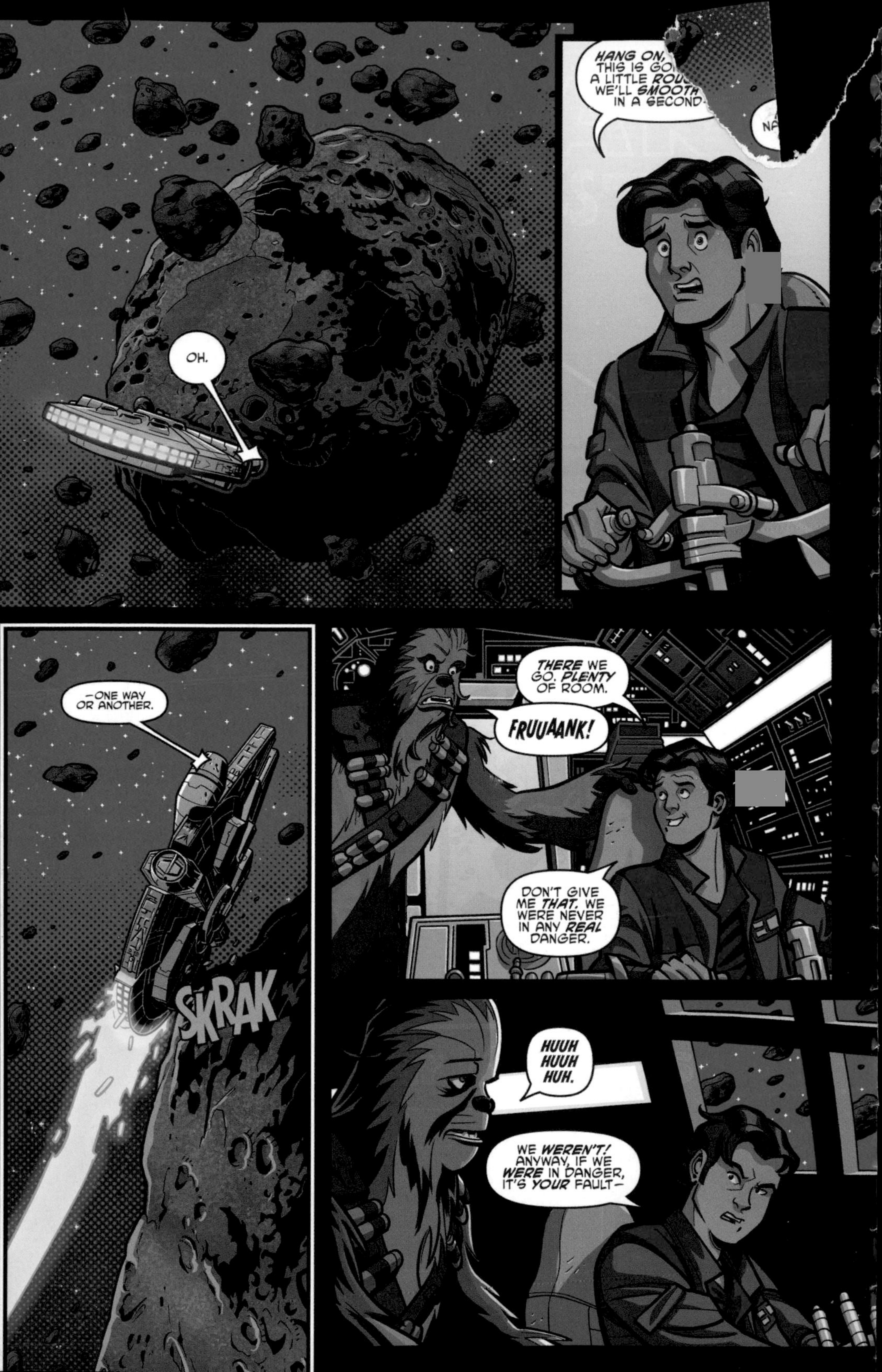

OH.
HANG ON, THIS IS GO A LITTLE ROU WE'LL SMOOTH IN A SECOND-
—ONE WAY OR ANOTHER.
SKRAK
THERE WE GO. PLENTY OF ROOM.
FRUUAANK!
DON'T GIVE ME THAT. WE WERE NEVER IN ANY REAL DANGER.
HUUH HUUH HUH.
WE WEREN'T! ANYWAY, IF WE WERE IN DANGER, IT'S YOUR FAULT—

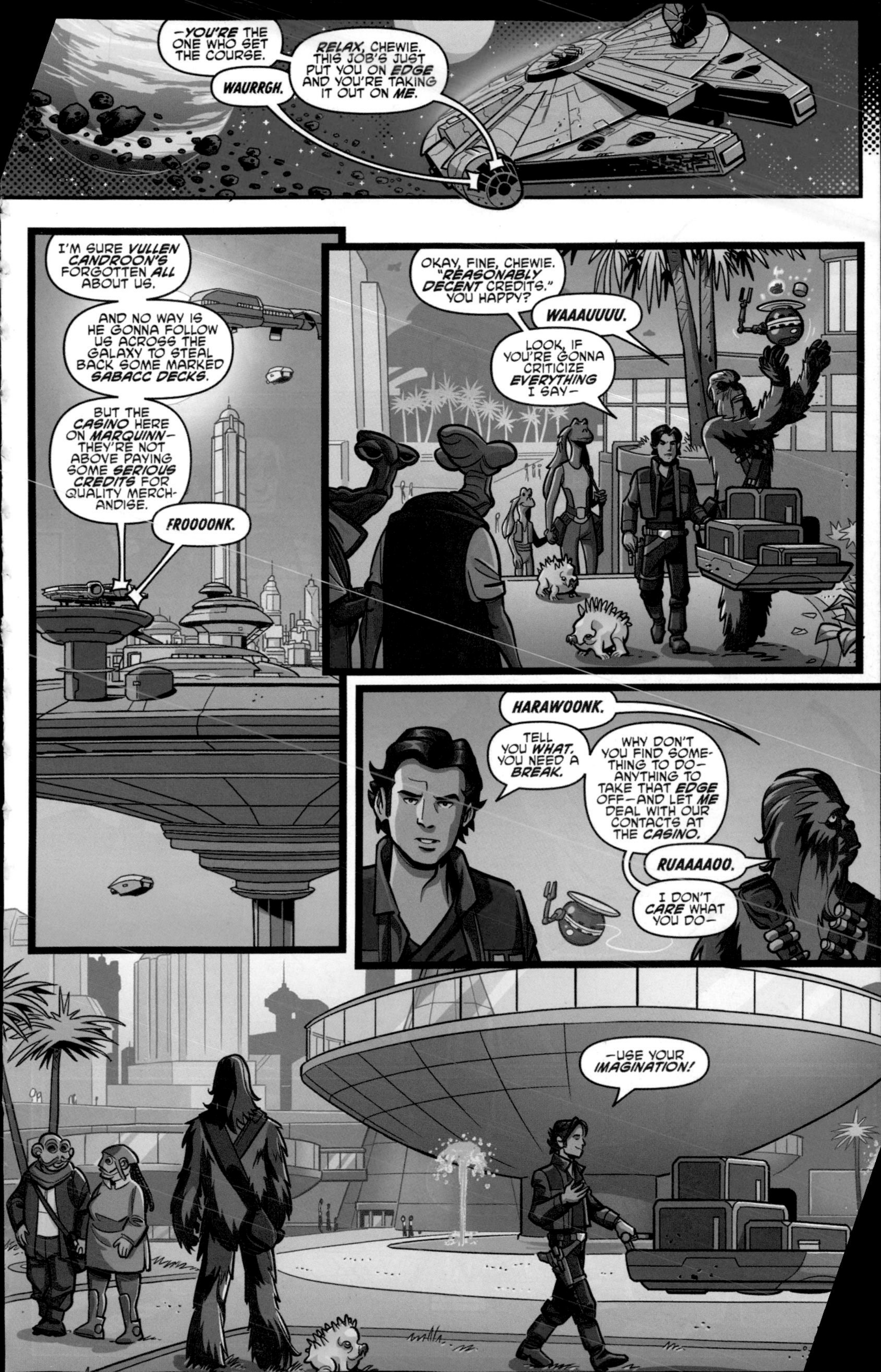

—YOU'RE THE ONE WHO SET THE COURSE.
WAURRGH.
RELAX, CHEWIE. THIS JOB'S JUST PUT YOU ON EDGE AND YOU'RE TAKING IT OUT ON ME.
I'M SURE VULLEN CANDROON'S FORGOTTEN ALL ABOUT US.
AND NO WAY IS HE GONNA FOLLOW US ACROSS THE GALAXY TO STEAL BACK SOME MARKED SABACC DECKS.
BUT THE CASINO HERE ON MARQUINN— THEY'RE NOT ABOVE PAYING SOME SERIOUS CREDITS FOR QUALITY MERCH-ANDISE.
FROOOONK.
OKAY, FINE, CHEWIE. "REASONABLY DECENT CREDITS." YOU HAPPY?
WAAAUUUU.
LOOK, IF YOU'RE GONNA CRITICIZE EVERYTHING I SAY—
HARAWOONK.
TELL YOU WHAT. YOU NEED A BREAK.
WHY DON'T YOU FIND SOME-THING TO DO— ANYTHING TO TAKE THAT EDGE OFF—AND LET ME DEAL WITH OUR CONTACTS AT THE CASINO.
RUAAAAOO.
I DON'T CARE WHAT YOU DO—
—USE YOUR IMAGINATION!

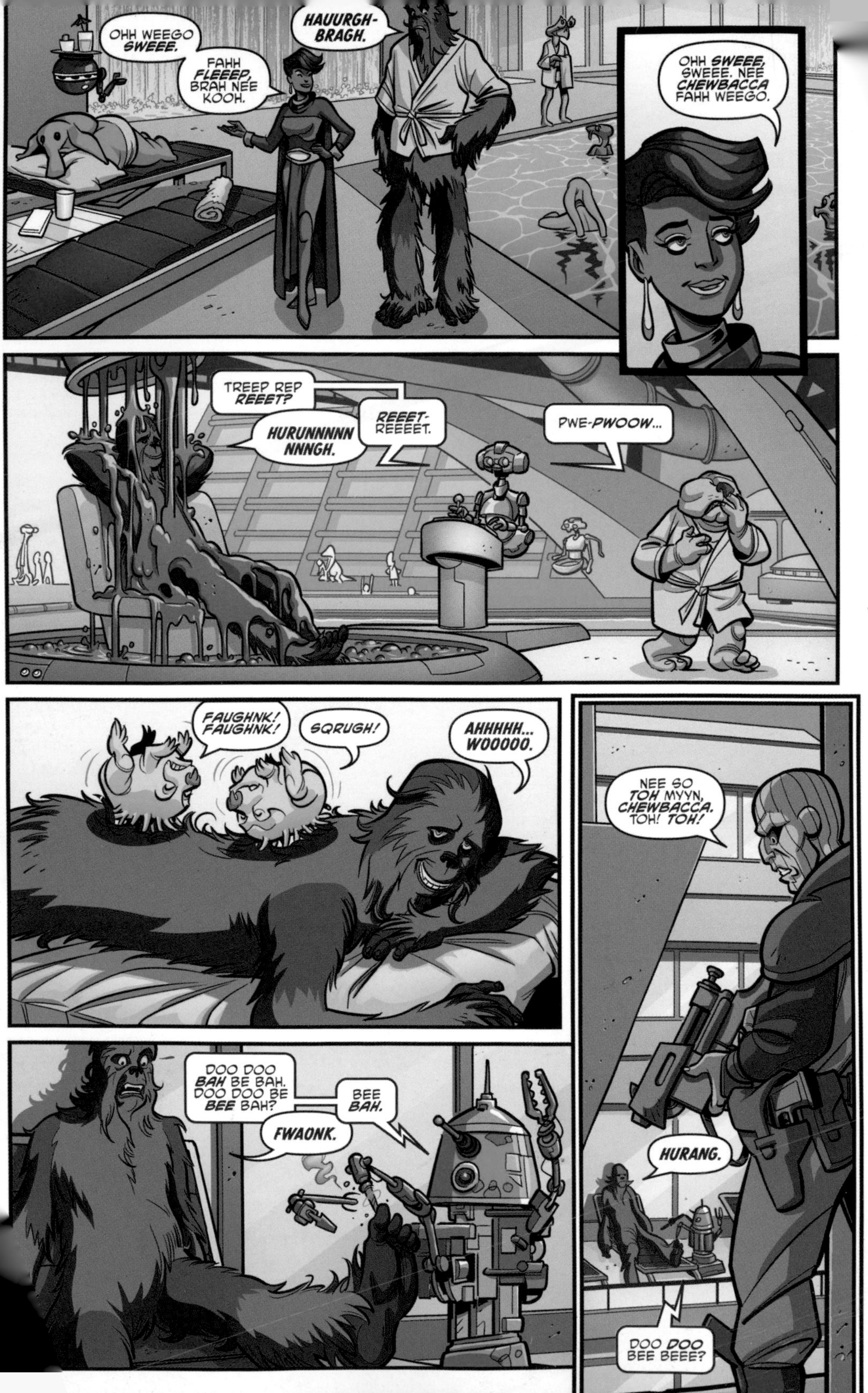
OHH WEEGO SWEEE.
FAHH FLEEEP, BRAH NEE KOOH.
HAUURGH-BRAGH.
OHH SWEEE, SWEEE. NEE CHEWBACCA FAHH WEEGO.
TREEP REP REEET?
HURUNNNNN NNNGH.
REEET-REEEET.
PWE-PWOOW...
FAUGHNK! FAUGHNK!
SQRUGH!
AHHHHH... WOOOOO.
NEE SO TOH MYYN, CHEWBACCA. TOH! TOH!
DOO DOO BAH BE BAH. DOO DOO BE BEE BAH?
BEE BAH.
FWAONK.
HURANG.
DOO DOO BEE BEEE?

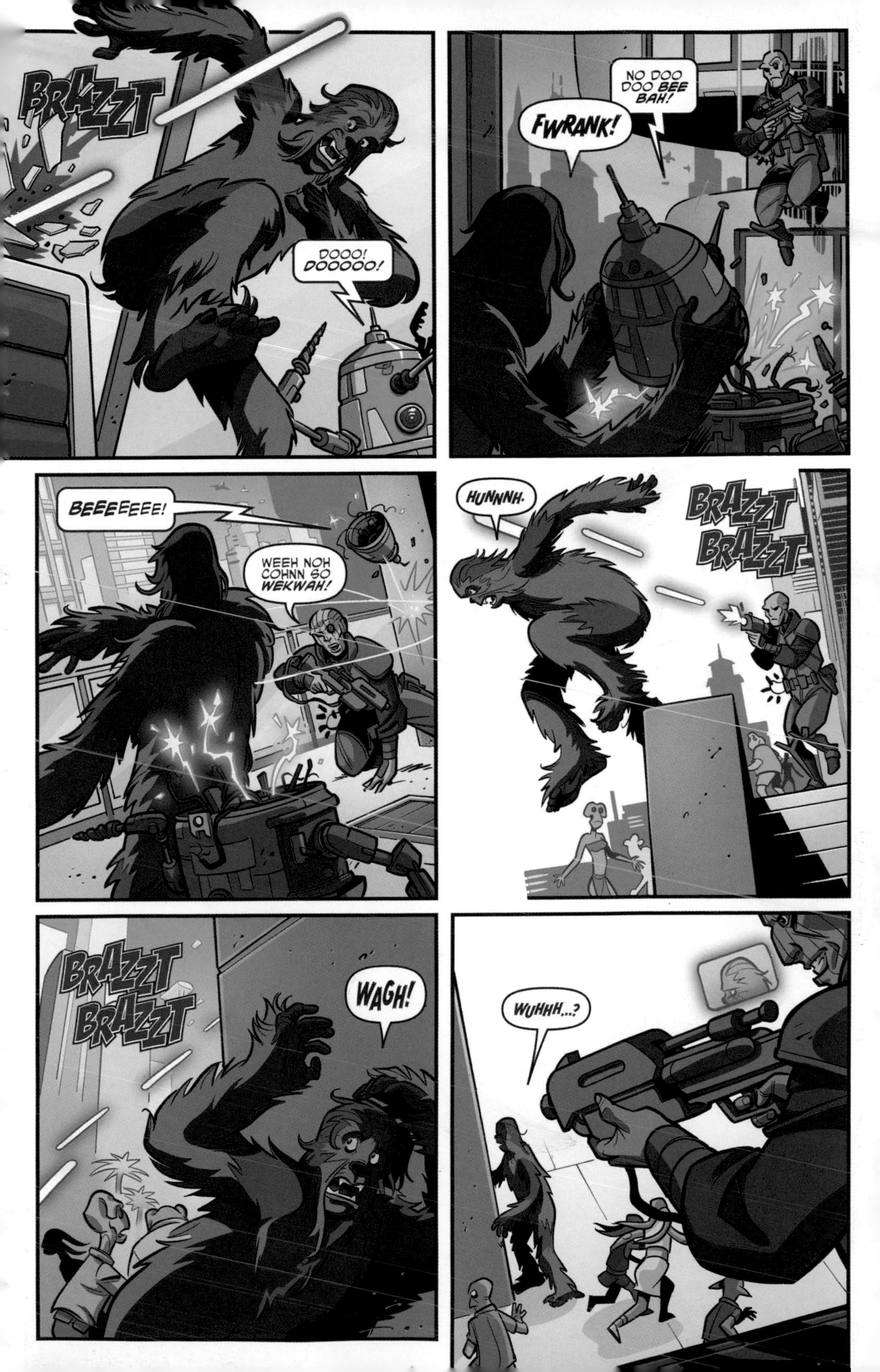
BRAZZT
DOOO! DOOOOOO!
NO DOO DOO BEE BAH!
FWRANK!
BEEEEEEE!
WEEH NOH COHNN SO WEKWAH!
HUNNNH.
BRAZZT BRAZZT
BRAZZT BRAZZT
WAGH!
WUHHH...?

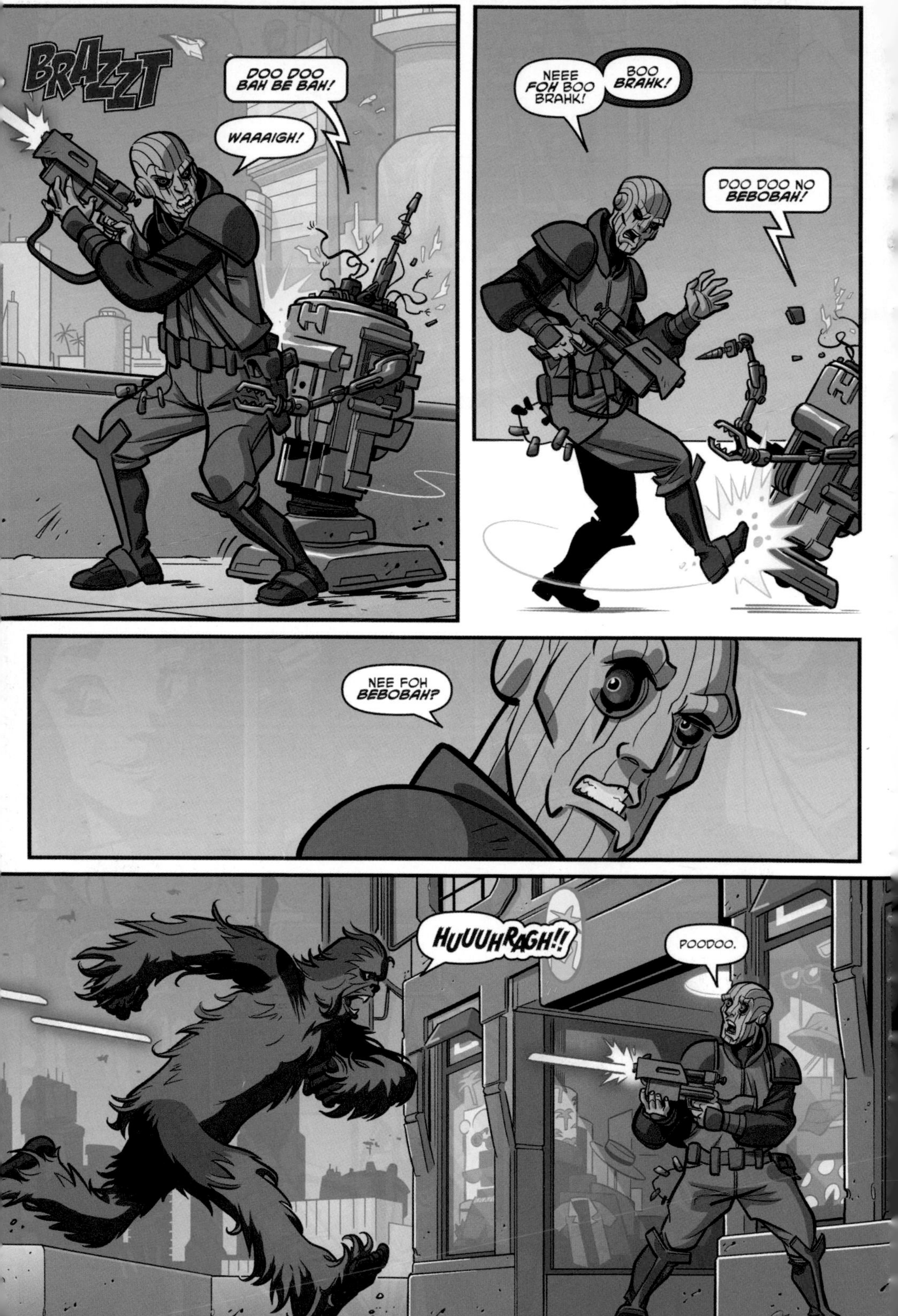
BRAZZT
DOO DOO BAH BE BAH!
WAAAIGH!
NEEE FOH BOO BRAHK!
BOO BRAHK!
DOO DOO NO BEBOBAH!
NEE FOH BEBOBAH?
HUUUHRAGH!!
POODOO.

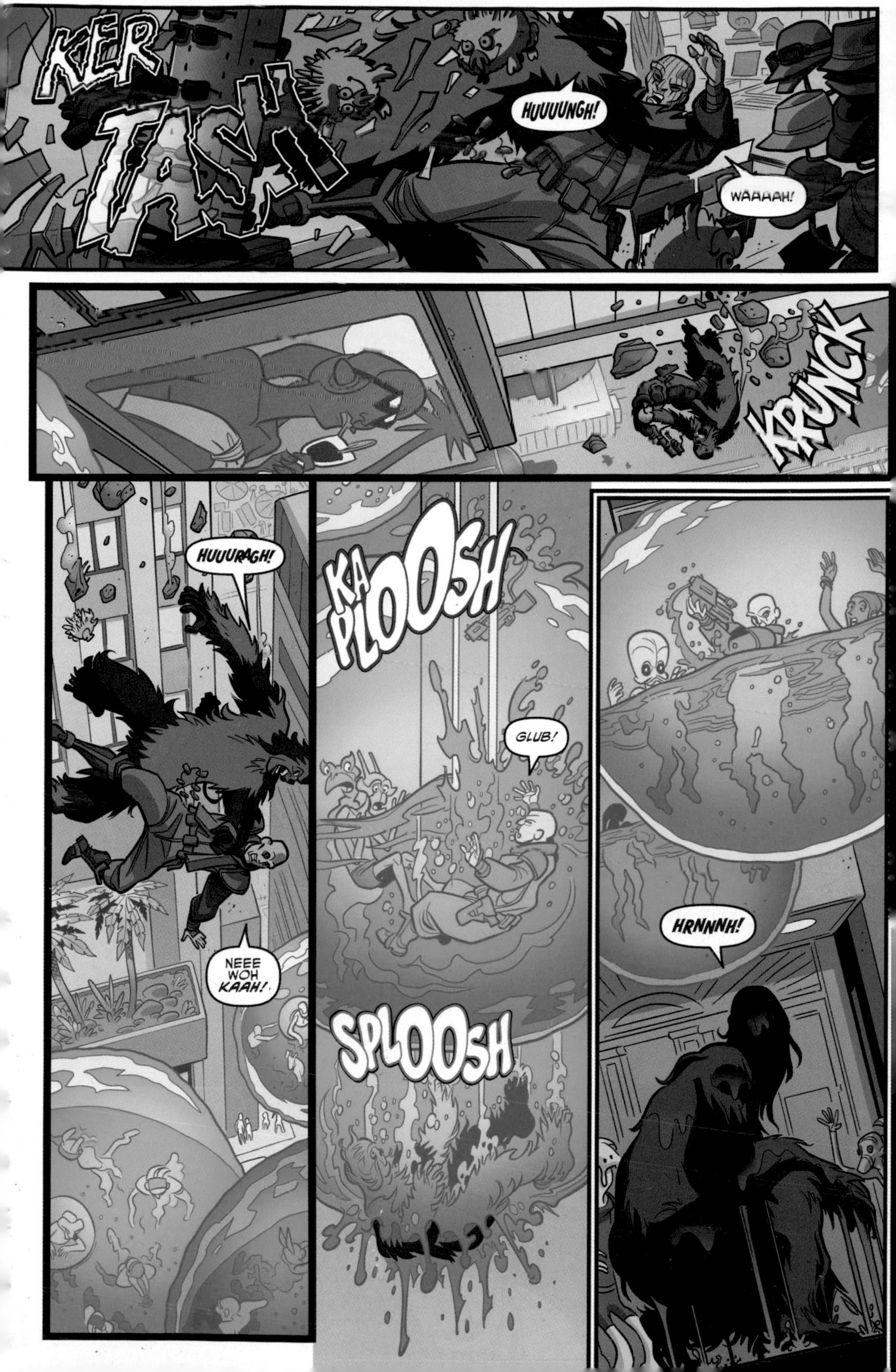
KER TASH
HUUUUNGH!
WAAAAH!
KRUNCK
HUUURAGH!
NEEE WOH KAAH!
KA PLOOSH
GLUB!
SPLOOSH
HRNNNH!

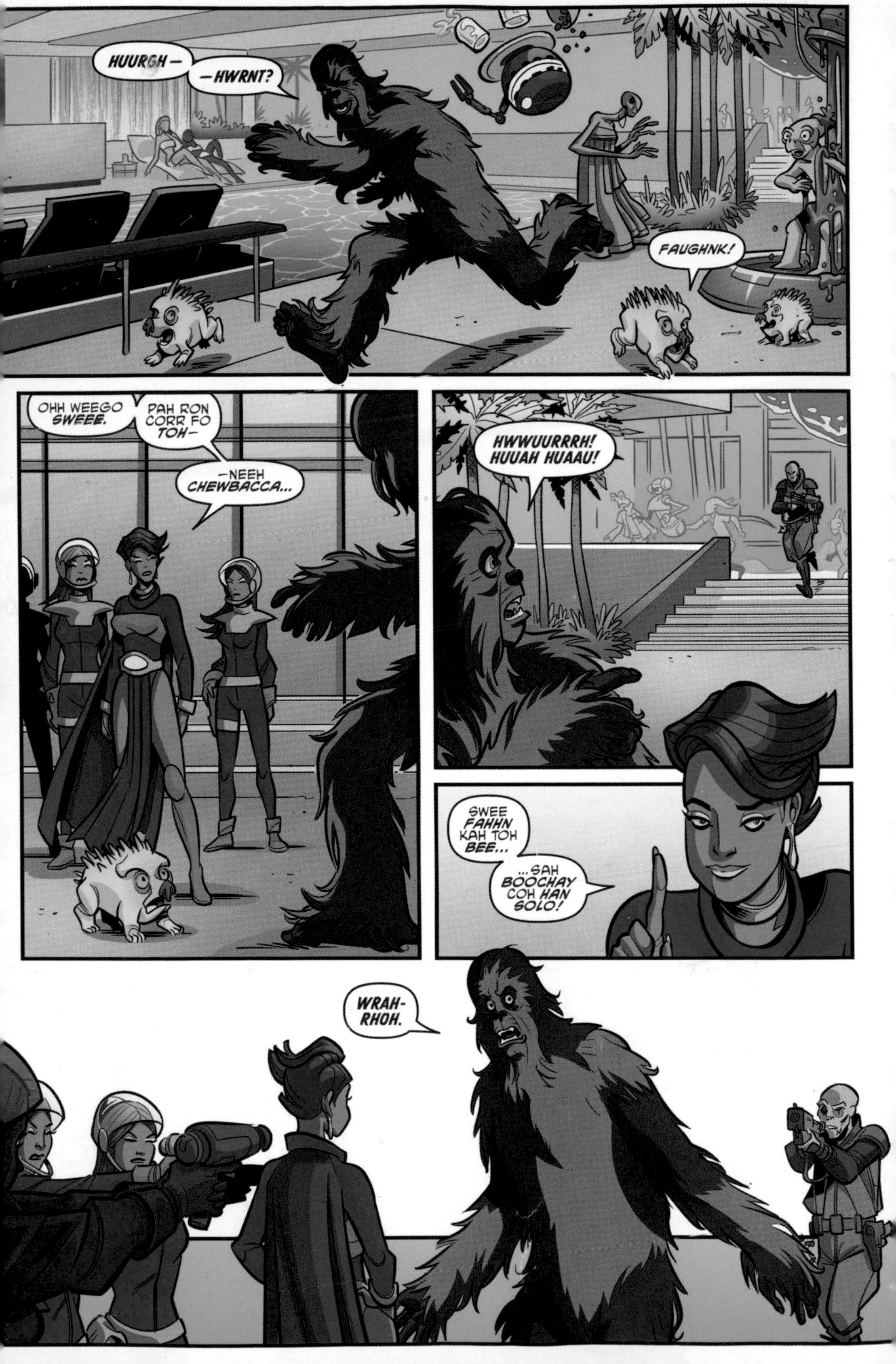
HUURGH—
—HWRNT?
FAUGHNK!
OHH WEEGO SWEEE.
PAH RON CORR FO TOH—
—NEEH CHEWBACCA...
HWWUURRRH! HUUAH HUAAU!
SWEE FAHHN KAH TOH BEE...
...SAH BOOCHAY COH HAN SOLO!
WRAH-RHOH.

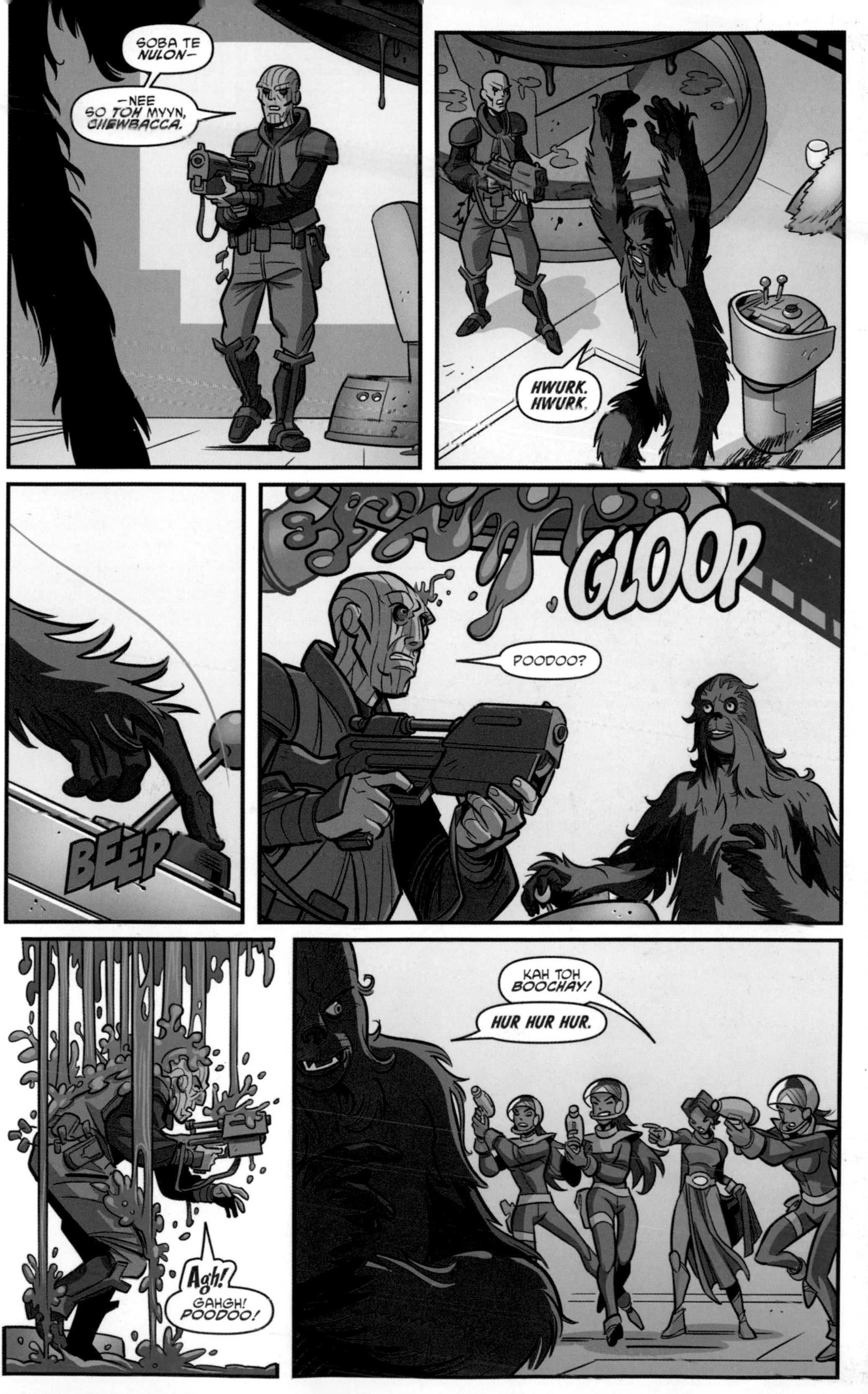
SOBA TE NULON—
—NEE SO TOH MYYN, CHEWBACCA.
HWURK. HWURK.
BEEP
GLOOP
POODOO?
Agh! GAGHH! POODOO!
KAH TOH BOOCHAY!
HUR HUR HUR.

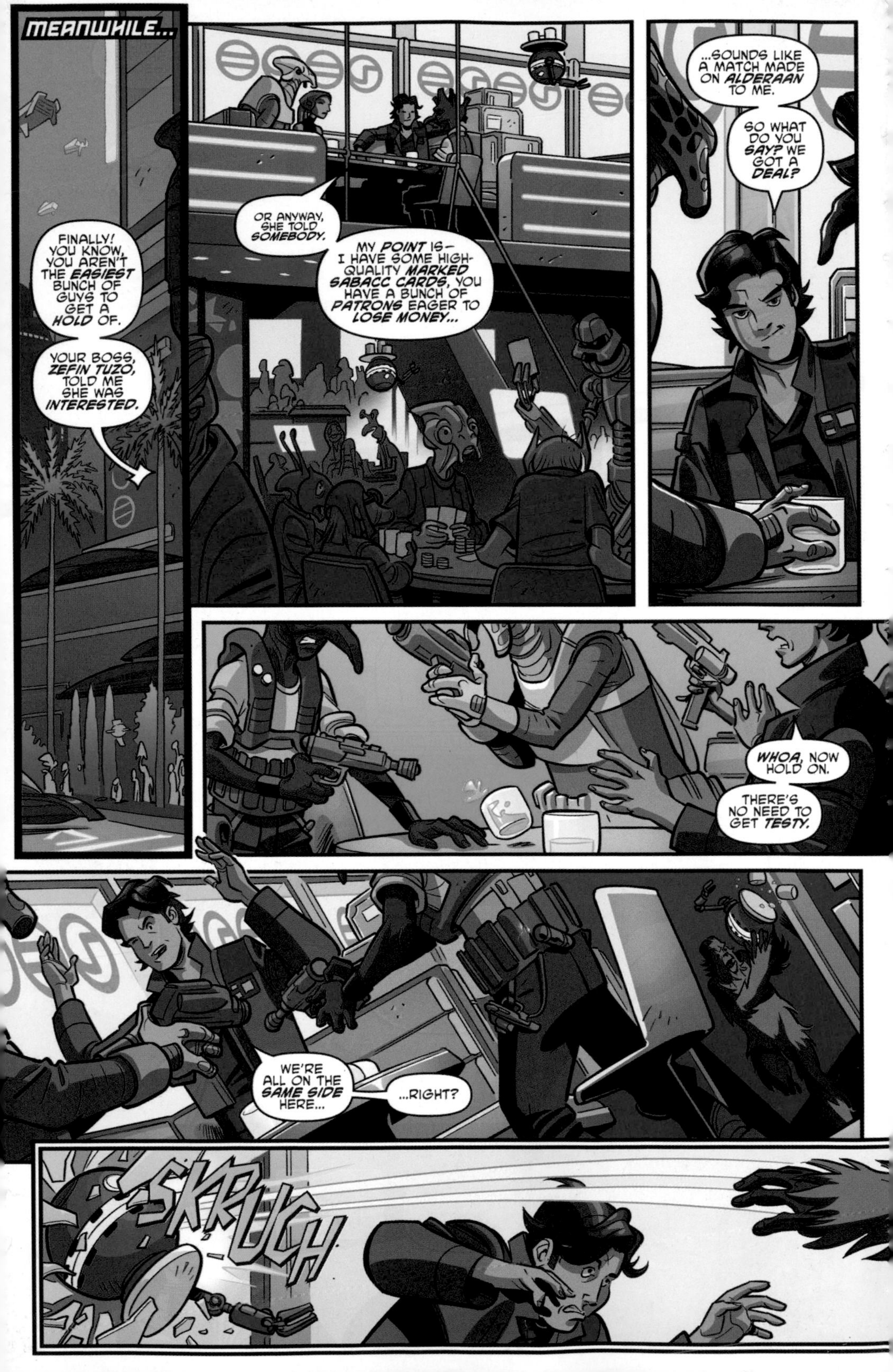
MEANWHILE...
FINALLY! YOU KNOW, YOU AREN'T THE EASIEST BUNCH OF GUYS TO GET A HOLD OF.
YOUR BOSS, ZEFIN TUZO, TOLD ME SHE WAS INTERESTED.
OR ANYWAY, SHE TOLD SOMEBODY.
MY POINT IS— I HAVE SOME HIGH-QUALITY MARKED SABACC CARDS, YOU HAVE A BUNCH OF PATRONS EAGER TO LOSE MONEY...
...SOUNDS LIKE A MATCH MADE ON ALDERAAN TO ME.
SO WHAT DO YOU SAY? WE GOT A DEAL?
WHOA, NOW HOLD ON.
THERE'S NO NEED TO GET TESTY.
WE'RE ALL ON THE SAME SIDE HERE...
...RIGHT?
SKRUCH

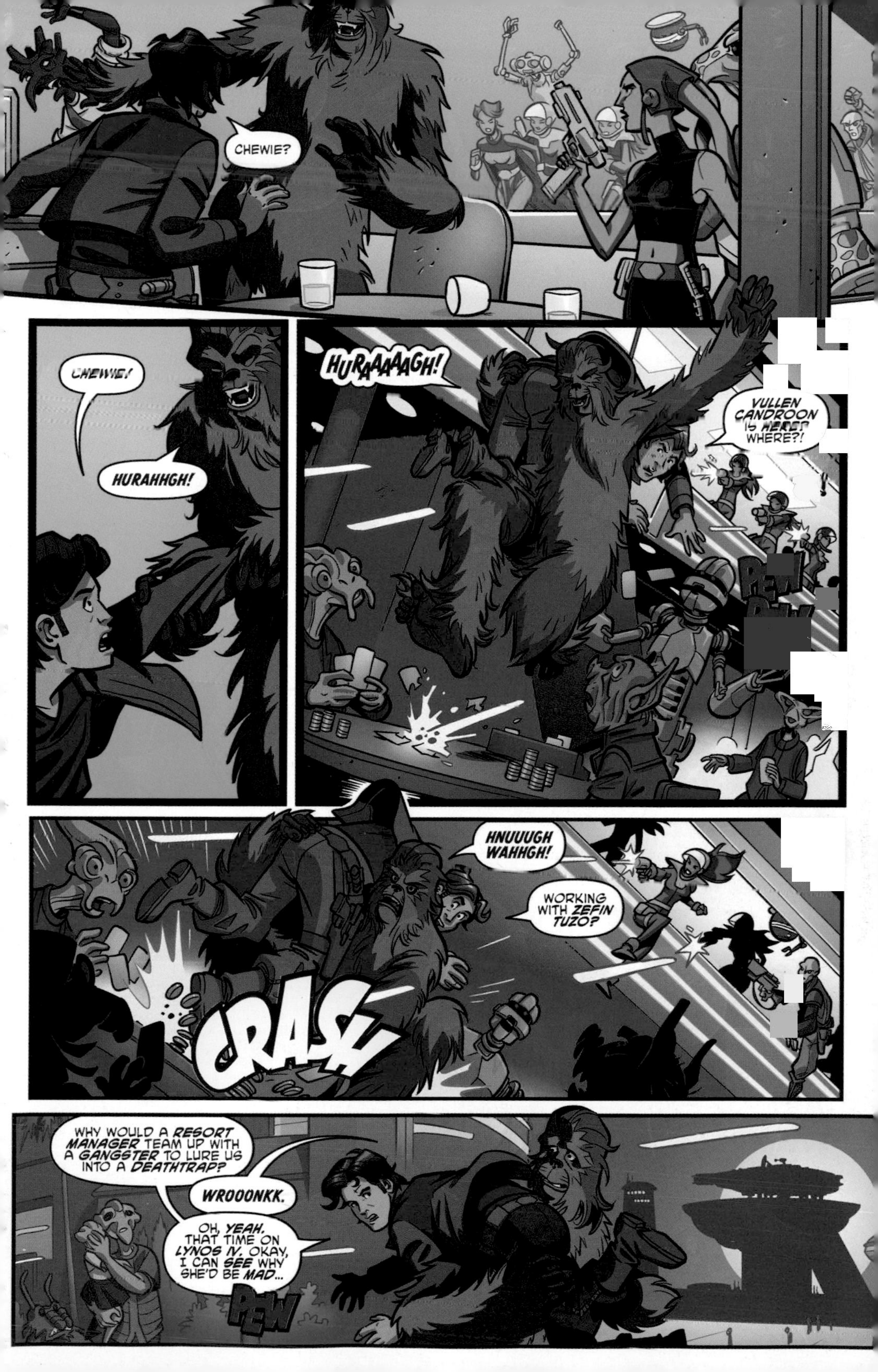
CHEWIE?
CHEWIE!
HURAHHGH!
HURAAAAAGH!
VULLEN CANDROON IS HERE?! WHERE?!
PEW
HNUUUGH WAHHGH!
WORKING WITH ZEFIN TUZO?
CRASH
WHY WOULD A RESORT MANAGER TEAM UP WITH A GANGSTER TO LURE US INTO A DEATHTRAP?
WROOONKK.
OH, YEAH. THAT TIME ON LYNOS IV. OKAY, I CAN SEE WHY SHE'D BE MAD...
PEW

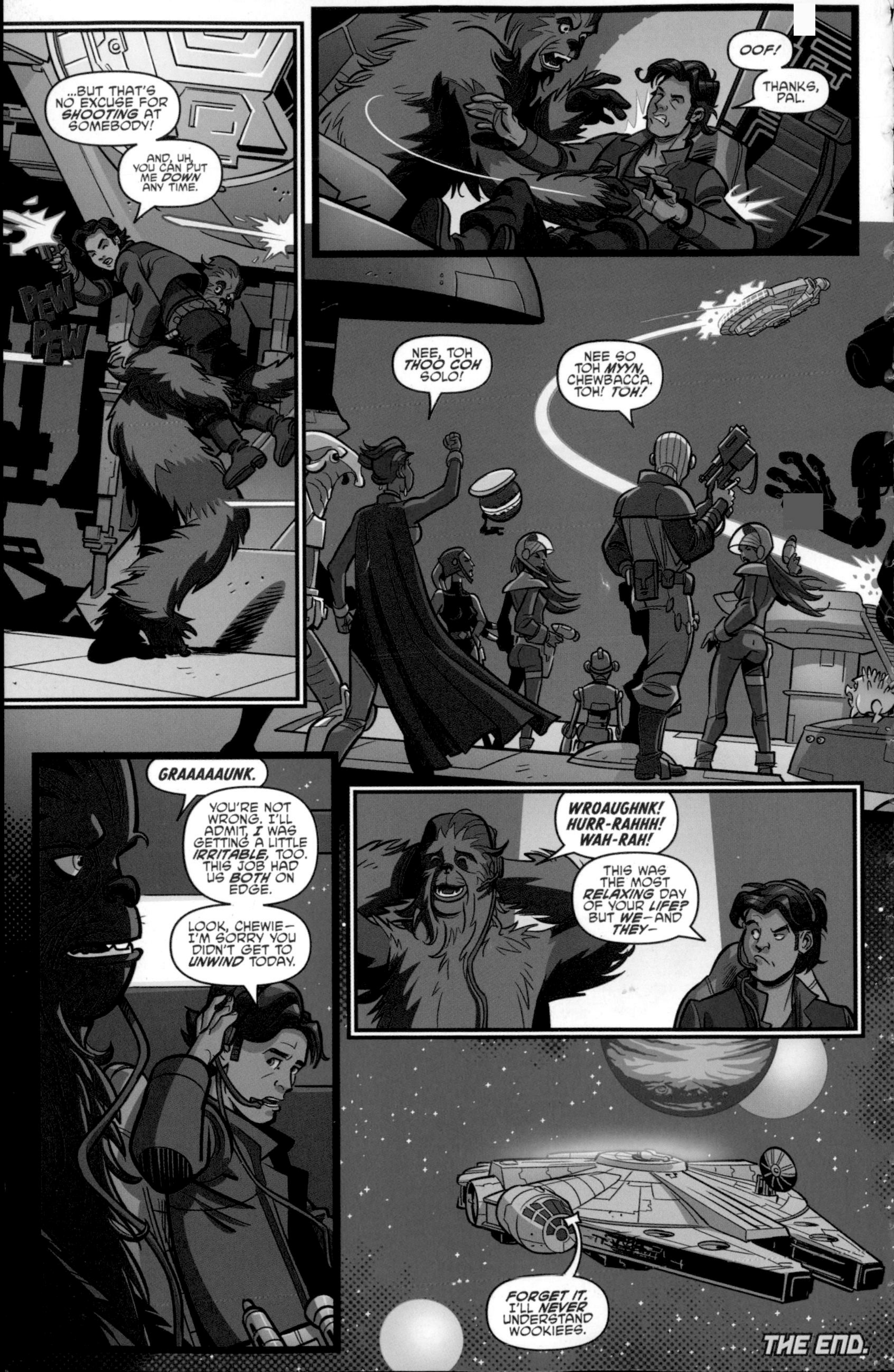
...BUT THAT'S NO EXCUSE FOR *SHOOTING* AT SOMEBODY!
AND, UH, YOU CAN PUT ME *DOWN* ANY TIME.
PEW PEW
OOF!
THANKS, PAL.
NEE, TOH *THOO COH* SOLO!
NEE SO TOH *MYYN*, CHEWBACCA. TOH! *TOH!*
GRAAAAAUNK.
YOU'RE NOT WRONG. I'LL ADMIT, *I* WAS GETTING A LITTLE *IRRITABLE*, TOO. THIS JOB HAD US *BOTH* ON EDGE.
LOOK, CHEWIE-- I'M SORRY YOU DIDN'T GET TO *UNWIND* TODAY.
WROAUGHNK! HURR-RAHHH! WAH-RAH!
THIS WAS THE MOST *RELAXING* DAY OF YOUR *LIFE?* BUT *WE*-- AND *THEY*--
FORGET IT. I'LL *NEVER* UNDERSTAND WOOKIEES.
THE END.

STAR WARS
ADVENTURES

An Unlikely Friendship

WRITER
JAMES GILARTE
ARTIST
MAURICET
COLORIST
CHARLIE KIRCHOFF

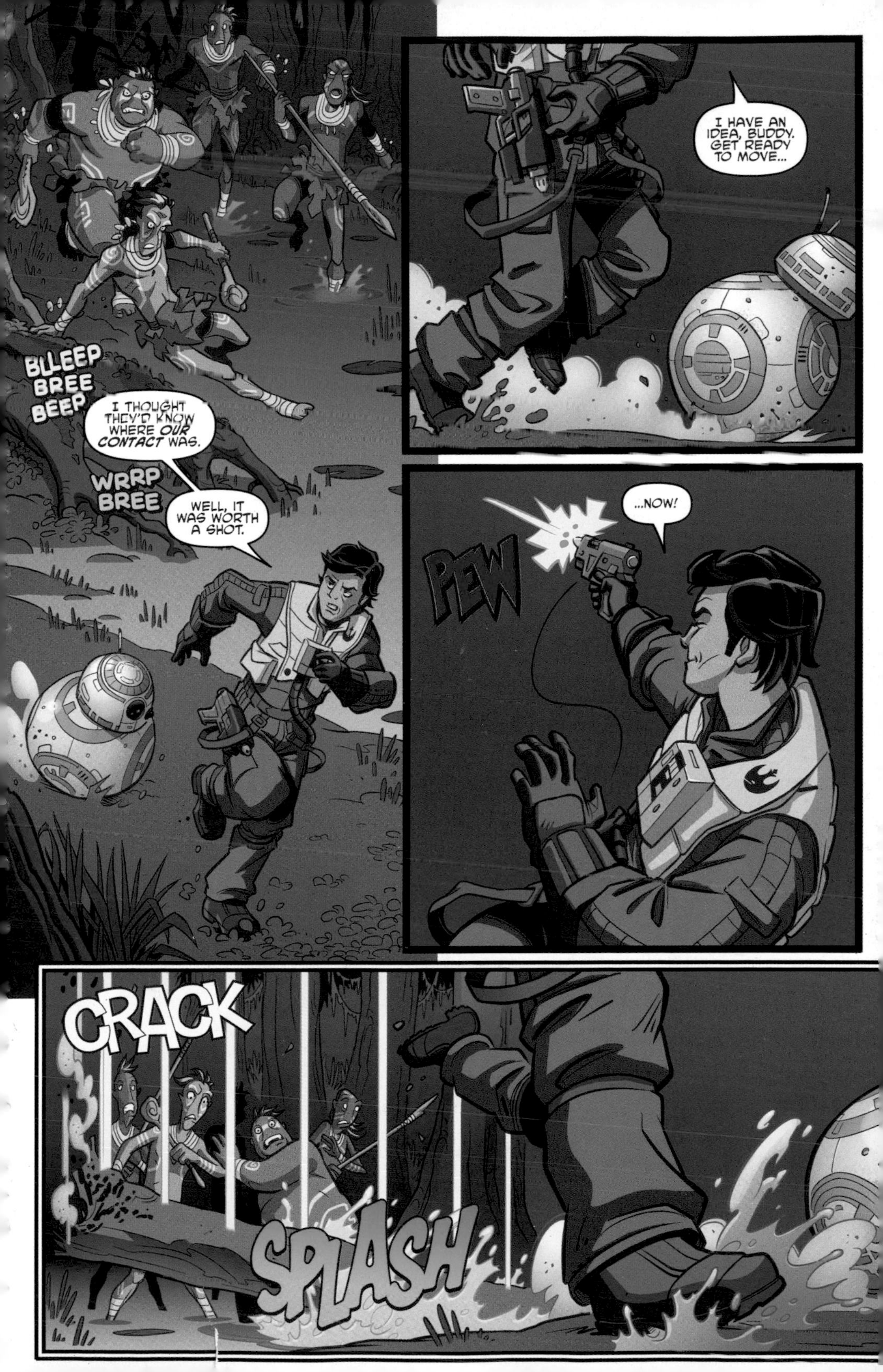
BLLEEP BREE BEEP
I THOUGHT THEY'D KNOW WHERE *OUR CONTACT* WAS.
WRRP BREE
WELL, IT WAS WORTH A SHOT.
I HAVE AN IDEA, BUDDY. GET READY TO MOVE...
PEW
...NOW!
CRACK
SPLASH

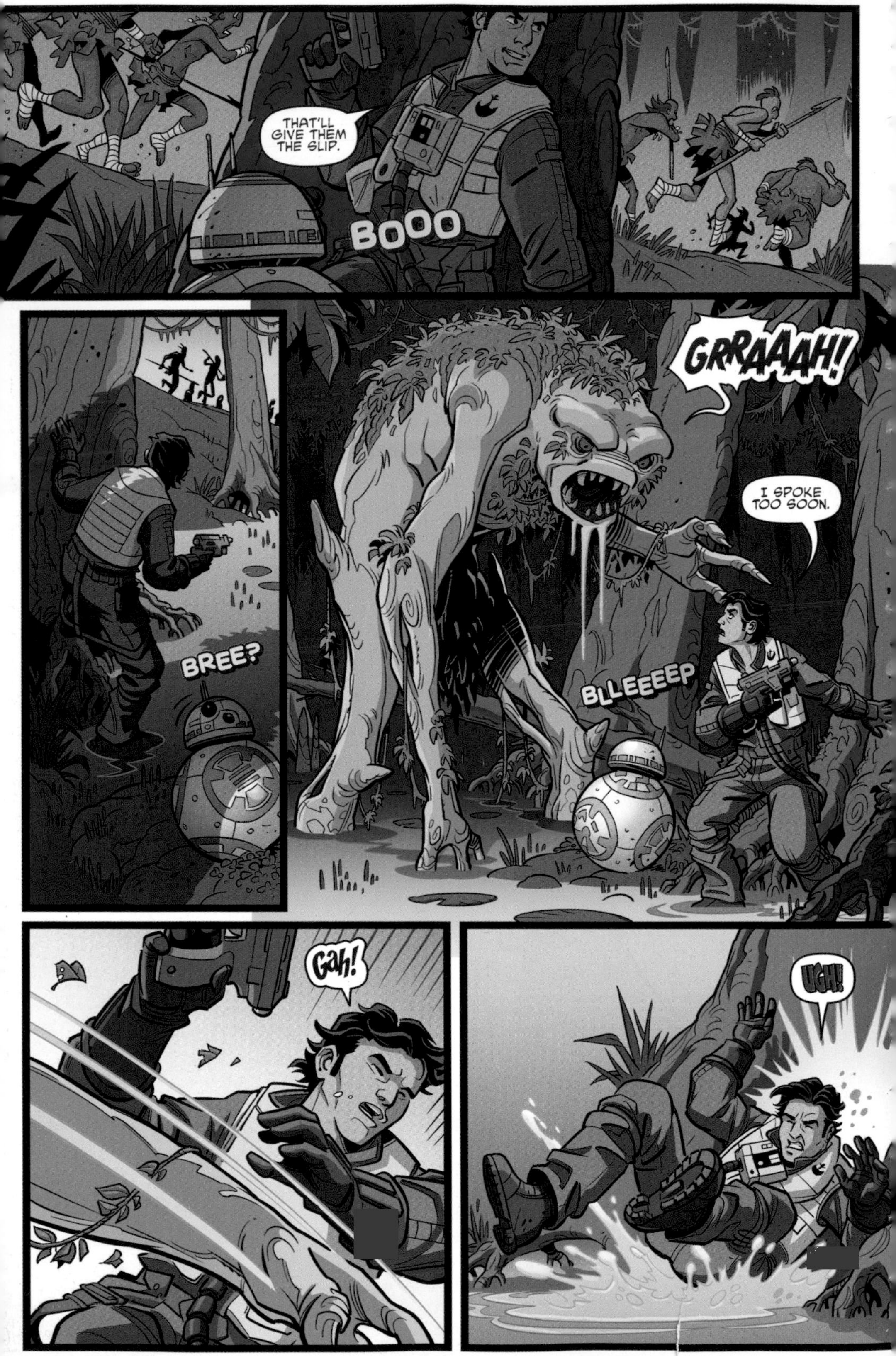
THAT'LL GIVE THEM THE SLIP.
BOOO
BREE?
GRRAAAH!
I SPOKE TOO SOON.
BLLEEEEP
Gah!
UGH!

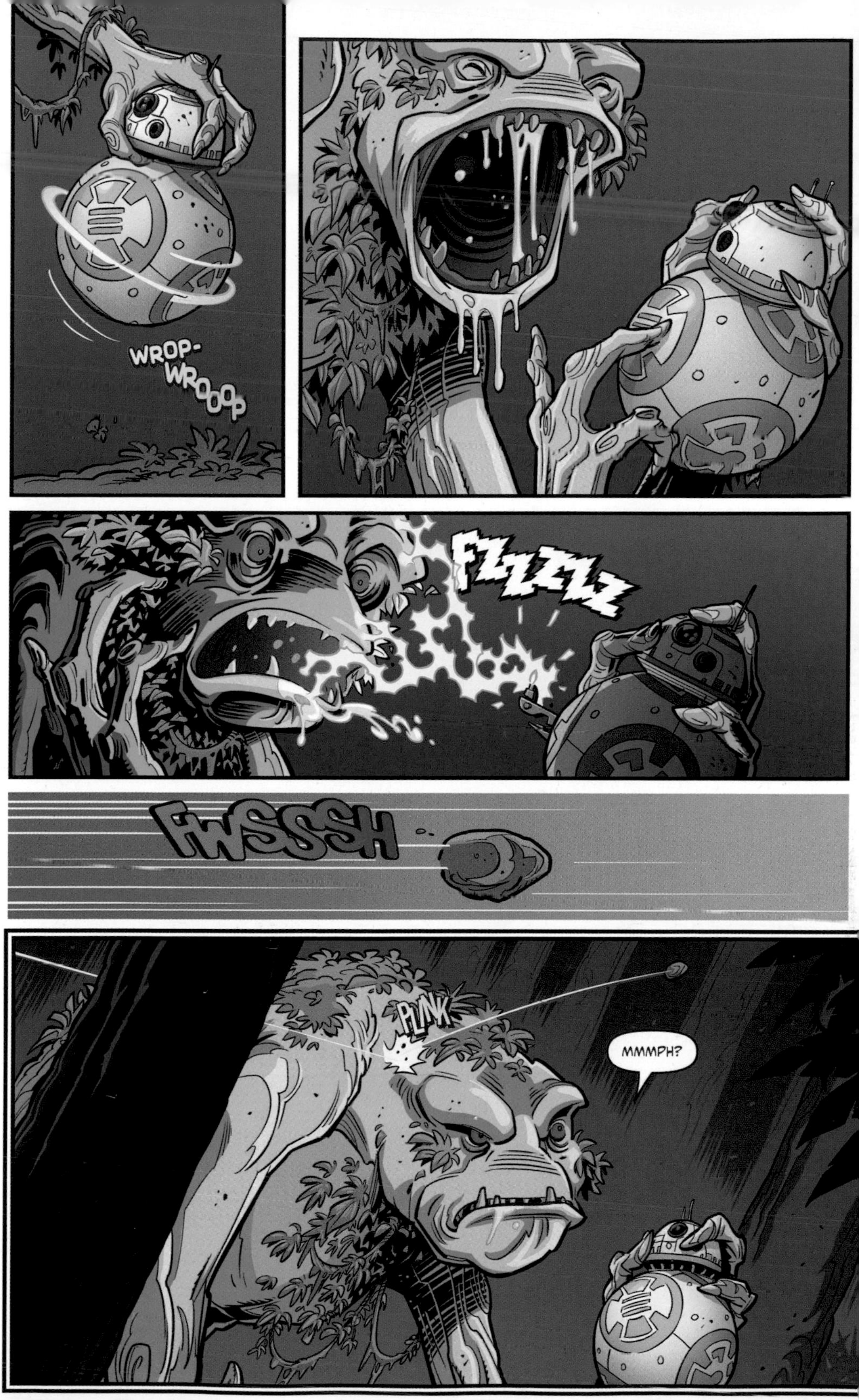
WROP-
WROOOP
FZZZZZZ
FWSSSH
PLINK
MMMPH?

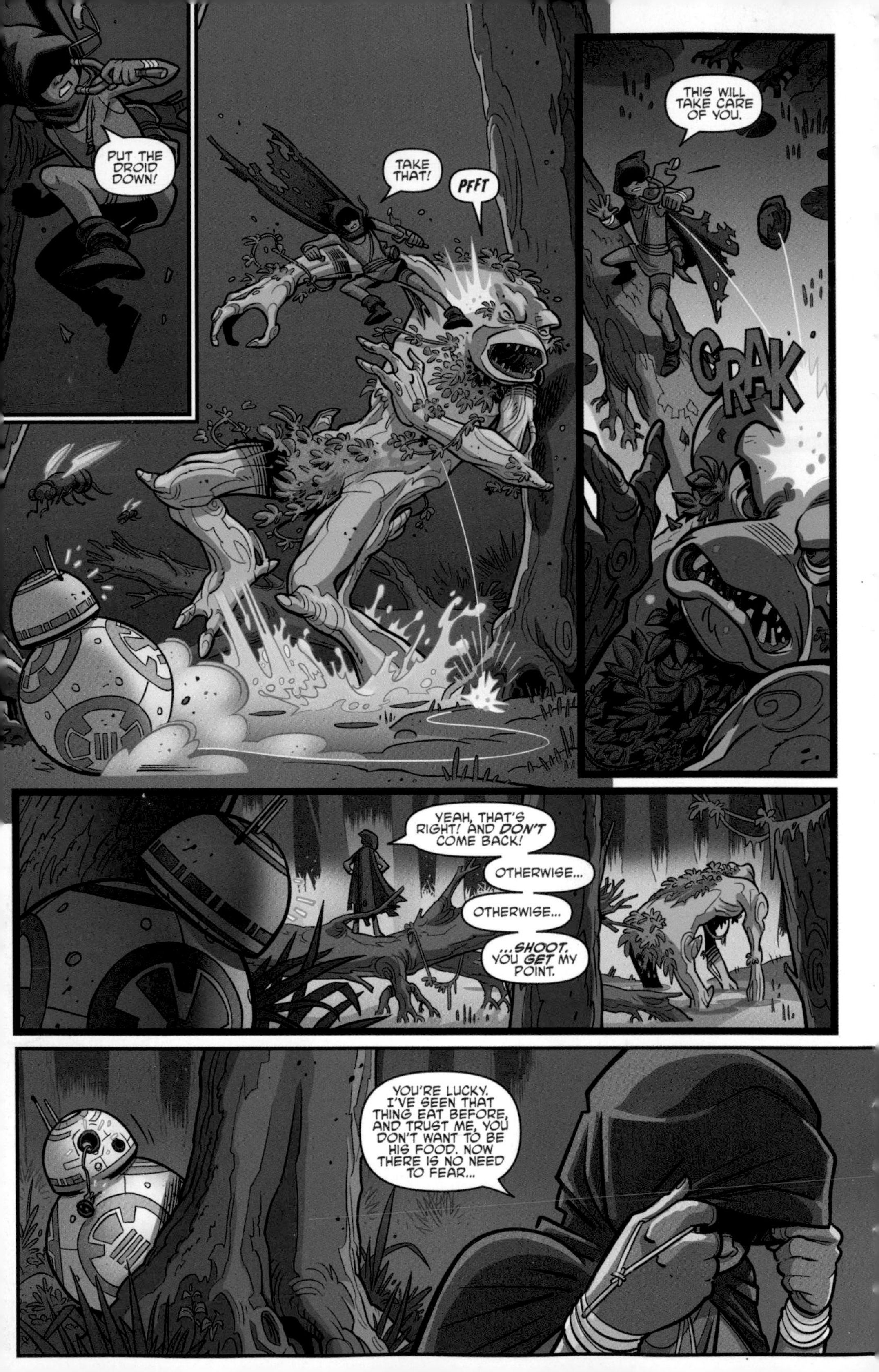
PUT THE DROID DOWN!
TAKE THAT!
PFFT
THIS WILL TAKE CARE OF YOU.
CRAK
YEAH, THAT'S RIGHT! AND DON'T COME BACK!
OTHERWISE...
OTHERWISE...
...SHOOT. YOU GET MY POINT.
YOU'RE LUCKY. I'VE SEEN THAT THING EAT BEFORE, AND TRUST ME, YOU DON'T WANT TO BE HIS FOOD. NOW THERE IS NO NEED TO FEAR...

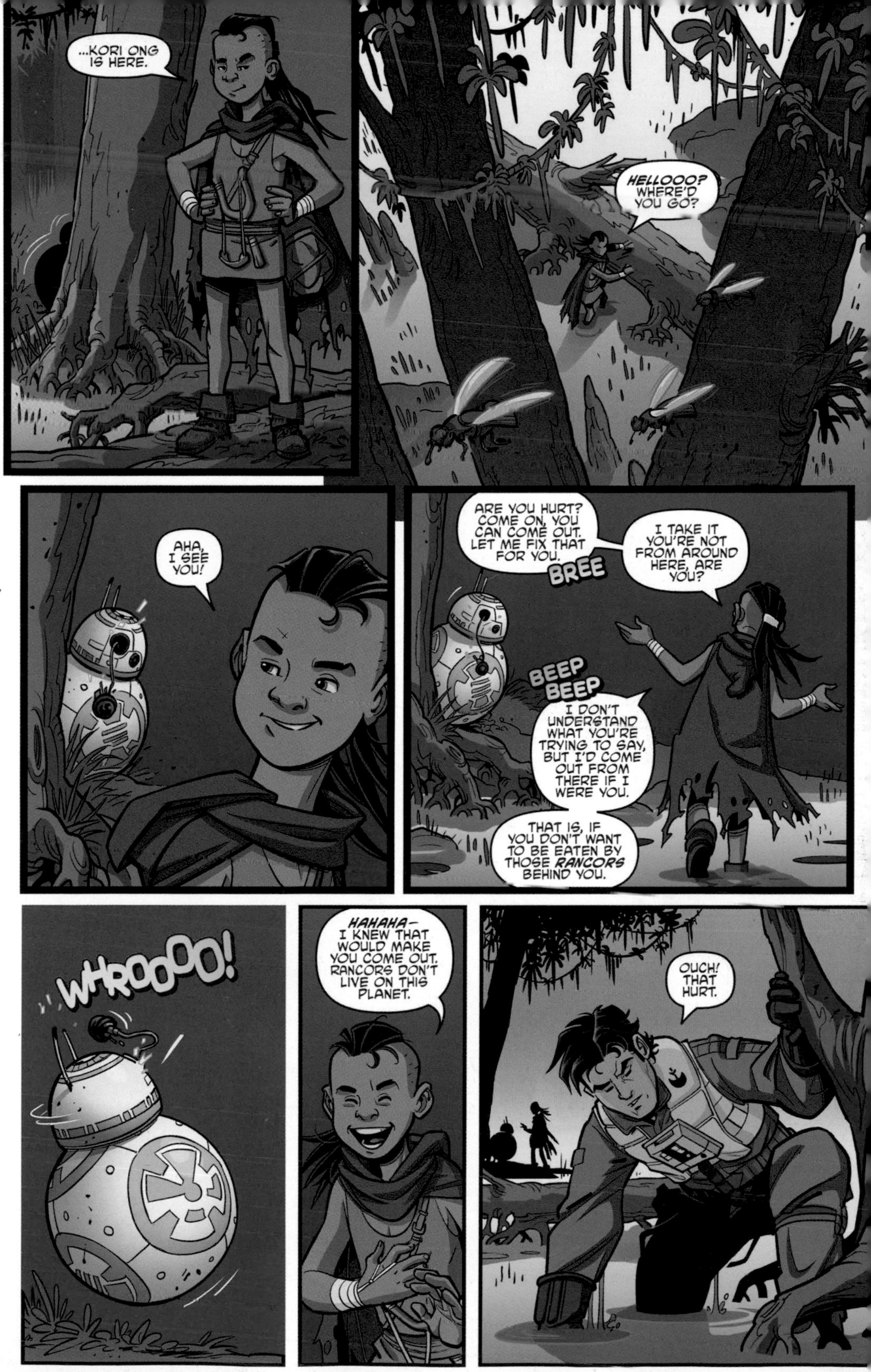
...KORI ONG IS HERE.
HELLOOO? WHERE'D YOU GO?
AHA, I SEE YOU!
ARE YOU HURT? COME ON, YOU CAN COME OUT. LET ME FIX THAT FOR YOU.
BREE
I TAKE IT YOU'RE NOT FROM AROUND HERE, ARE YOU?
BEEP BEEP
I DON'T UNDERSTAND WHAT YOU'RE TRYING TO SAY, BUT I'D COME OUT FROM THERE IF I WERE YOU.
THAT IS, IF YOU DON'T WANT TO BE EATEN BY THOSE RANCORS BEHIND YOU.
WHROOOO!
HAHAHA— I KNEW THAT WOULD MAKE YOU COME OUT. RANCORS DON'T LIVE ON THIS PLANET.
OUCH! THAT HURT.

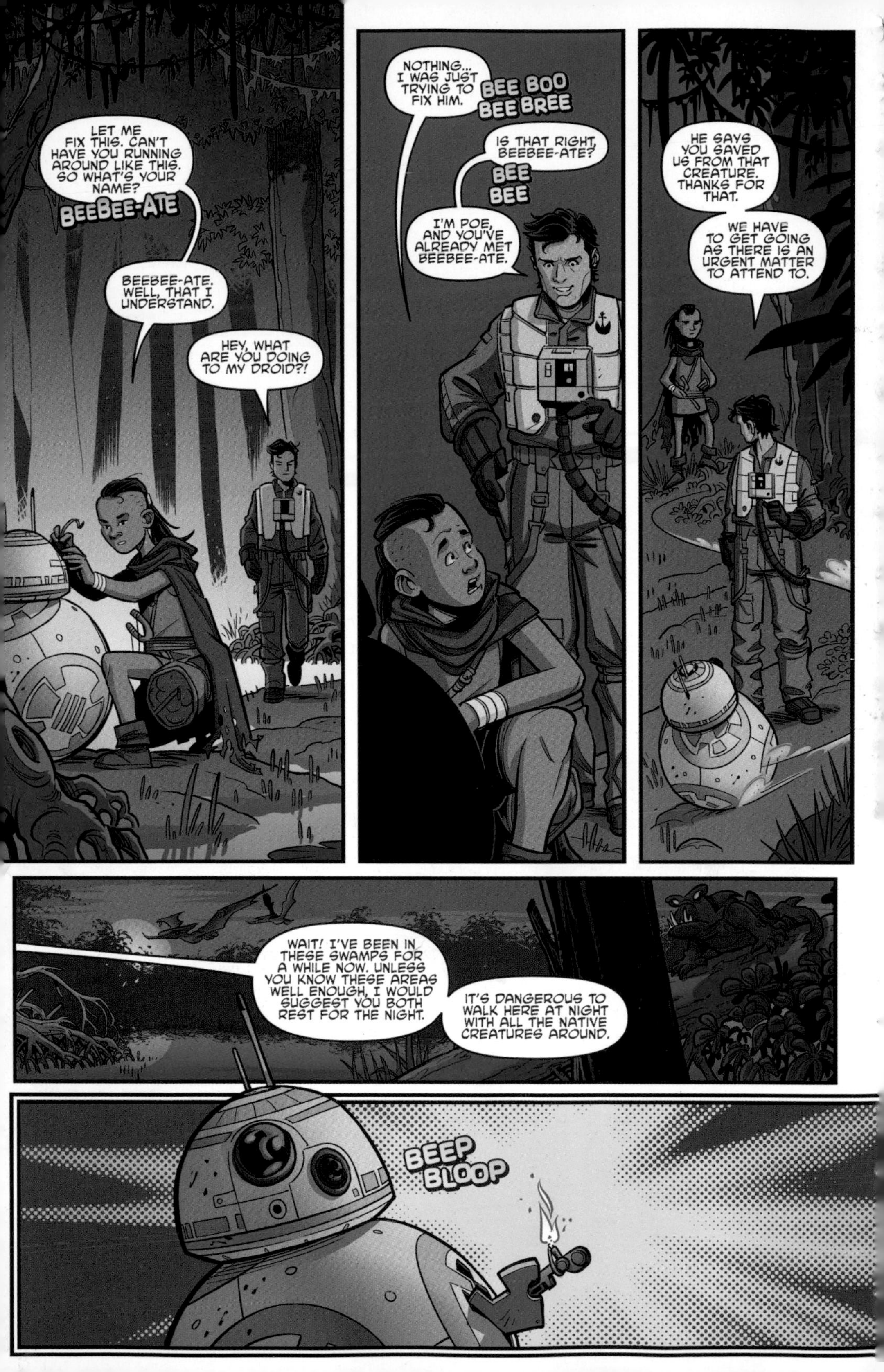
LET ME FIX THIS. CAN'T HAVE YOU RUNNING AROUND LIKE THIS. SO WHAT'S YOUR NAME?
BEEBEE-ATE
BEEBEE-ATE. WELL, THAT I UNDERSTAND.
HEY, WHAT ARE YOU DOING TO MY DROID?!
NOTHING... I WAS JUST TRYING TO FIX HIM.
BEE BOO BEE BREE
IS THAT RIGHT, BEEBEE-ATE?
BEE BEE
I'M POE, AND YOU'VE ALREADY MET BEEBEE-ATE.
HE SAYS YOU SAVED US FROM THAT CREATURE. THANKS FOR THAT.
WE HAVE TO GET GOING AS THERE IS AN URGENT MATTER TO ATTEND TO.
WAIT! I'VE BEEN IN THESE SWAMPS FOR A WHILE NOW. UNLESS YOU KNOW THESE AREAS WELL ENOUGH, I WOULD SUGGEST YOU BOTH REST FOR THE NIGHT.
IT'S DANGEROUS TO WALK HERE AT NIGHT WITH ALL THE NATIVE CREATURES AROUND.
BEEP BLOOP

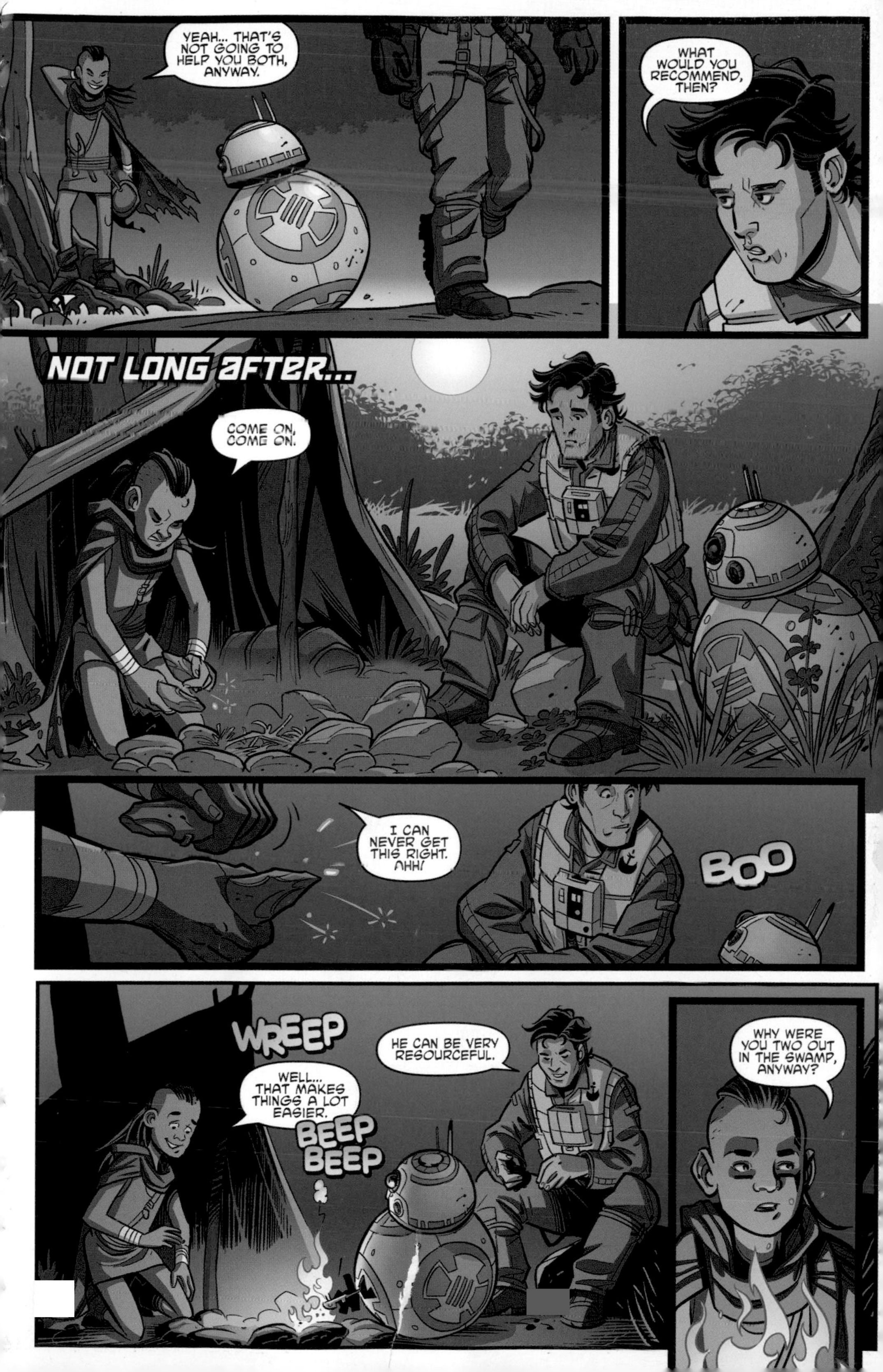
YEAH... THAT'S NOT GOING TO HELP YOU BOTH, ANYWAY.
WHAT WOULD YOU RECOMMEND, THEN?
NOT LONG AFTER...
COME ON, COME ON.
I CAN NEVER GET THIS RIGHT. AHH!
BOO
WREEP
WELL... THAT MAKES THINGS A LOT EASIER.
BEEP BEEP
HE CAN BE VERY RESOURCEFUL.
WHY WERE YOU TWO OUT IN THE SWAMP, ANYWAY?

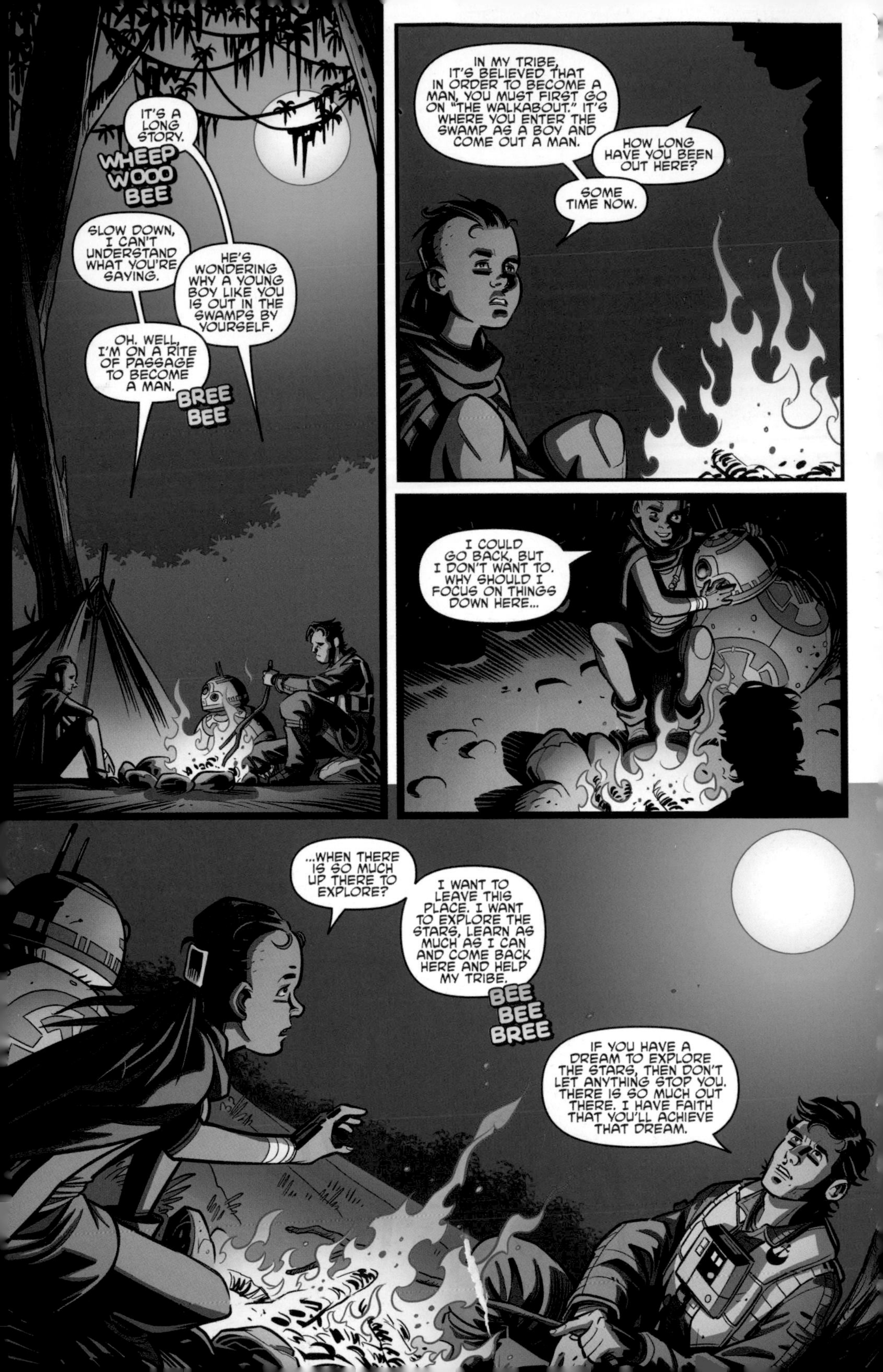
IT'S A LONG STORY.
WHEEP WOOO BEE
SLOW DOWN, I CAN'T UNDERSTAND WHAT YOU'RE SAYING.
HE'S WONDERING WHY A YOUNG BOY LIKE YOU IS OUT IN THE SWAMPS BY YOURSELF.
OH. WELL, I'M ON A RITE OF PASSAGE TO BECOME A MAN.
BREE BEE
IN MY TRIBE, IT'S BELIEVED THAT IN ORDER TO BECOME A MAN, YOU MUST FIRST GO ON "THE WALKABOUT." IT'S WHERE YOU ENTER THE SWAMP AS A BOY AND COME OUT A MAN.
HOW LONG HAVE YOU BEEN OUT HERE?
SOME TIME NOW.
I COULD GO BACK, BUT I DON'T WANT TO. WHY SHOULD I FOCUS ON THINGS DOWN HERE...
...WHEN THERE IS SO MUCH UP THERE TO EXPLORE?
I WANT TO LEAVE THIS PLACE. I WANT TO EXPLORE THE STARS, LEARN AS MUCH AS I CAN AND COME BACK HERE AND HELP MY TRIBE.
BEE BEE BREE
IF YOU HAVE A DREAM TO EXPLORE THE STARS, THEN DON'T LET ANYTHING STOP YOU. THERE IS SO MUCH OUT THERE. I HAVE FAITH THAT YOU'LL ACHIEVE THAT DREAM.

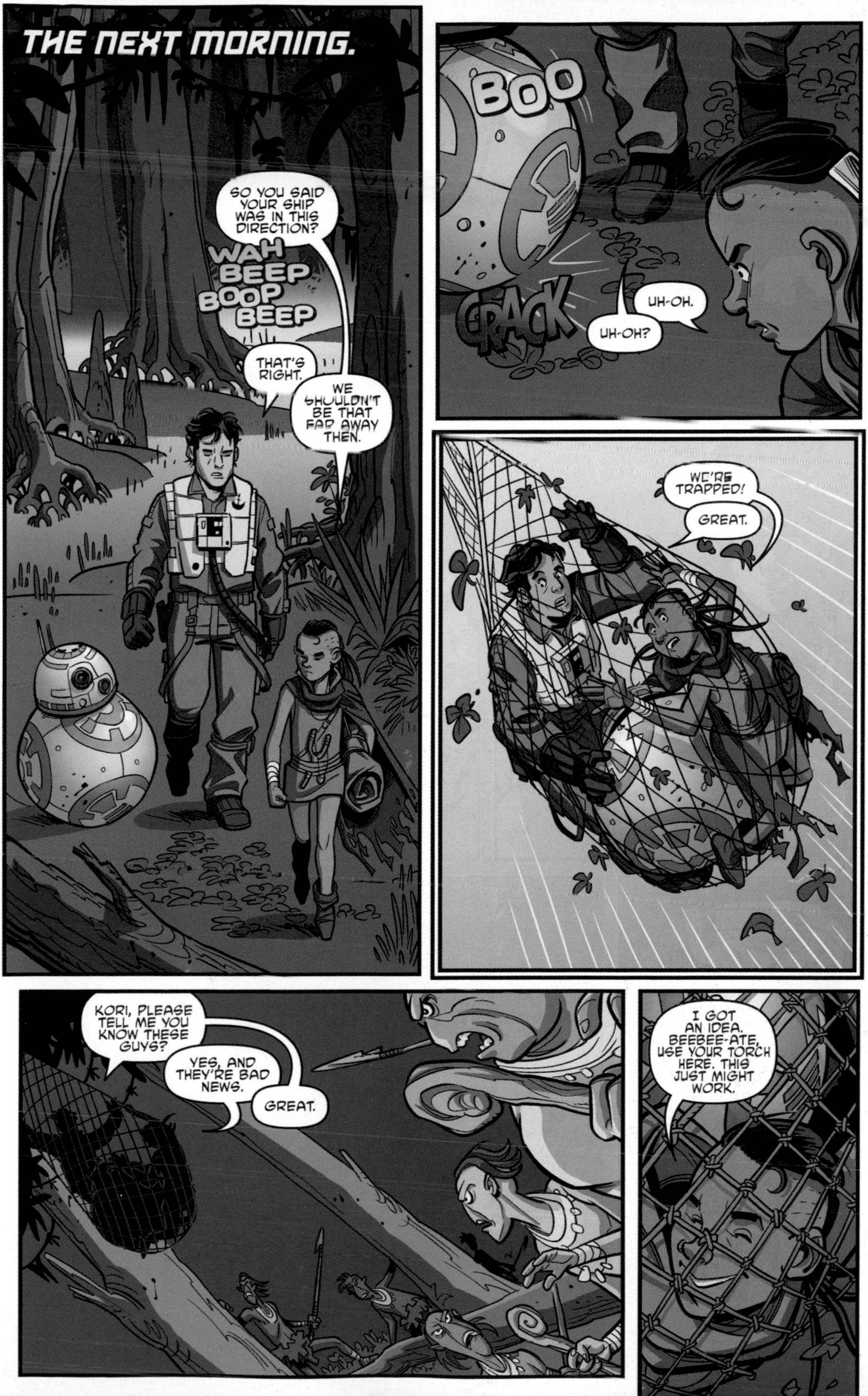
THE NEXT MORNING.
SO YOU SAID YOUR SHIP WAS IN THIS DIRECTION?
WAH BEEP BOOP BEEP
THAT'S RIGHT.
WE SHOULDN'T BE THAT FAR AWAY THEN.
BOO
CRACK
UH-OH.
UH-OH?
WE'RE TRAPPED!
GREAT.
KORI, PLEASE TELL ME YOU KNOW THESE GUYS?
YES, AND THEY'RE BAD NEWS.
GREAT.
I GOT AN IDEA. BEEBEE-ATE, USE YOUR TORCH HERE. THIS JUST MIGHT WORK.

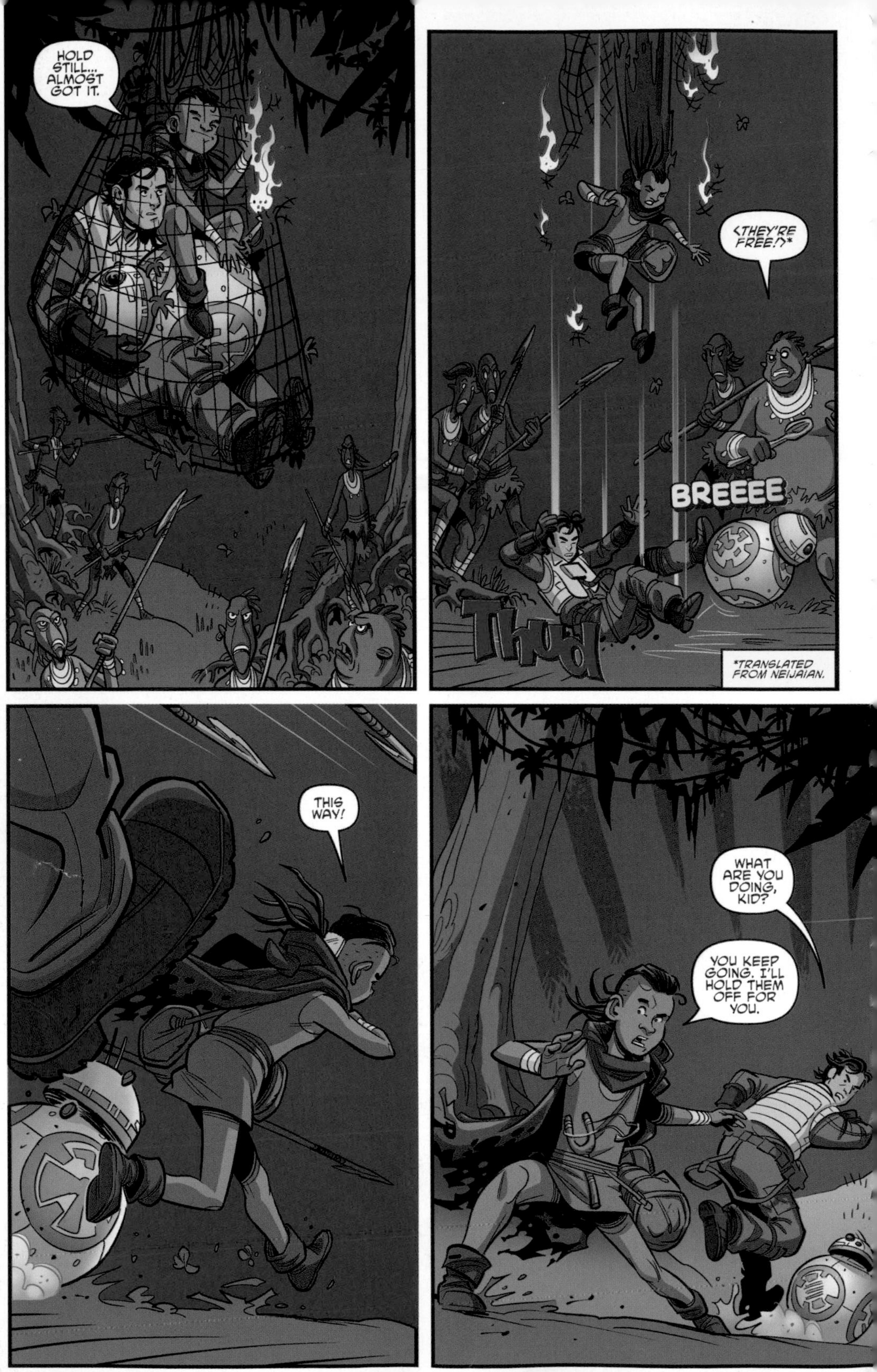
HOLD STILL... ALMOST GOT IT.
<THEY'RE FREE!>*
BREEEE
THUD
*TRANSLATED FROM NEIJAIAN.
THIS WAY!
WHAT ARE YOU DOING, KID?
YOU KEEP GOING. I'LL HOLD THEM OFF FOR YOU.

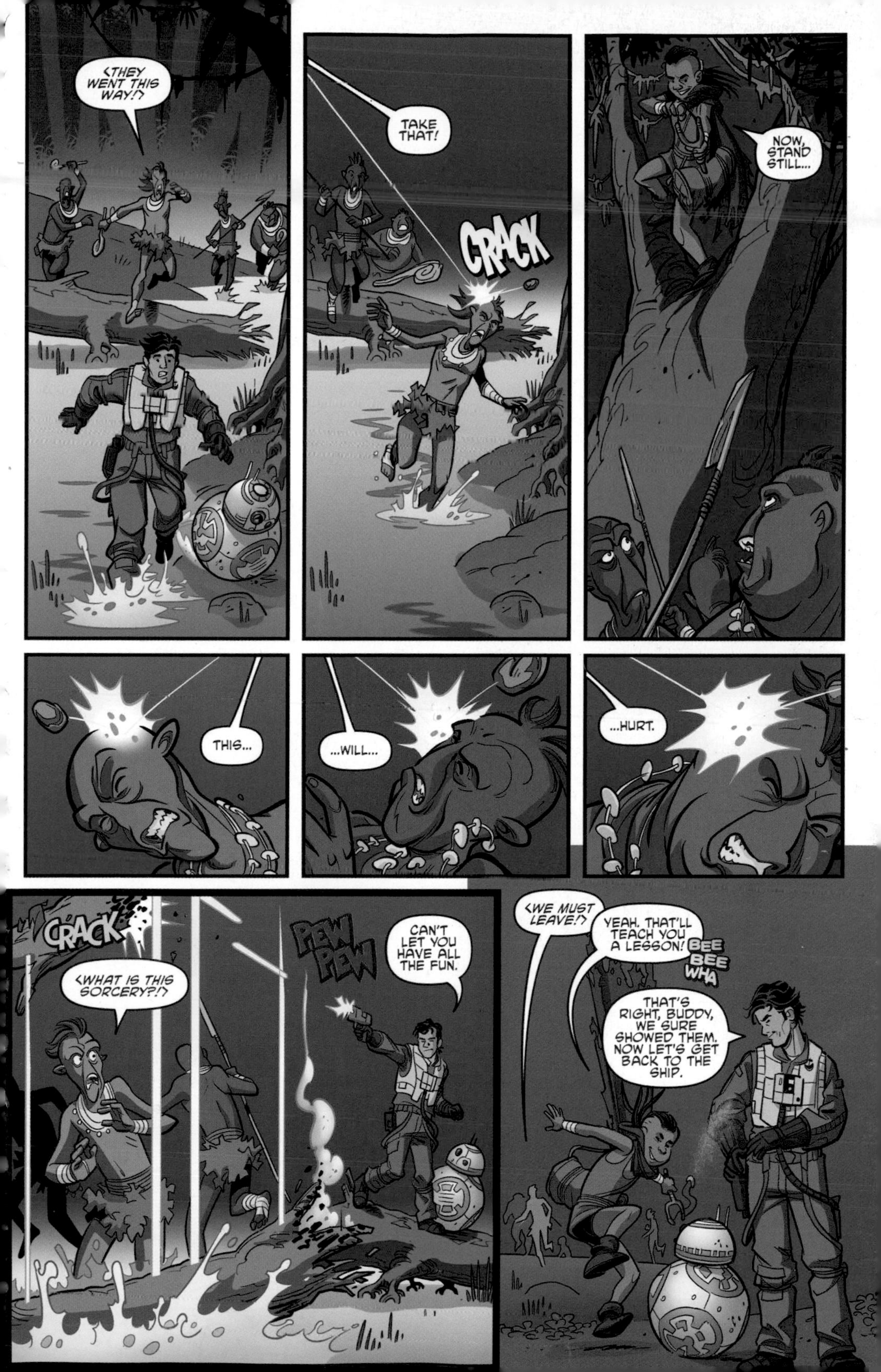

<THEY WENT THIS WAY!>
TAKE THAT!
CRACK
NOW, STAND STILL...
THIS...
...WILL...
...HURT.
CRACK
<WHAT IS THIS SORCERY?!>
PEW PEW
CAN'T LET YOU HAVE ALL THE FUN.
<WE MUST LEAVE!>
YEAH. THAT'LL TEACH YOU A LESSON!
BEE BEE WHA
THAT'S RIGHT, BUDDY, WE SURE SHOWED THEM. NOW LET'S GET BACK TO THE SHIP.

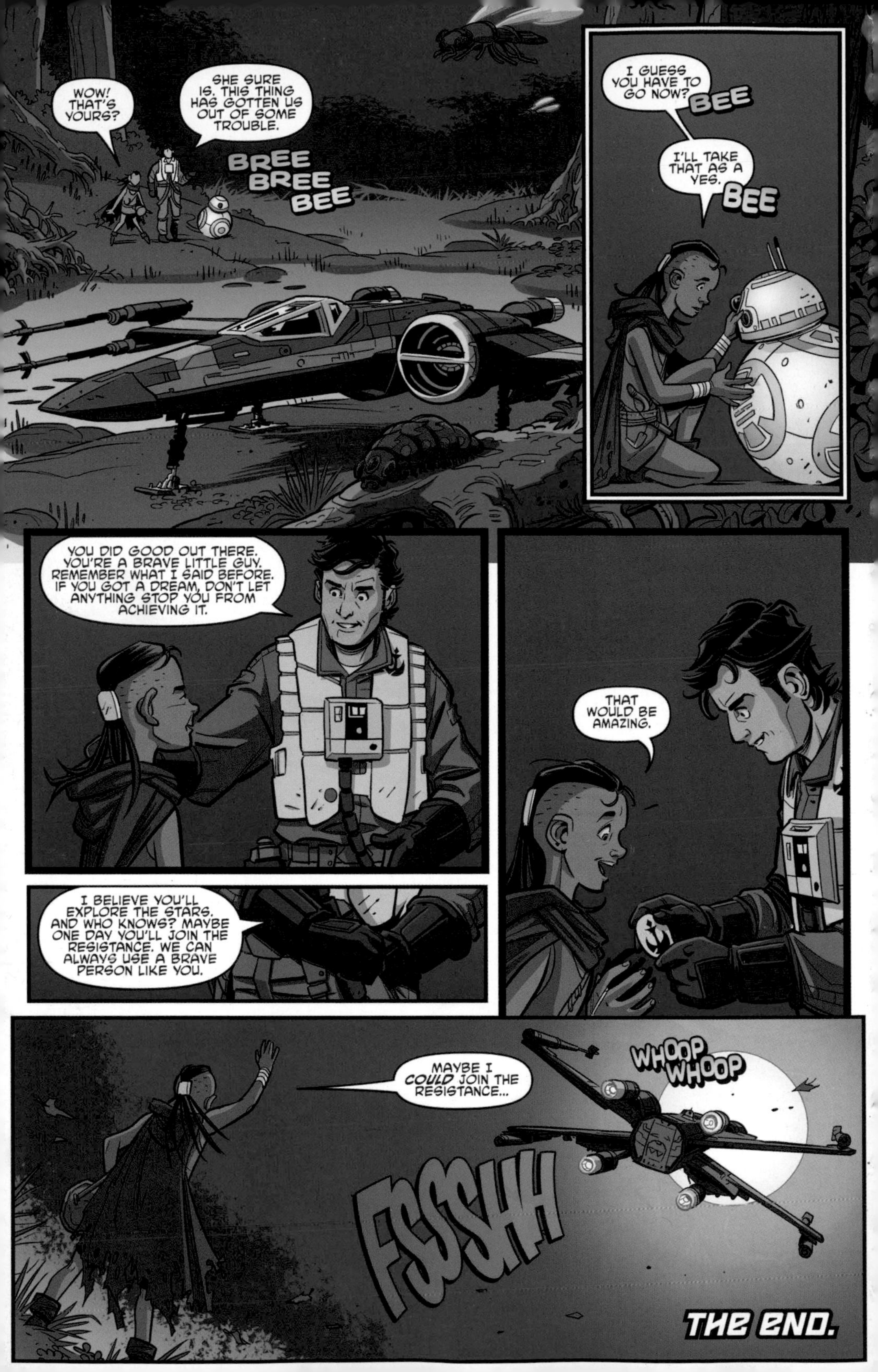
WOW! THAT'S YOURS?
SHE SURE IS. THIS THING HAS GOTTEN US OUT OF SOME TROUBLE.
BREE BREE BEE
I GUESS YOU HAVE TO GO NOW?
BEE
I'LL TAKE THAT AS A YES.
BEE
YOU DID GOOD OUT THERE. YOU'RE A BRAVE LITTLE GUY. REMEMBER WHAT I SAID BEFORE. IF YOU GOT A DREAM, DON'T LET ANYTHING STOP YOU FROM ACHIEVING IT.
I BELIEVE YOU'LL EXPLORE THE STARS. AND WHO KNOWS? MAYBE ONE DAY YOU'LL JOIN THE RESISTANCE. WE CAN ALWAYS USE A BRAVE PERSON LIKE YOU.
THAT WOULD BE AMAZING.
MAYBE I *COULD* JOIN THE RESISTANCE...
WHOOP WHOOP
FSSSHH
THE END.

STAR WARS

ADVENTURES

All Aces Battle Royale

WRITERS
**KEVIN BURKE
& CHRIS "DOC" WYATT**

ARTIST & COLORIST
VALENTINA PINTO

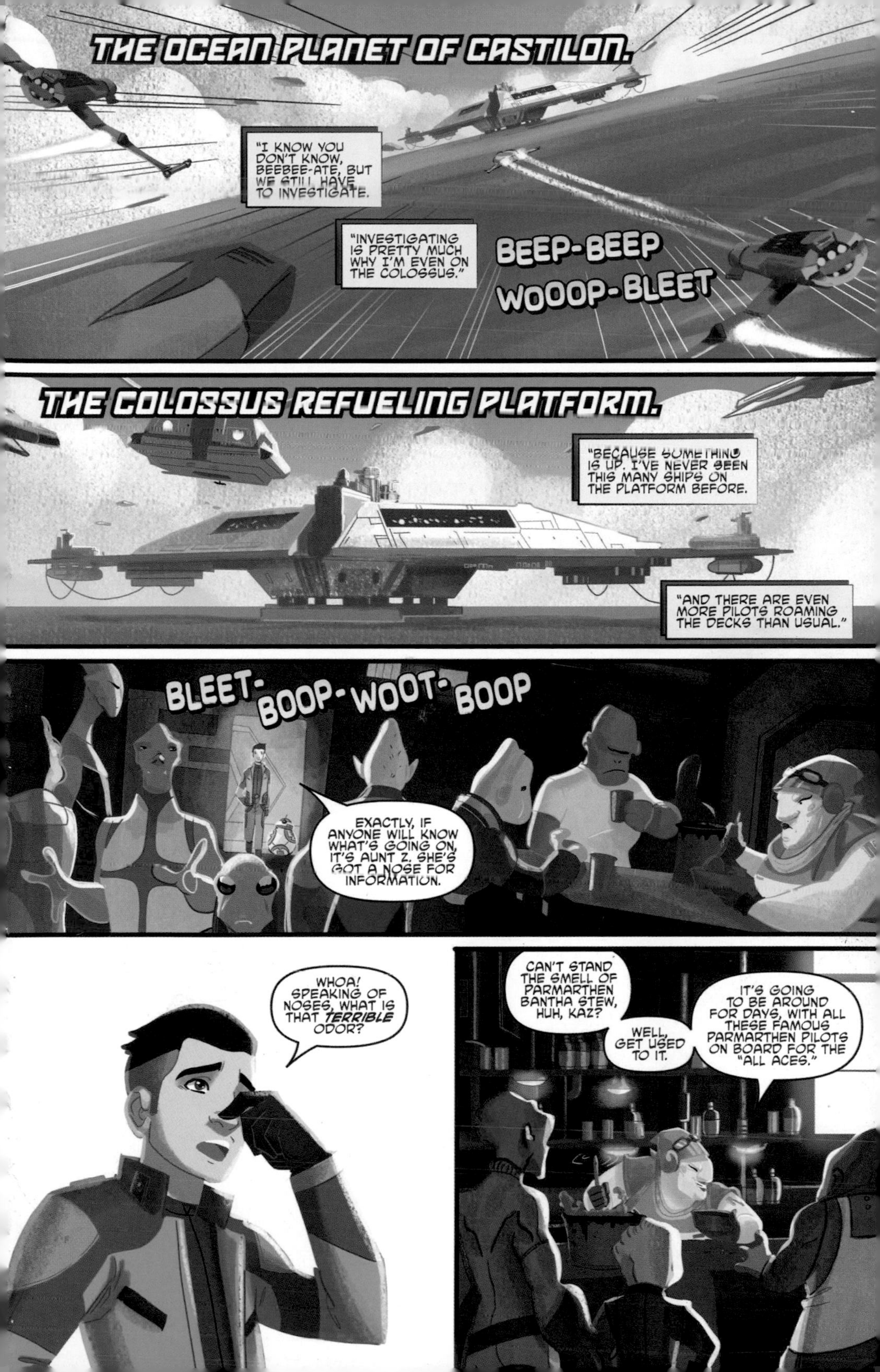
THE OCEAN PLANET OF CASTILON.
"I KNOW YOU DON'T KNOW, BEEBEE-ATE, BUT WE STILL HAVE TO INVESTIGATE.
"INVESTIGATING IS PRETTY MUCH WHY I'M EVEN ON THE COLOSSUS."
BEEP-BEEP
WOOOP-BLEET
THE COLOSSUS REFUELING PLATFORM.
"BECAUSE SOMETHING IS UP. I'VE NEVER SEEN THIS MANY SHIPS ON THE PLATFORM BEFORE.
"AND THERE ARE EVEN MORE PILOTS ROAMING THE DECKS THAN USUAL."
BLEET-BOOP-WOOT-BOOP
EXACTLY, IF ANYONE WILL KNOW WHAT'S GOING ON, IT'S AUNT Z. SHE'S GOT A NOSE FOR INFORMATION.
WHOA! SPEAKING OF NOSES, WHAT IS THAT *TERRIBLE* ODOR?
CAN'T STAND THE SMELL OF PARMARTHEN BANTHA STEW, HUH, KAZ?
WELL, GET USED TO IT.
IT'S GOING TO BE AROUND FOR DAYS, WITH ALL THESE FAMOUS PARMARTHEN PILOTS ON BOARD FOR THE "ALL ACES."

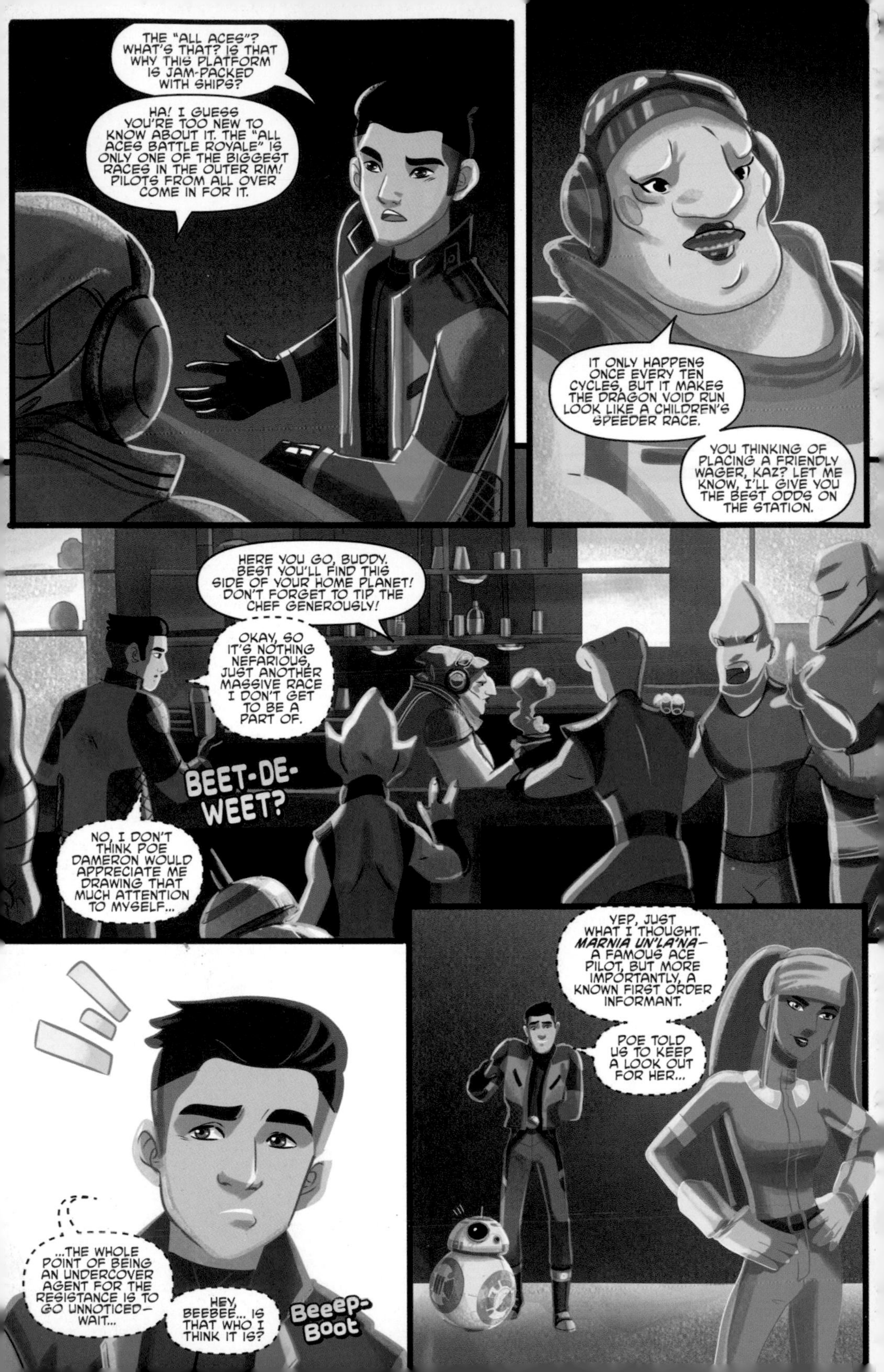
THE "ALL ACES"? WHAT'S THAT? IS THAT WHY THIS PLATFORM IS JAM-PACKED WITH SHIPS?
HA! I GUESS YOU'RE TOO NEW TO KNOW ABOUT IT. THE "ALL ACES BATTLE ROYALE" IS ONLY ONE OF THE BIGGEST RACES IN THE OUTER RIM! PILOTS FROM ALL OVER COME IN FOR IT.
IT ONLY HAPPENS ONCE EVERY TEN CYCLES, BUT IT MAKES THE DRAGON VOID RUN LOOK LIKE A CHILDREN'S SPEEDER RACE.
YOU THINKING OF PLACING A FRIENDLY WAGER, KAZ? LET ME KNOW, I'LL GIVE YOU THE BEST ODDS ON THE STATION.
HERE YOU GO, BUDDY. BEST YOU'LL FIND THIS SIDE OF YOUR HOME PLANET! DON'T FORGET TO TIP THE CHEF GENEROUSLY!
OKAY, SO IT'S NOTHING NEFARIOUS, JUST ANOTHER MASSIVE RACE I DON'T GET TO BE A PART OF.
BEET-DE-WEET?
NO, I DON'T THINK POE DAMERON WOULD APPRECIATE ME DRAWING THAT MUCH ATTENTION TO MYSELF...
...THE WHOLE POINT OF BEING AN UNDERCOVER AGENT FOR THE RESISTANCE IS TO GO UNNOTICED— WAIT...
HEY, BEEBEE... IS THAT WHO I THINK IT IS?
Beeep-Boot
YEP, JUST WHAT I THOUGHT. MARNIA UN'LA'NA— A FAMOUS ACE PILOT, BUT MORE IMPORTANTLY, A KNOWN FIRST ORDER INFORMANT.
POE TOLD US TO KEEP A LOOK OUT FOR HER...

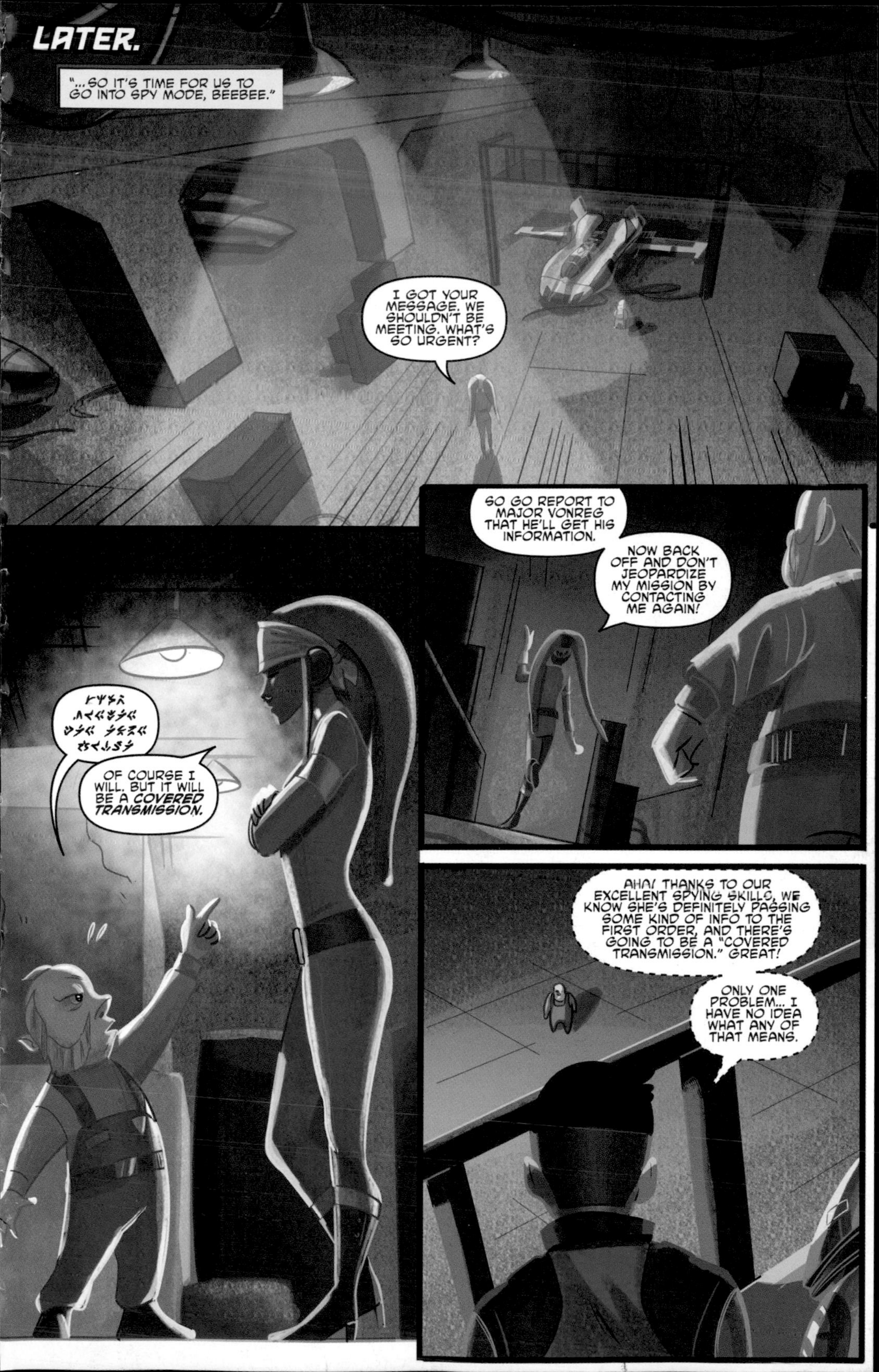
LATER.
"...SO IT'S TIME FOR US TO GO INTO SPY MODE, BEEBEE."
I GOT YOUR MESSAGE. WE SHOULDN'T BE MEETING. WHAT'S SO URGENT?
OF COURSE I WILL. BUT IT WILL BE A COVERED TRANSMISSION.
SO GO REPORT TO MAJOR VONREG THAT HE'LL GET HIS INFORMATION.
NOW BACK OFF AND DON'T JEOPARDIZE MY MISSION BY CONTACTING ME AGAIN!
AHA! THANKS TO OUR EXCELLENT SPYING SKILLS, WE KNOW SHE'S DEFINITELY PASSING SOME KIND OF INFO TO THE FIRST ORDER, AND THERE'S GOING TO BE A "COVERED TRANSMISSION." GREAT!
ONLY ONE PROBLEM... I HAVE NO IDEA WHAT ANY OF THAT MEANS.

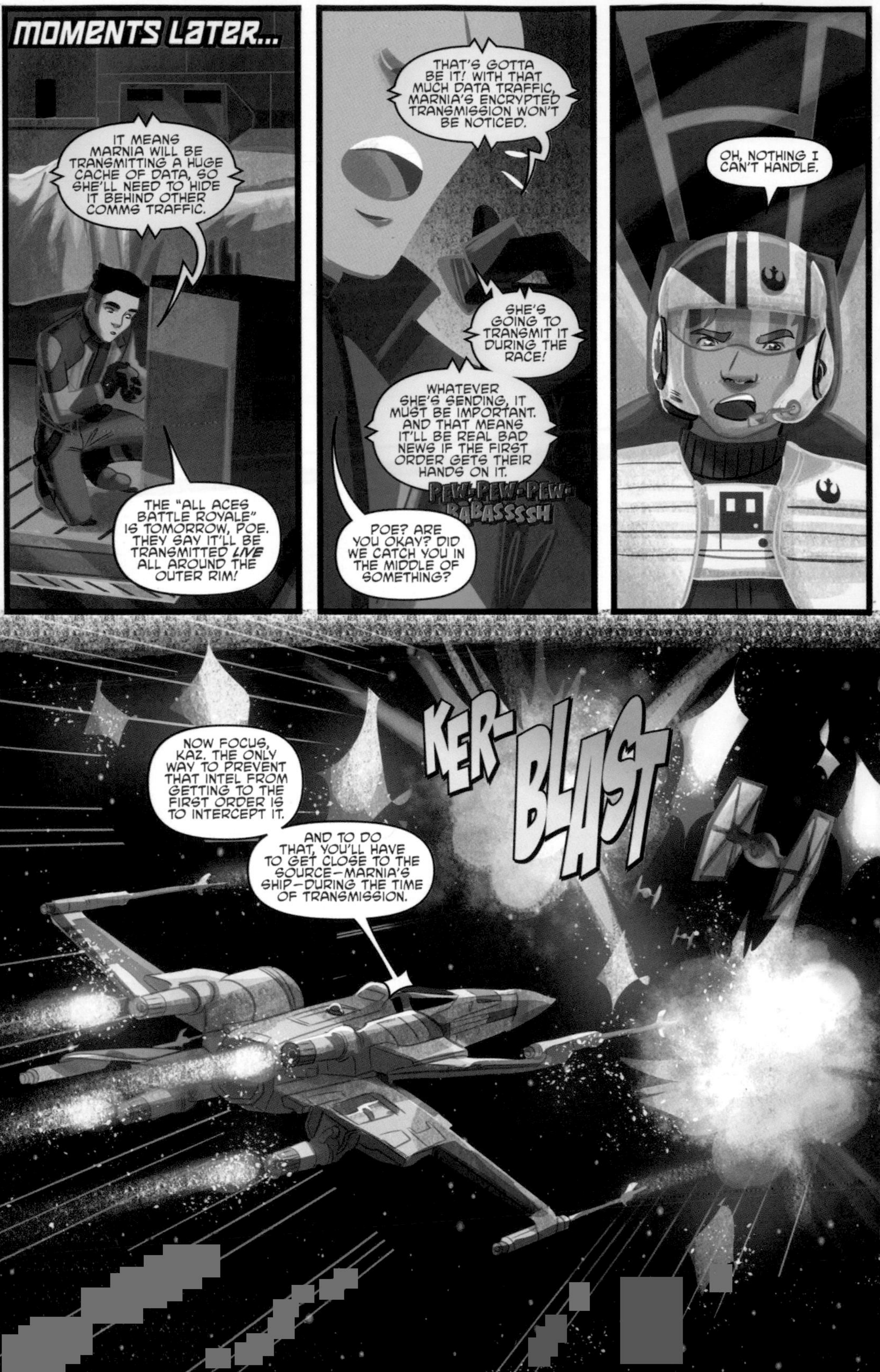
MOMENTS LATER...
IT MEANS MARNIA WILL BE TRANSMITTING A HUGE CACHE OF DATA, SO SHE'LL NEED TO HIDE IT BEHIND OTHER COMMS TRAFFIC.
THE "ALL ACES BATTLE ROYALE" IS TOMORROW, POE. THEY SAY IT'LL BE TRANSMITTED *LIVE* ALL AROUND THE OUTER RIM!
THAT'S GOTTA BE IT! WITH THAT MUCH DATA TRAFFIC, MARNIA'S ENCRYPTED TRANSMISSION WON'T BE NOTICED.
SHE'S GOING TO TRANSMIT IT DURING THE RACE!
WHATEVER SHE'S SENDING, IT MUST BE IMPORTANT. AND THAT MEANS IT'LL BE REAL BAD NEWS IF THE FIRST ORDER GETS THEIR HANDS ON IT.
PEW-PEW-PEW-BABASSSSH
POE? ARE YOU OKAY? DID WE CATCH YOU IN THE MIDDLE OF SOMETHING?
OH, NOTHING I CAN'T HANDLE.
KER-BLAST
NOW FOCUS, KAZ. THE ONLY WAY TO PREVENT THAT INTEL FROM GETTING TO THE FIRST ORDER IS TO INTERCEPT IT.
AND TO DO THAT, YOU'LL HAVE TO GET CLOSE TO THE SOURCE—MARNIA'S SHIP—DURING THE TIME OF TRANSMISSION.

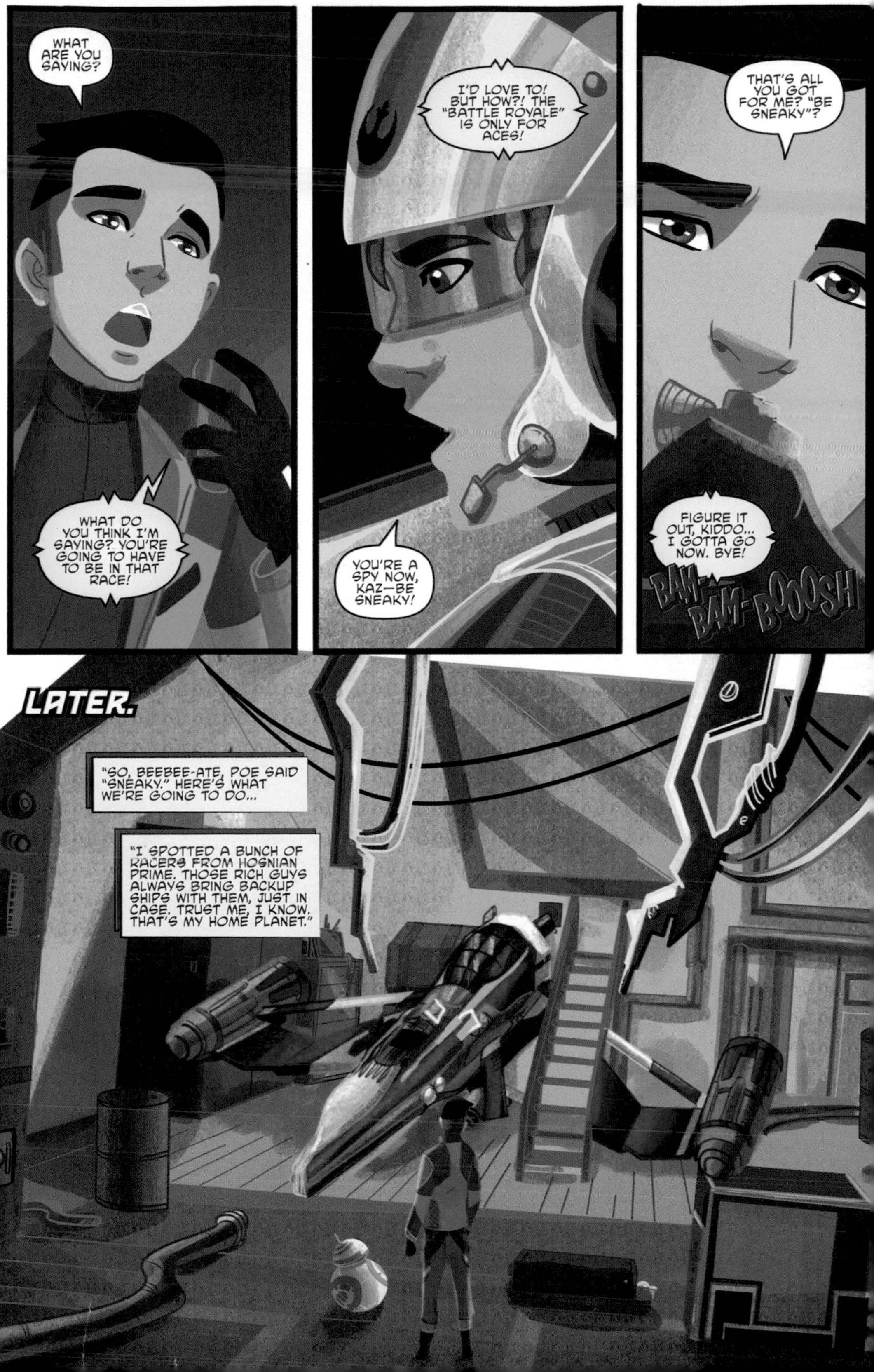
WHAT ARE YOU SAYING?
WHAT DO YOU THINK I'M SAYING? YOU'RE GOING TO HAVE TO BE IN THAT RACE!
I'D LOVE TO! BUT HOW?! THE "BATTLE ROYALE" IS ONLY FOR ACES!
YOU'RE A SPY NOW, KAZ—BE SNEAKY!
THAT'S ALL YOU GOT FOR ME? "BE SNEAKY"?
FIGURE IT OUT, KIDDO... I GOTTA GO NOW. BYE!
BAM-BAM-BOOOSH
LATER.
"SO, BEEBEE-ATE, POE SAID "SNEAKY." HERE'S WHAT WE'RE GOING TO DO...
"I SPOTTED A BUNCH OF RACERS FROM HOSNIAN PRIME. THOSE RICH GUYS ALWAYS BRING BACKUP SHIPS WITH THEM, JUST IN CASE. TRUST ME, I KNOW. THAT'S MY HOME PLANET."

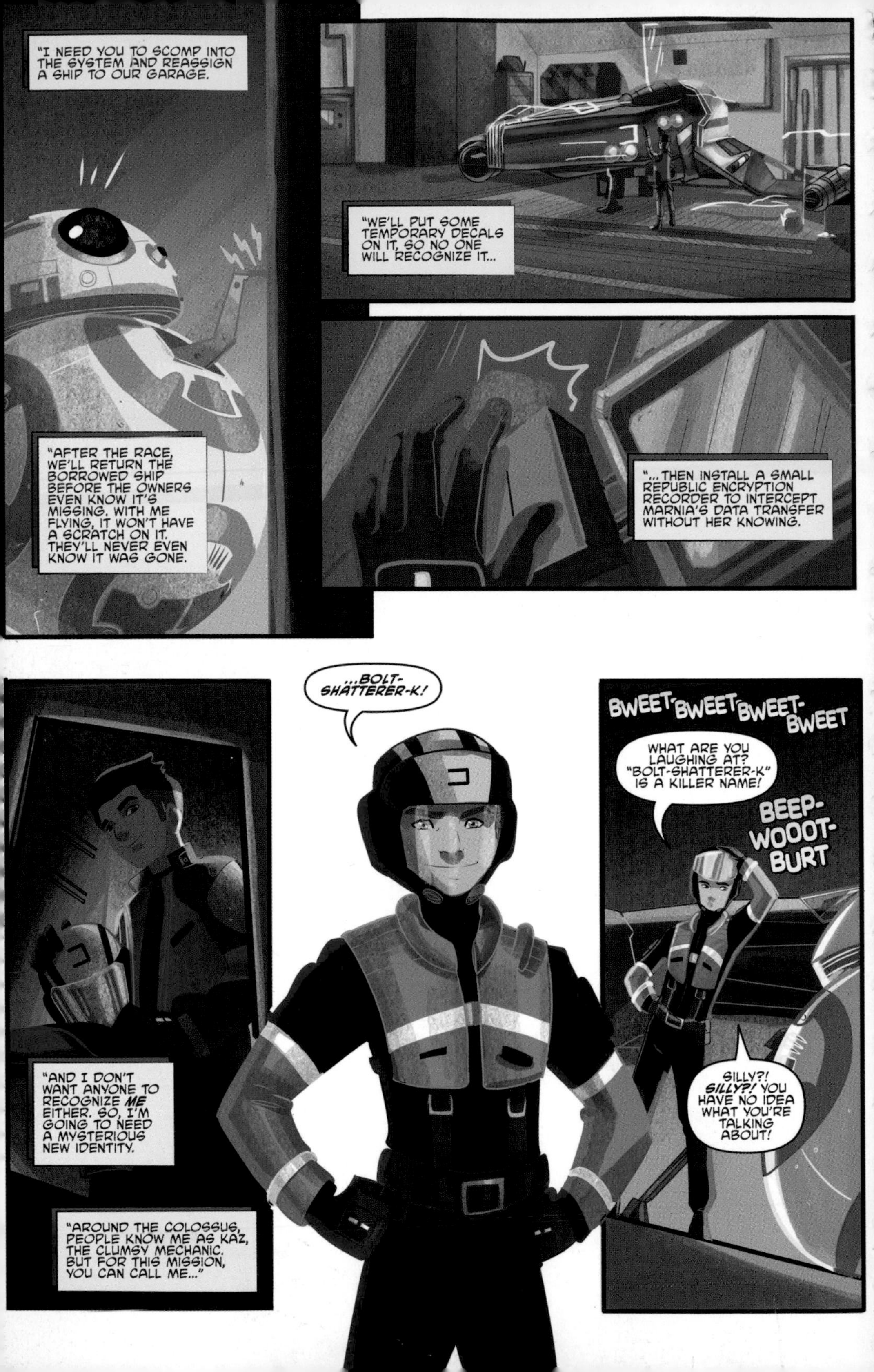
"I NEED YOU TO SCOMP INTO THE SYSTEM AND REASSIGN A SHIP TO OUR GARAGE.
"WE'LL PUT SOME TEMPORARY DECALS ON IT, SO NO ONE WILL RECOGNIZE IT...
"AFTER THE RACE, WE'LL RETURN THE BORROWED SHIP BEFORE THE OWNERS EVEN KNOW IT'S MISSING. WITH ME FLYING, IT WON'T HAVE A SCRATCH ON IT. THEY'LL NEVER EVEN KNOW IT WAS GONE.
"...THEN INSTALL A SMALL REPUBLIC ENCRYPTION RECORDER TO INTERCEPT MARNIA'S DATA TRANSFER WITHOUT HER KNOWING.
"AND I DON'T WANT ANYONE TO RECOGNIZE *ME* EITHER. SO, I'M GOING TO NEED A MYSTERIOUS NEW IDENTITY.
"AROUND THE COLOSSUS, PEOPLE KNOW ME AS KAZ, THE CLUMSY MECHANIC. BUT FOR THIS MISSION, YOU CAN CALL ME..."
...BOLT-SHATTERER-K!
BWEET-BWEET-BWEET-BWEET
WHAT ARE YOU LAUGHING AT? "BOLT-SHATTERER-K" IS A KILLER NAME!
BEEP-WOOOT-BURT
SILLY?! *SILLY?!* YOU HAVE NO IDEA WHAT YOU'RE TALKING ABOUT!

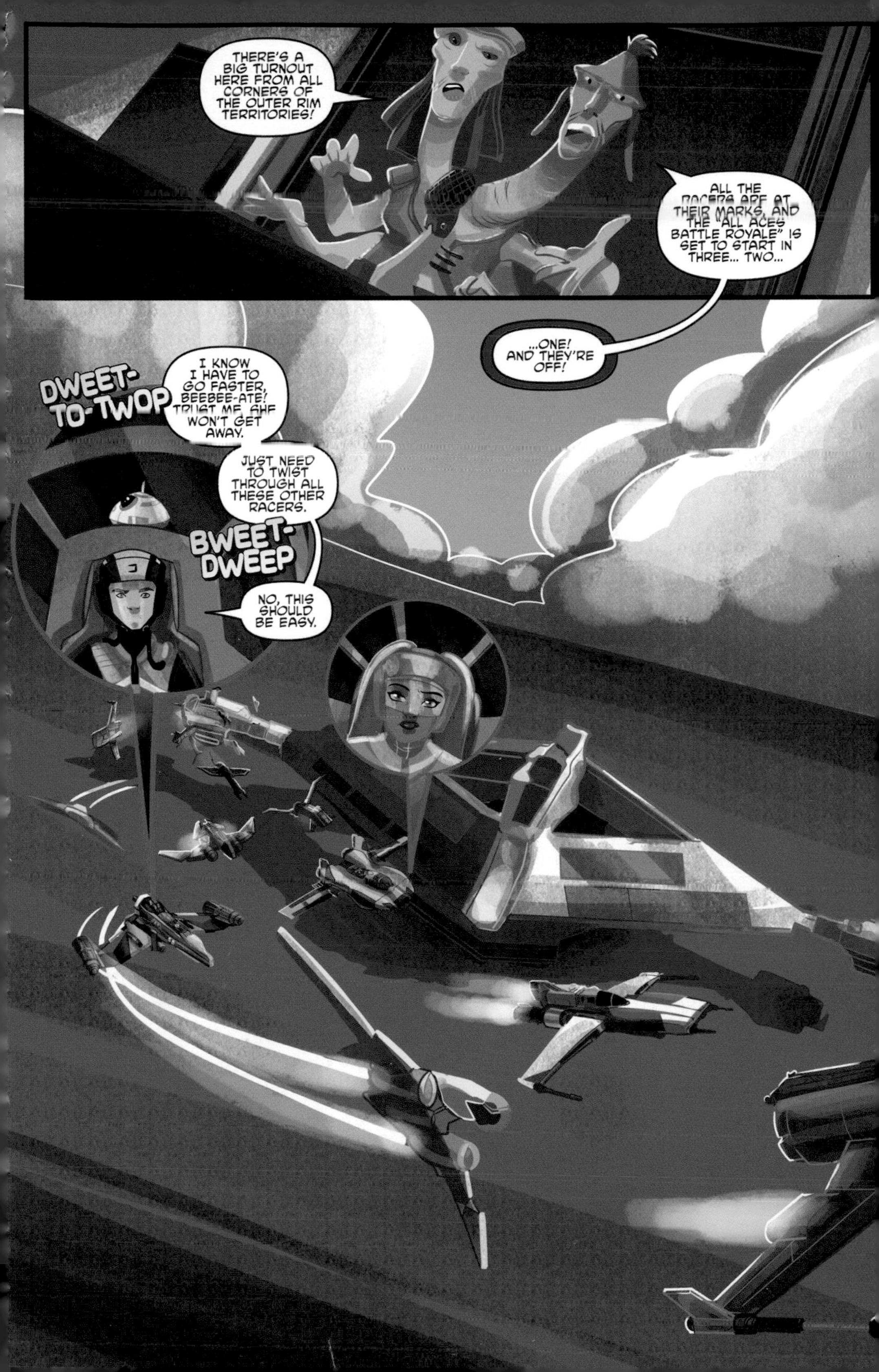
THERE'S A BIG TURNOUT HERE FROM ALL CORNERS OF THE OUTER RIM TERRITORIES!
ALL THE RACERS ARE AT THEIR MARKS, AND THE "ALL ACES BATTLE ROYALE" IS SET TO START IN THREE... TWO...
...ONE! AND THEY'RE OFF!
DWEET-TO-TWOP
I KNOW I HAVE TO GO FASTER, BEEBEE-ATE! TRUST ME, SHE WON'T GET AWAY.
JUST NEED TO TWIST THROUGH ALL THESE OTHER RACERS.
BWEET-DWEEP
NO, THIS SHOULD BE EASY.

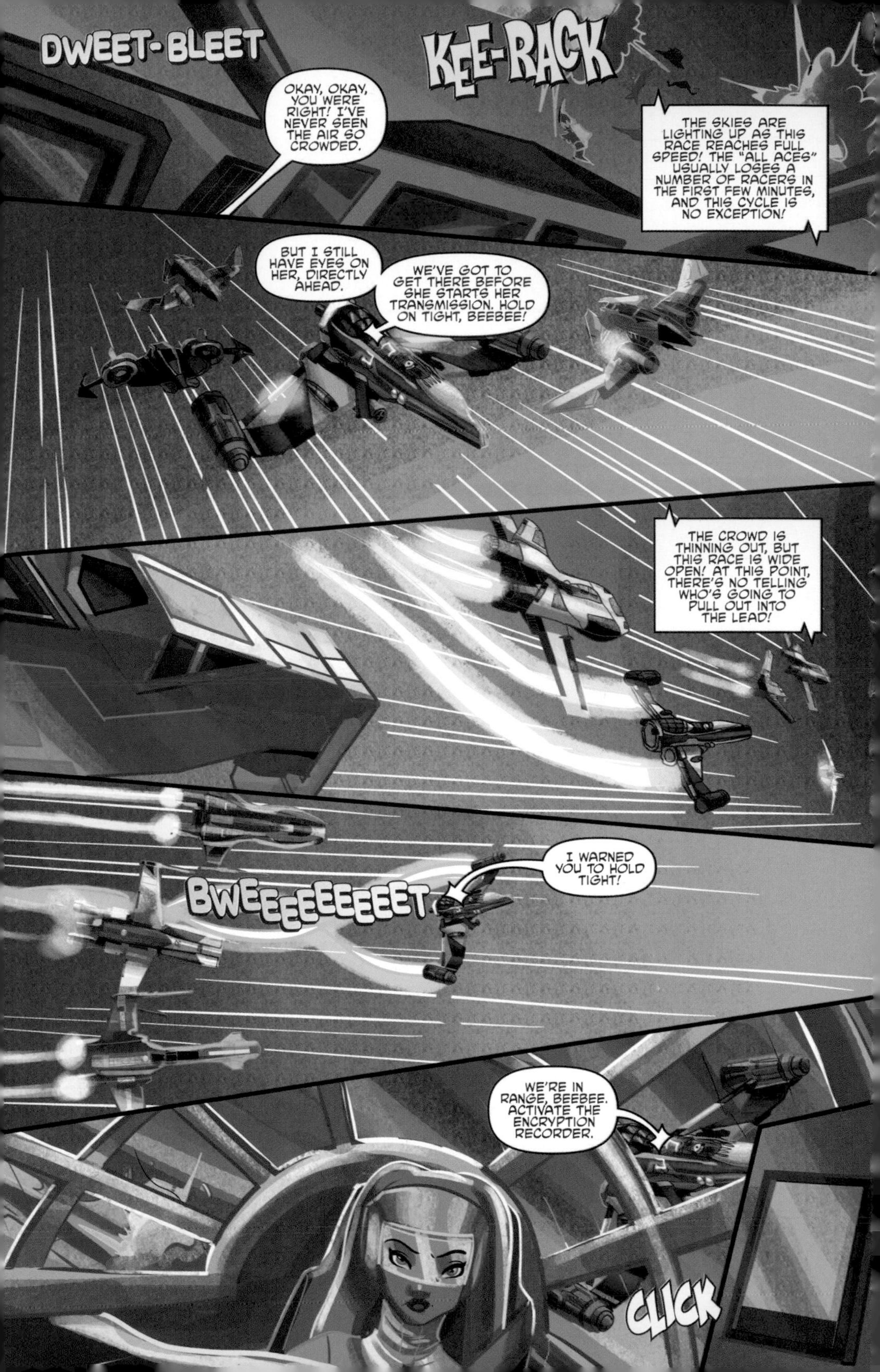
DWEET-BLEET
KEE-RACK
OKAY, OKAY, YOU WERE RIGHT! I'VE NEVER SEEN THE AIR SO CROWDED.
THE SKIES ARE LIGHTING UP AS THIS RACE REACHES FULL SPEED! THE "ALL ACES" USUALLY LOSES A NUMBER OF RACERS IN THE FIRST FEW MINUTES, AND THIS CYCLE IS NO EXCEPTION!
BUT I STILL HAVE EYES ON HER, DIRECTLY AHEAD.
WE'VE GOT TO GET THERE BEFORE SHE STARTS HER TRANSMISSION. HOLD ON TIGHT, BEEBEE!
THE CROWD IS THINNING OUT, BUT THIS RACE IS WIDE OPEN! AT THIS POINT, THERE'S NO TELLING WHO'S GOING TO PULL OUT INTO THE LEAD!
BWEEEEEEEEEET
I WARNED YOU TO HOLD TIGHT!
WE'RE IN RANGE, BEEBEE. ACTIVATE THE ENCRYPTION RECORDER.
CLICK

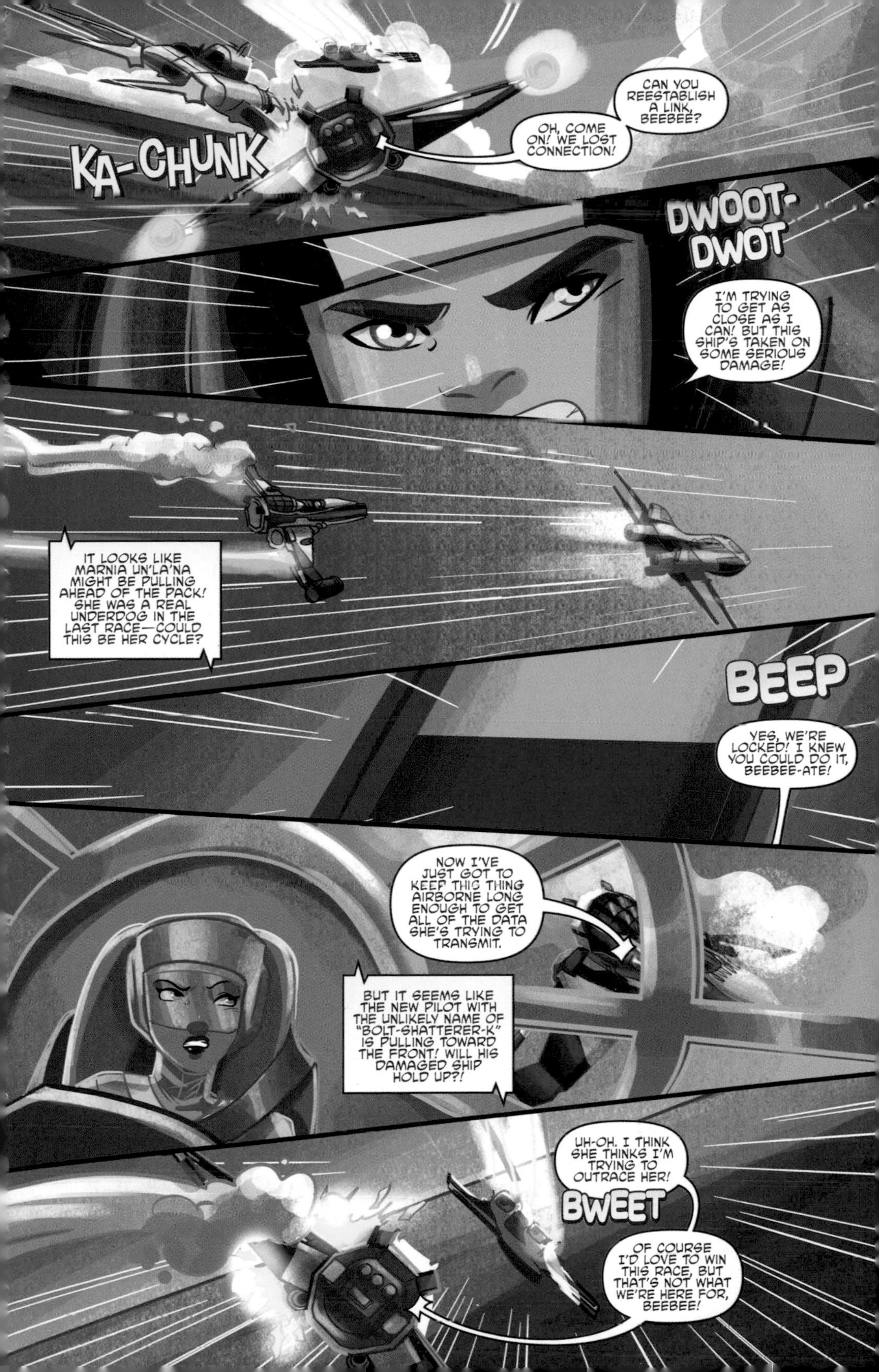
KA-CHUNK
CAN YOU REESTABLISH A LINK, BEEBEE?
OH, COME ON! WE LOST CONNECTION!
DWOOT-DWOT
I'M TRYING TO GET AS CLOSE AS I CAN! BUT THIS SHIP'S TAKEN ON SOME SERIOUS DAMAGE!
IT LOOKS LIKE MARNIA UN'LA'NA MIGHT BE PULLING AHEAD OF THE PACK! SHE WAS A REAL UNDERDOG IN THE LAST RACE—COULD THIS BE HER CYCLE?
BEEP
YES, WE'RE LOCKED! I KNEW YOU COULD DO IT, BEEBEE-ATE!
NOW I'VE JUST GOT TO KEEP THIS THING AIRBORNE LONG ENOUGH TO GET ALL OF THE DATA SHE'S TRYING TO TRANSMIT.
BUT IT SEEMS LIKE THE NEW PILOT WITH THE UNLIKELY NAME OF "BOLT-SHATTERER-K" IS PULLING TOWARD THE FRONT! WILL HIS DAMAGED SHIP HOLD UP?!
UH-OH. I THINK SHE THINKS I'M TRYING TO OUTRACE HER!
BWEET
OF COURSE I'D LOVE TO WIN THIS RACE, BUT THAT'S NOT WHAT WE'RE HERE FOR, BEEBEE!

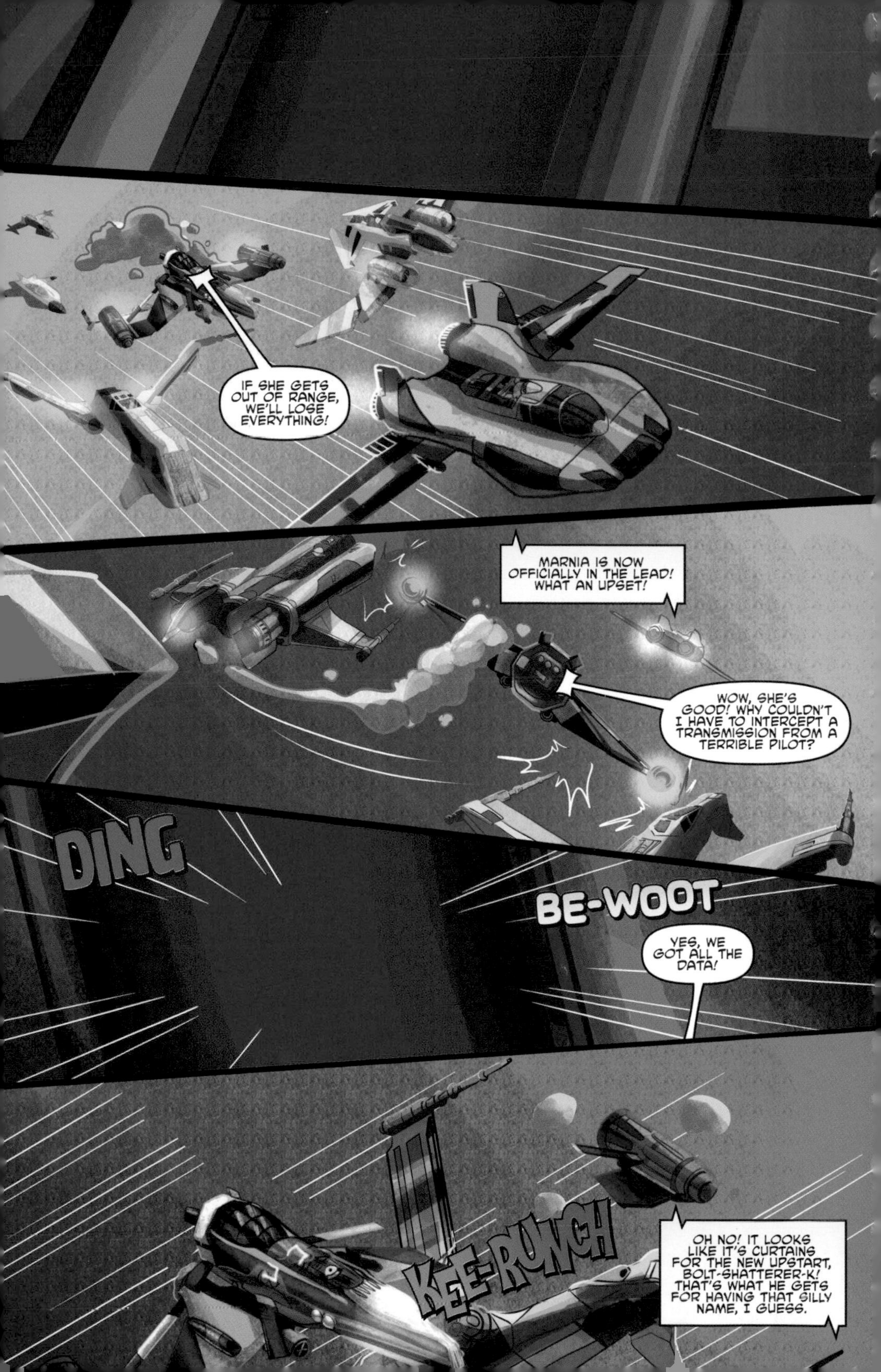
IF SHE GETS OUT OF RANGE, WE'LL LOSE EVERYTHING!
MARNIA IS NOW OFFICIALLY IN THE LEAD! WHAT AN UPSET!
WOW, SHE'S GOOD! WHY COULDN'T I HAVE TO INTERCEPT A TRANSMISSION FROM A TERRIBLE PILOT?
DING
BE-WOOT
YES, WE GOT ALL THE DATA!
KEE-RUNCH
OH NO! IT LOOKS LIKE IT'S CURTAINS FOR THE NEW UPSTART, BOLT-SHATTERER-K! THAT'S WHAT HE GETS FOR HAVING THAT SILLY NAME, I GUESS.

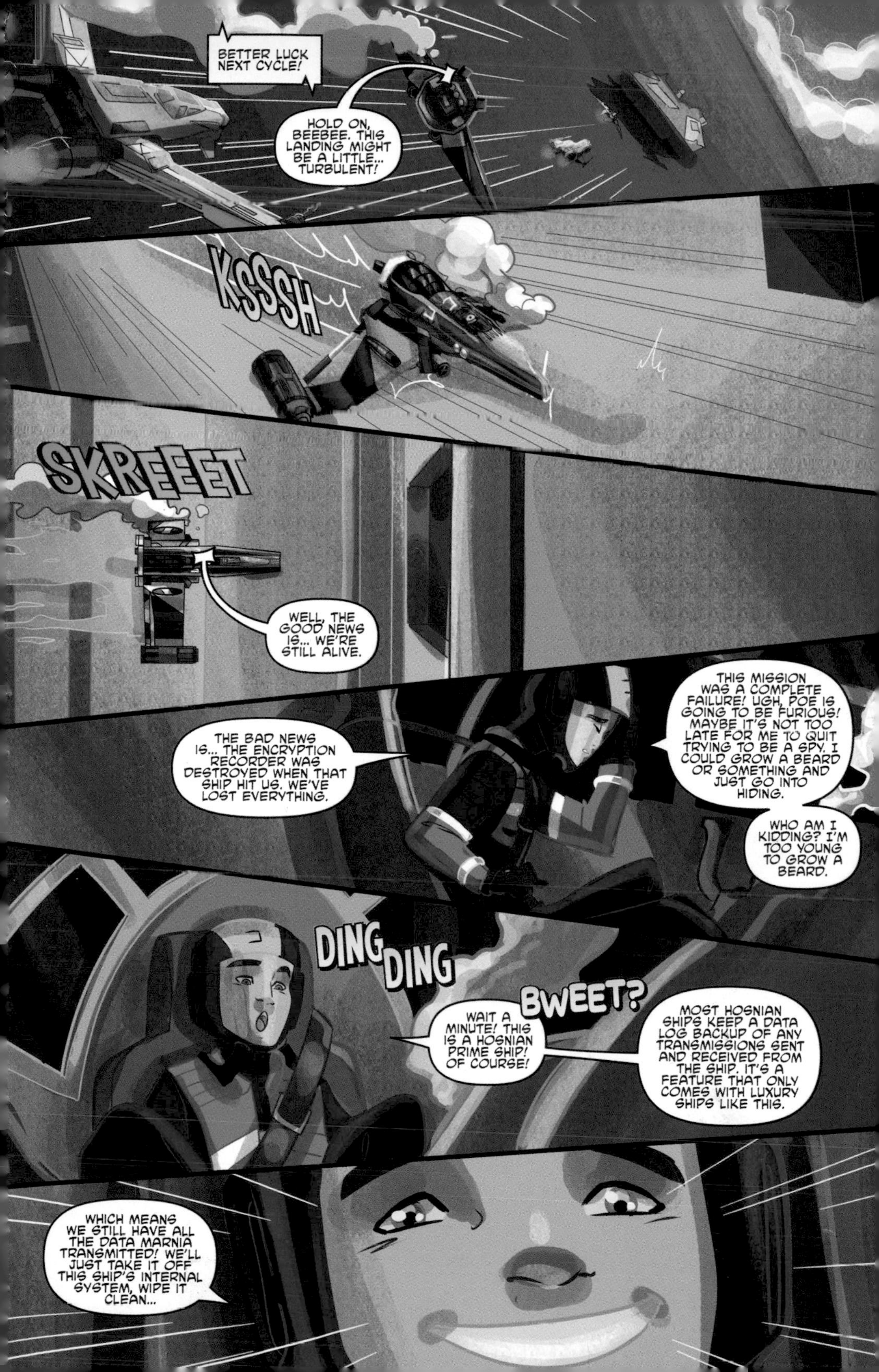
BETTER LUCK NEXT CYCLE!
HOLD ON, BEEBEE. THIS LANDING MIGHT BE A LITTLE... TURBULENT!
KSSSH
SKREEEET
WELL, THE GOOD NEWS IS... WE'RE STILL ALIVE.
THE BAD NEWS IS... THE ENCRYPTION RECORDER WAS DESTROYED WHEN THAT SHIP HIT US. WE'VE LOST EVERYTHING.
THIS MISSION WAS A COMPLETE FAILURE! UGH, POE IS GOING TO BE FURIOUS! MAYBE IT'S NOT TOO LATE FOR ME TO QUIT TRYING TO BE A SPY. I COULD GROW A BEARD OR SOMETHING AND JUST GO INTO HIDING.
WHO AM I KIDDING? I'M TOO YOUNG TO GROW A BEARD.
DING DING
BWEET?
WAIT A MINUTE! THIS IS A HOSNIAN PRIME SHIP! OF COURSE!
MOST HOSNIAN SHIPS KEEP A DATA LOG BACKUP OF ANY TRANSMISSIONS SENT AND RECEIVED FROM THE SHIP. IT'S A FEATURE THAT ONLY COMES WITH LUXURY SHIPS LIKE THIS.
WHICH MEANS WE STILL HAVE ALL THE DATA MARNIA TRANSMITTED! WE'LL JUST TAKE IT OFF THIS SHIP'S INTERNAL SYSTEM, WIPE IT CLEAN...

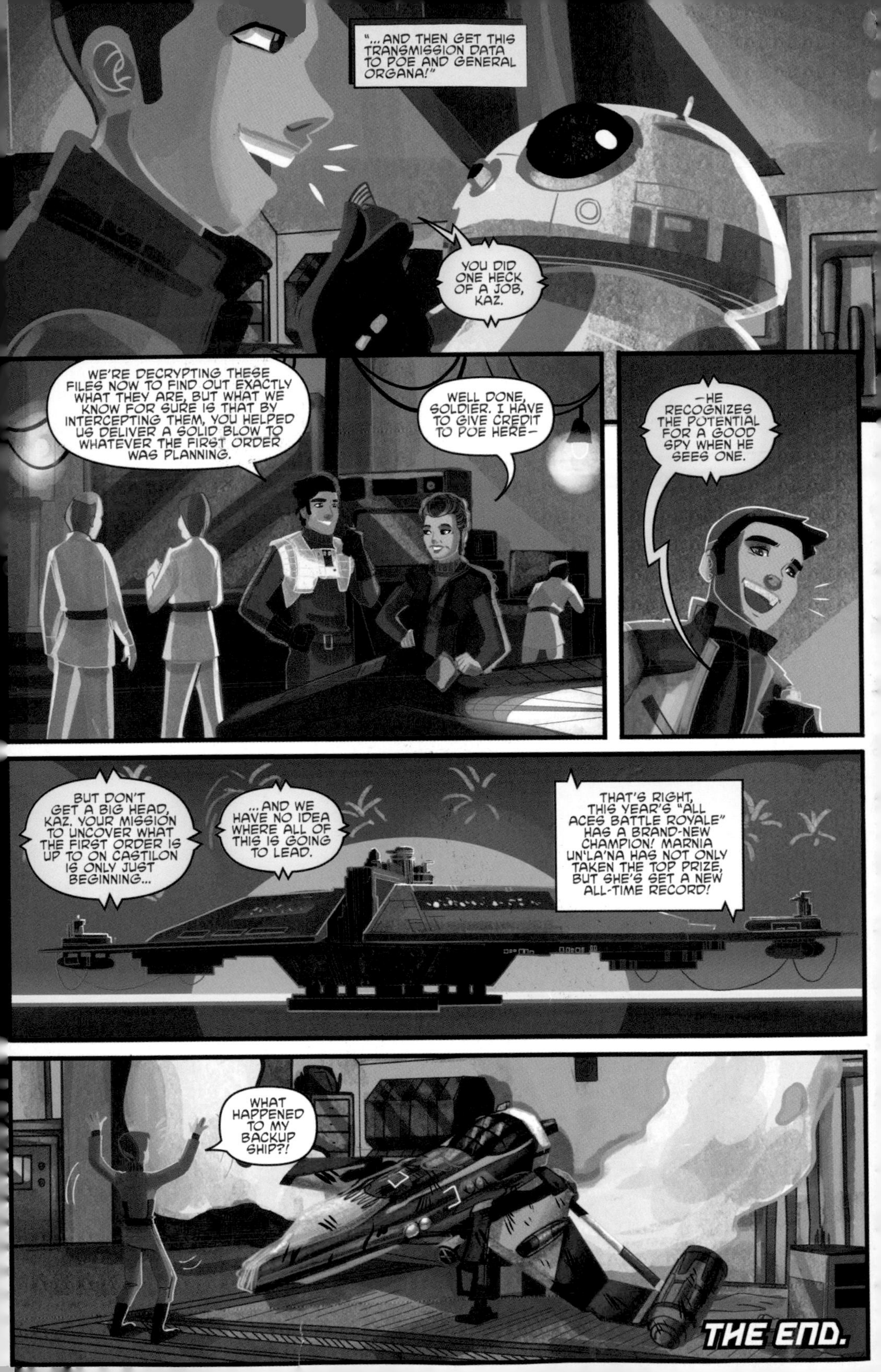
"...AND THEN GET THIS TRANSMISSION DATA TO POE AND GENERAL ORGANA!"
YOU DID ONE HECK OF A JOB, KAZ.
WE'RE DECRYPTING THESE FILES NOW TO FIND OUT EXACTLY WHAT THEY ARE, BUT WHAT WE KNOW FOR SURE IS THAT BY INTERCEPTING THEM, YOU HELPED US DELIVER A SOLID BLOW TO WHATEVER THE FIRST ORDER WAS PLANNING.
WELL DONE, SOLDIER. I HAVE TO GIVE CREDIT TO POE HERE—
—HE RECOGNIZES THE POTENTIAL FOR A GOOD SPY WHEN HE SEES ONE.
BUT DON'T GET A BIG HEAD, KAZ. YOUR MISSION TO UNCOVER WHAT THE FIRST ORDER IS UP TO ON CASTILON IS ONLY JUST BEGINNING...
...AND WE HAVE NO IDEA WHERE ALL OF THIS IS GOING TO LEAD.
THAT'S RIGHT, THIS YEAR'S "ALL ACES BATTLE ROYALE" HAS A BRAND-NEW CHAMPION! MARNIA UN'LA'NA HAS NOT ONLY TAKEN THE TOP PRIZE, BUT SHE'S SET A NEW ALL-TIME RECORD!
WHAT HAPPENED TO MY BACKUP SHIP?!
THE END.

STAR WARS

ADVENTURES

Sector 7-E

WRITERS
**KEVIN BURKE
& CHRIS "DOC" WYATT**

ARTIST & COLORIST
VALENTINA PINTO

LAYOUT ASSISTANT
LUCA COLANDREA

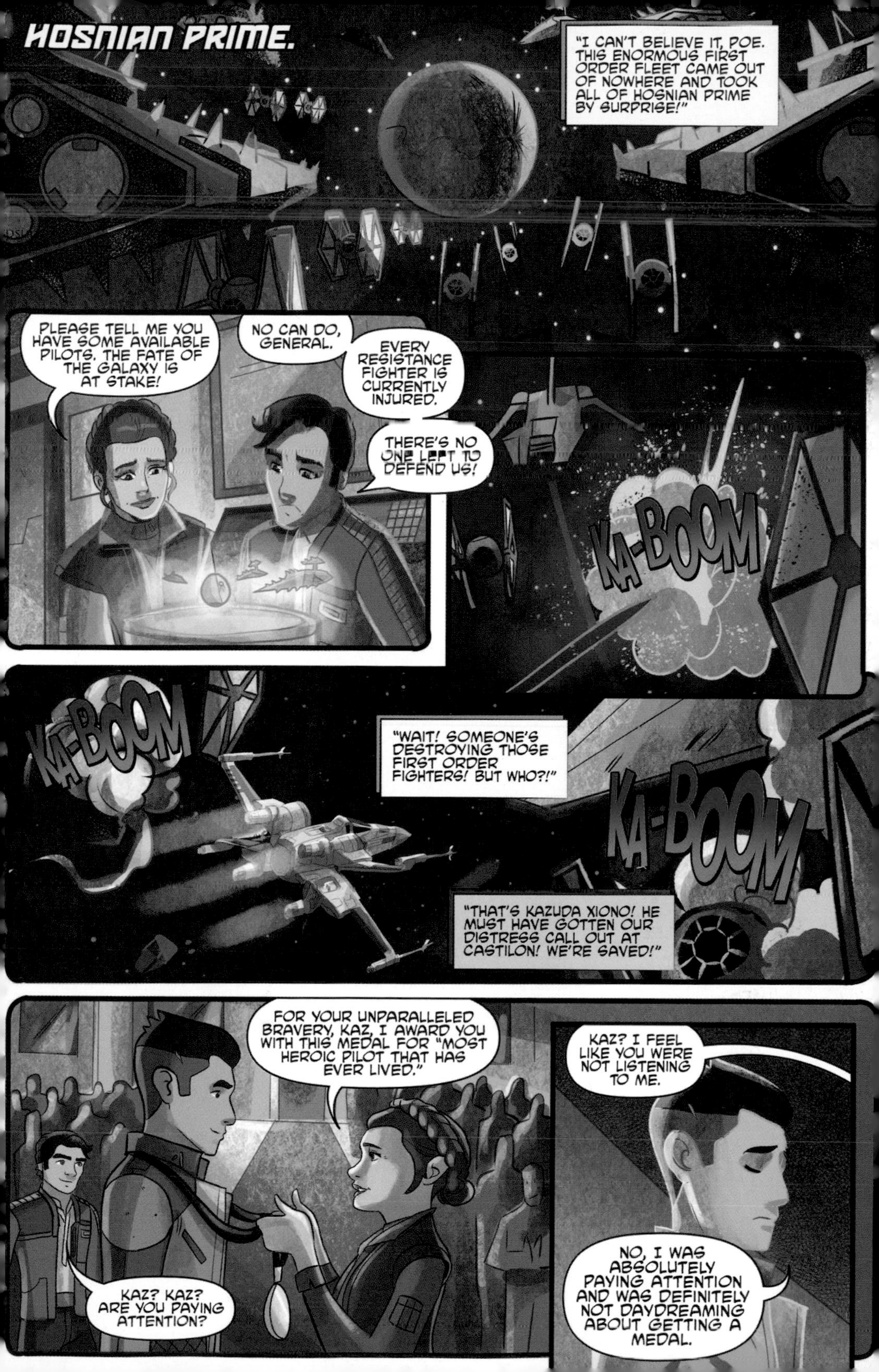
HOSNIAN PRIME.
"I CAN'T BELIEVE IT, POE. THIS ENORMOUS FIRST ORDER FLEET CAME OUT OF NOWHERE AND TOOK ALL OF HOSNIAN PRIME BY SURPRISE!"
PLEASE TELL ME YOU HAVE SOME AVAILABLE PILOTS. THE FATE OF THE GALAXY IS AT STAKE!
NO CAN DO, GENERAL.
EVERY RESISTANCE FIGHTER IS CURRENTLY INJURED.
THERE'S NO ONE LEFT TO DEFEND US!
KA-BOOM
KA-BOOM
"WAIT! SOMEONE'S DESTROYING THOSE FIRST ORDER FIGHTERS! BUT WHO?!"
KA-BOOM
"THAT'S KAZUDA XIONO! HE MUST HAVE GOTTEN OUR DISTRESS CALL OUT AT CASTILON! WE'RE SAVED!"
FOR YOUR UNPARALLELED BRAVERY, KAZ, I AWARD YOU WITH THIS MEDAL FOR "MOST HEROIC PILOT THAT HAS EVER LIVED."
KAZ? KAZ? ARE YOU PAYING ATTENTION?
KAZ? I FEEL LIKE YOU WERE NOT LISTENING TO ME.
NO, I WAS ABSOLUTELY PAYING ATTENTION AND WAS DEFINITELY NOT DAYDREAMING ABOUT GETTING A MEDAL.

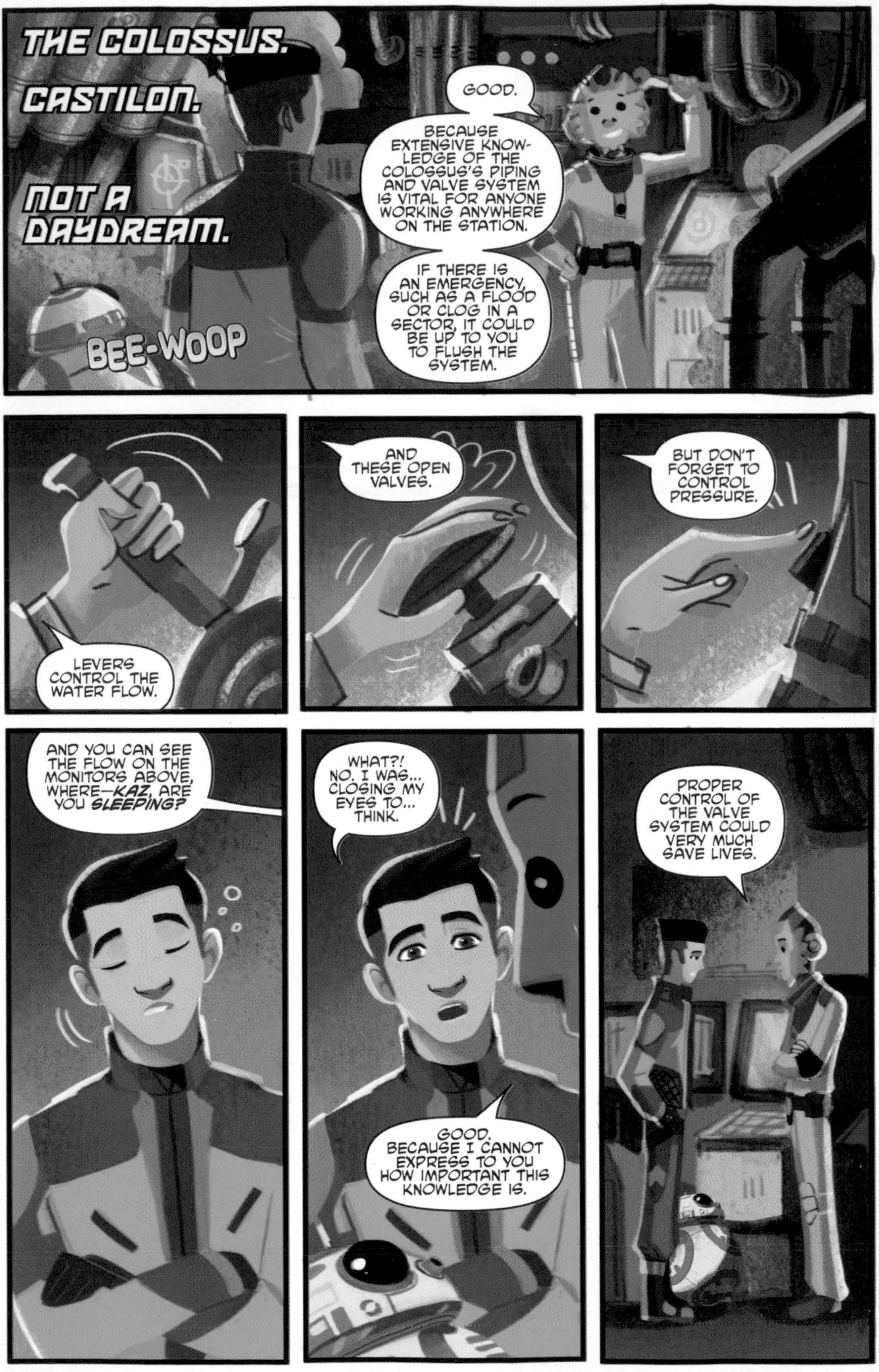
THE COLOSSUS.
CASTILON.
NOT A DAYDREAM.
GOOD.
BECAUSE EXTENSIVE KNOWLEDGE OF THE COLOSSUS'S PIPING AND VALVE SYSTEM IS VITAL FOR ANYONE WORKING ANYWHERE ON THE STATION.
IF THERE IS AN EMERGENCY, SUCH AS A FLOOD OR CLOG IN A SECTOR, IT COULD BE UP TO YOU TO FLUSH THE SYSTEM.
BEE-WOOP
LEVERS CONTROL THE WATER FLOW.
AND THESE OPEN VALVES.
BUT DON'T FORGET TO CONTROL PRESSURE.
AND YOU CAN SEE THE FLOW ON THE MONITORS ABOVE, WHERE—*KAZ*, ARE YOU *SLEEPING?*
WHAT?! NO. I WAS... CLOSING MY EYES TO... THINK.
GOOD. BECAUSE I CANNOT EXPRESS TO YOU HOW IMPORTANT THIS KNOWLEDGE IS.
PROPER CONTROL OF THE VALVE SYSTEM COULD VERY MUCH SAVE LIVES.

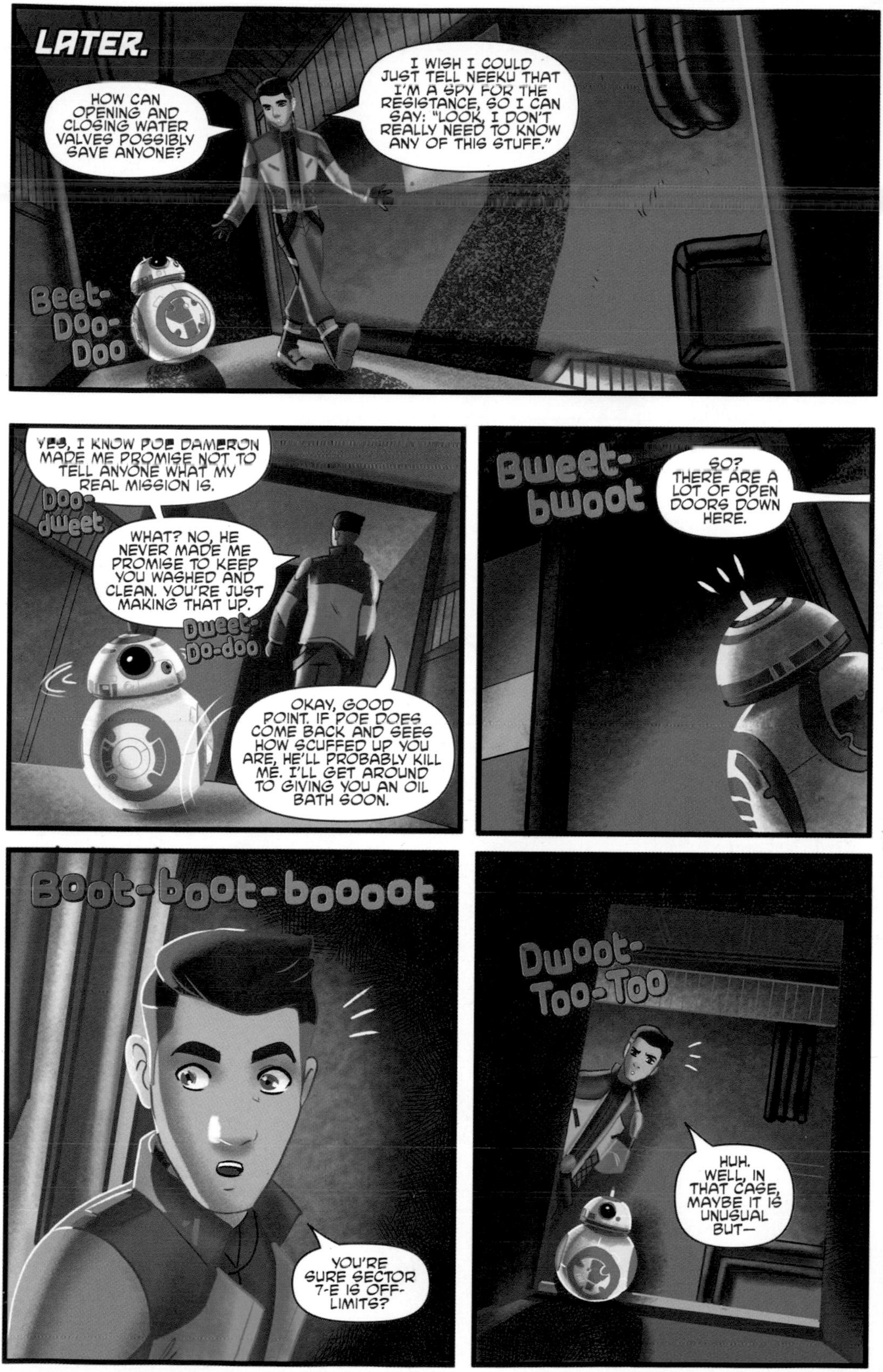
LATER.
HOW CAN OPENING AND CLOSING WATER VALVES POSSIBLY SAVE ANYONE?
I WISH I COULD JUST TELL NEEKU THAT I'M A SPY FOR THE RESISTANCE, SO I CAN SAY: "LOOK, I DON'T REALLY NEED TO KNOW ANY OF THIS STUFF."
Beet-Doo-Doo
YES, I KNOW POE DAMERON MADE ME PROMISE NOT TO TELL ANYONE WHAT MY REAL MISSION IS.
Doo-dweet
WHAT? NO, HE NEVER MADE ME PROMISE TO KEEP YOU WASHED AND CLEAN. YOU'RE JUST MAKING THAT UP.
Dweet-Do-doo
OKAY, GOOD POINT. IF POE DOES COME BACK AND SEES HOW SCUFFED UP YOU ARE, HE'LL PROBABLY KILL ME. I'LL GET AROUND TO GIVING YOU AN OIL BATH SOON.
Bweet-bwoot
SO? THERE ARE A LOT OF OPEN DOORS DOWN HERE.
Boot-boot-booooot
YOU'RE SURE SECTOR 7-E IS OFF-LIMITS?
Dwoot-Too-Too
HUH. WELL, IN THAT CASE, MAYBE IT IS UNUSUAL BUT—

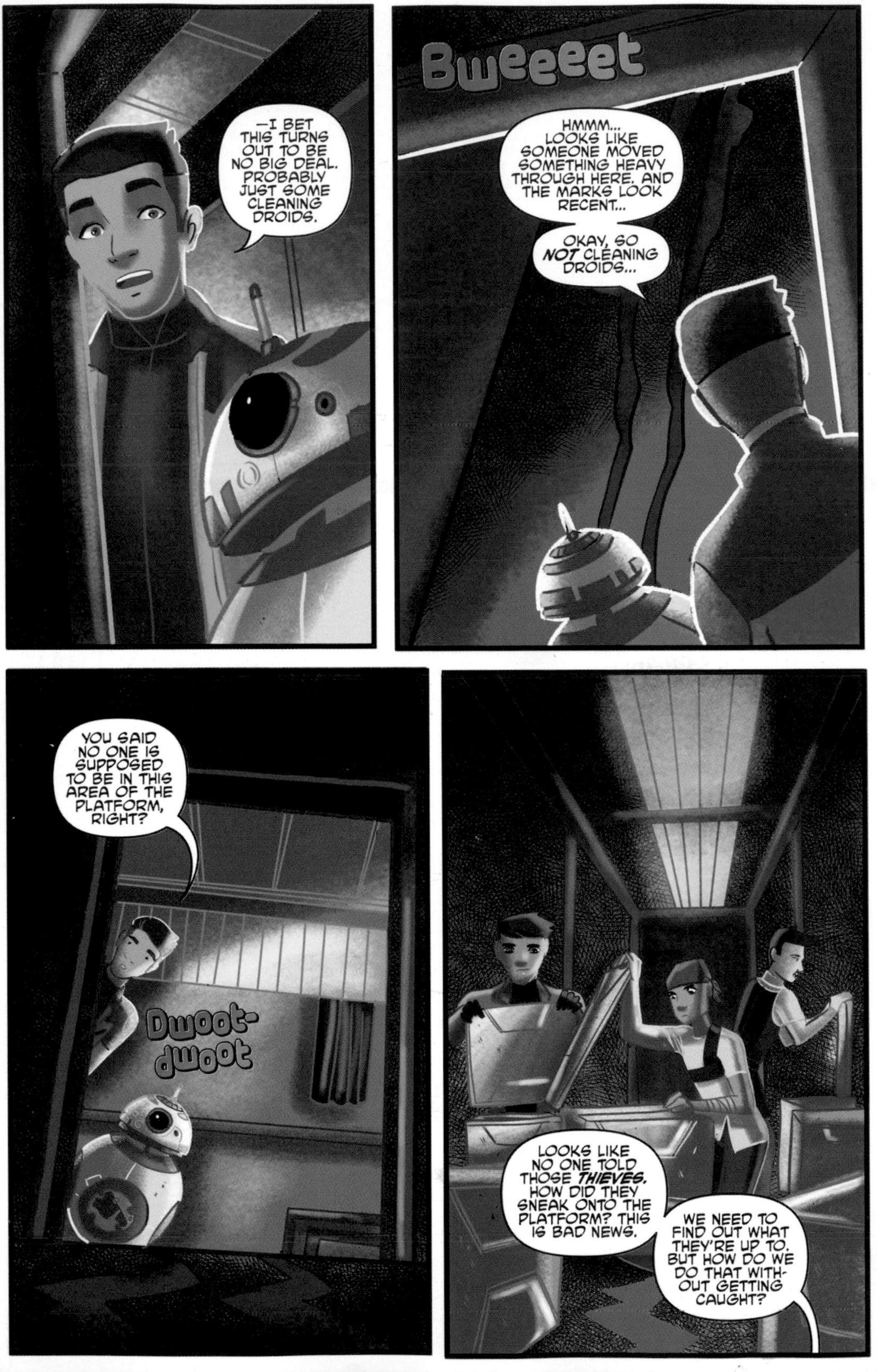
—I BET THIS TURNS OUT TO BE NO BIG DEAL. PROBABLY JUST SOME CLEANING DROIDS.
Bweeeet
HMMM... LOOKS LIKE SOMEONE MOVED SOMETHING HEAVY THROUGH HERE. AND THE MARKS LOOK RECENT...
OKAY, SO NOT CLEANING DROIDS...
YOU SAID NO ONE IS SUPPOSED TO BE IN THIS AREA OF THE PLATFORM, RIGHT?
Dwoot-dwoot
LOOKS LIKE NO ONE TOLD THOSE THIEVES. HOW DID THEY SNEAK ONTO THE PLATFORM? THIS IS BAD NEWS.
WE NEED TO FIND OUT WHAT THEY'RE UP TO. BUT HOW DO WE DO THAT WITHOUT GETTING CAUGHT?

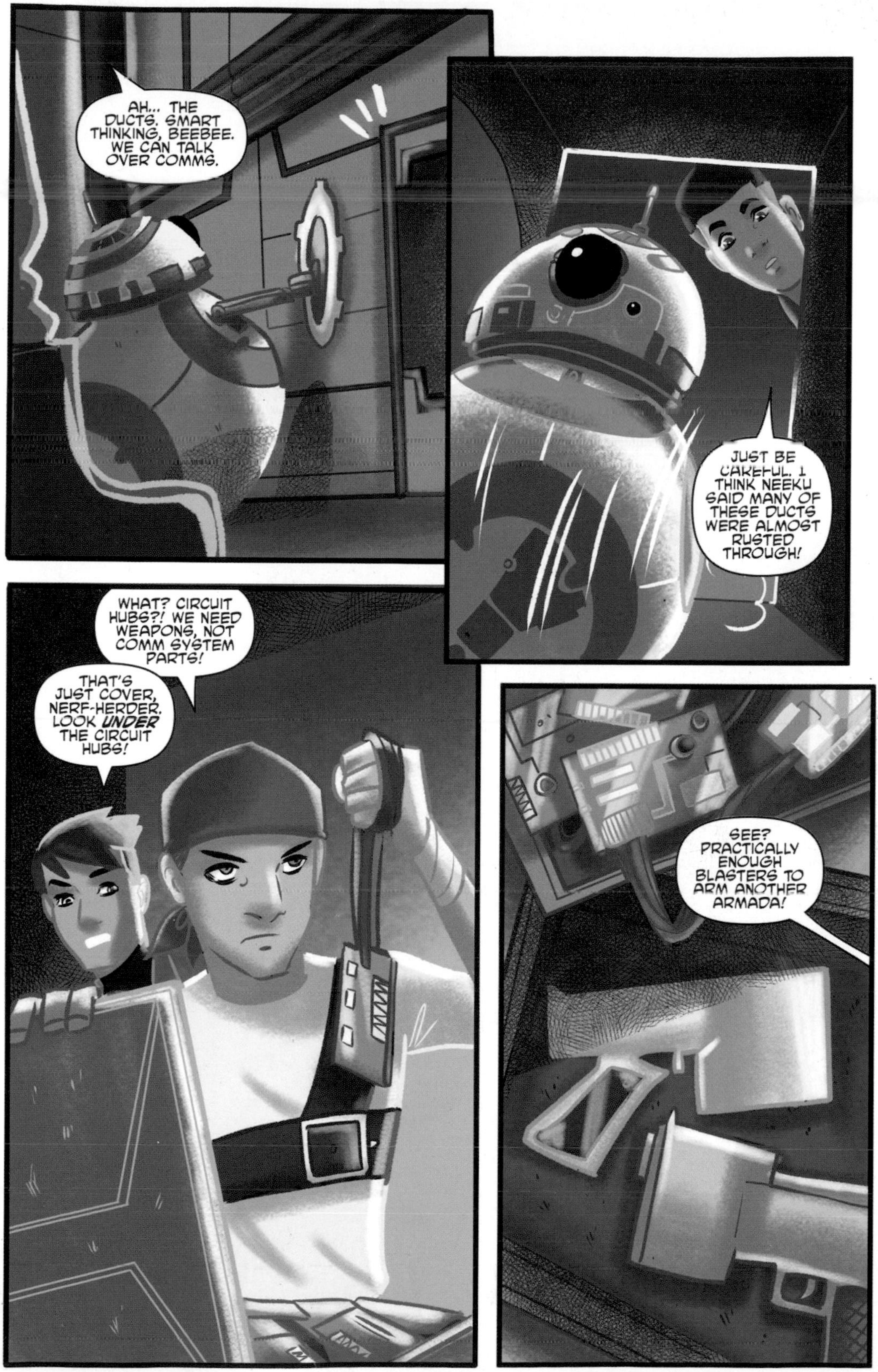
AH... THE DUCTS. SMART THINKING, BEEBEE. WE CAN TALK OVER COMMS.
JUST BE CAREFUL. I THINK NEEKU SAID MANY OF THESE DUCTS WERE ALMOST RUSTED THROUGH!
WHAT? CIRCUIT HUBS?! WE NEED WEAPONS, NOT COMM SYSTEM PARTS!
THAT'S JUST COVER, NERF-HERDER. LOOK *UNDER* THE CIRCUIT HUBS!
SEE? PRACTICALLY ENOUGH BLASTERS TO ARM ANOTHER ARMADA!

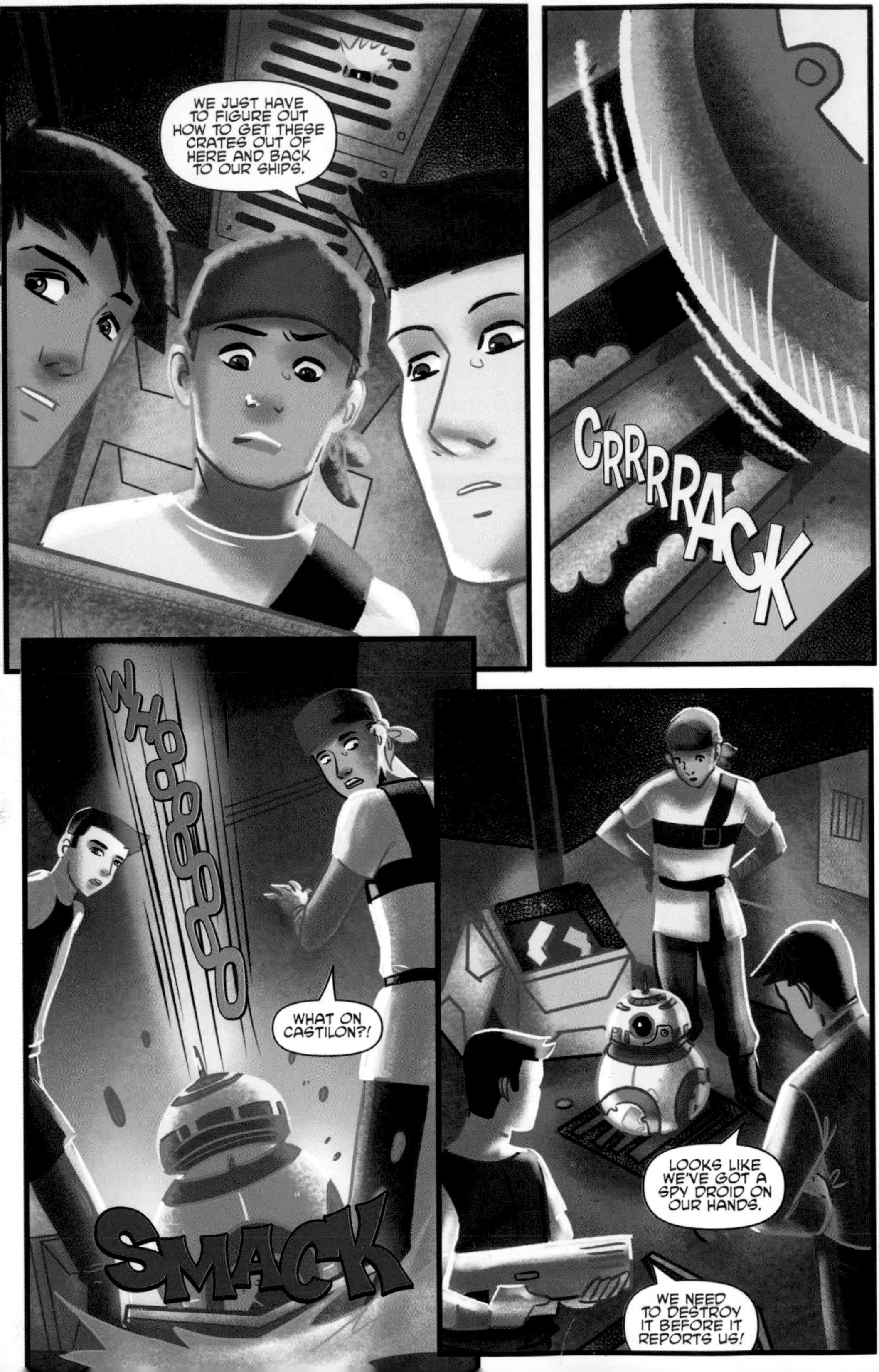
WE JUST HAVE TO FIGURE OUT HOW TO GET THESE CRATES OUT OF HERE AND BACK TO OUR SHIPS.
CRRRRACK
WHOOOOOOO
WHAT ON CASTILON?!
SMACK
LOOKS LIKE WE'VE GOT A SPY DROID ON OUR HANDS.
WE NEED TO DESTROY IT BEFORE IT REPORTS US!

OH, NO! WHAT DO I DO?

WAIT, IS THAT...?

A PUMP INTAKE VALVE, LIKE NEEKU WAS SHOWING ME.

HOLD ON, BEEBEE-EIGHT! I'VE GOT A PLAN!

LET'S SEE... SECTOR 7-E, SECTOR 7-E— THERE! NOW HOW DID NEEKU DO THIS AGAIN?

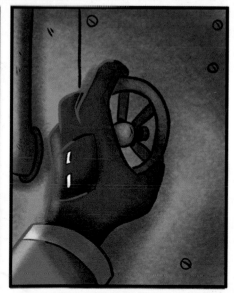

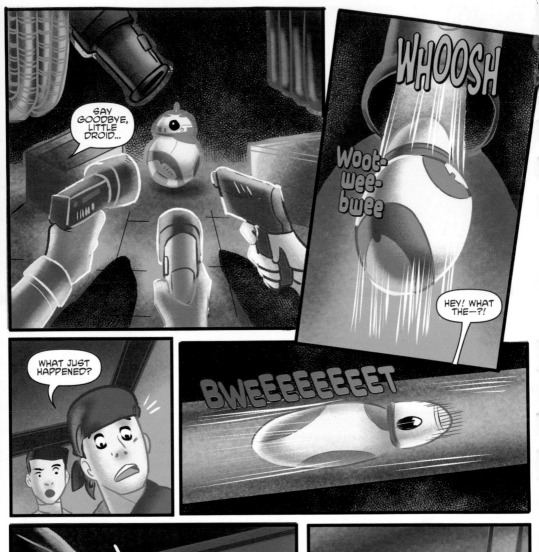

SAY GOODBYE, LITTLE DROID...

WHOOSH

Woot-wee-bwee

HEY! WHAT THE—?!

WHAT JUST HAPPENED?

BWEEEEEEEEET

Bweet-boop-bee

I DON'T KNOW WHAT YOU'RE COMPLAINING ABOUT. IS IT WORSE THAN GETTING BLASTED?

Brrt-bbt-berrrr

WHAT DO YOU MEAN "GETTING HOTTER"?

OH, NO! YOU'RE HEADED FOR THE FURNACE!

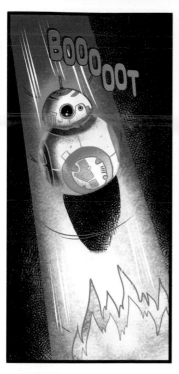

BOOOOOT

HOLD ON, BEEBEE!

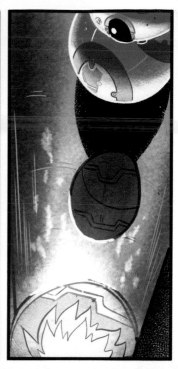

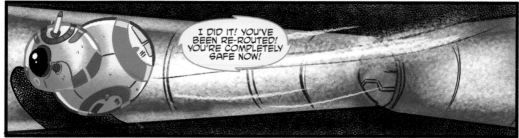

I DID IT! YOU'VE BEEN RE-ROUTED! YOU'RE COMPLETELY SAFE NOW!

ARE YOU CRAZY? YOU'VE ARMED THOSE THERMAL DETONATORS!

YEAH, ON A TIME DELAY... AND THEY SHOULD MAKE SHORT WORK OF THAT SPY DROID!

UH... BEEBEE? WHEN I SAID "COMPLETELY" SAFE, I MAY HAVE BEEN A LITTLE HASTY.
WHAT DID NEEKU SAY WHEN I WAS TOTALLY PAYING ATTENTION?
I GOTTA CONTROL THE FLOW, OPEN THESE VALVES, BUT DON'T FORGET THE PRESSURE!
BEEEEEEET
GOT IT!

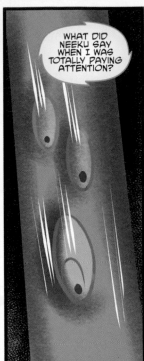

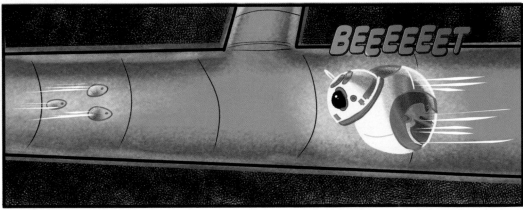

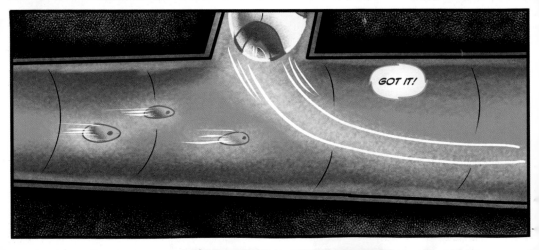

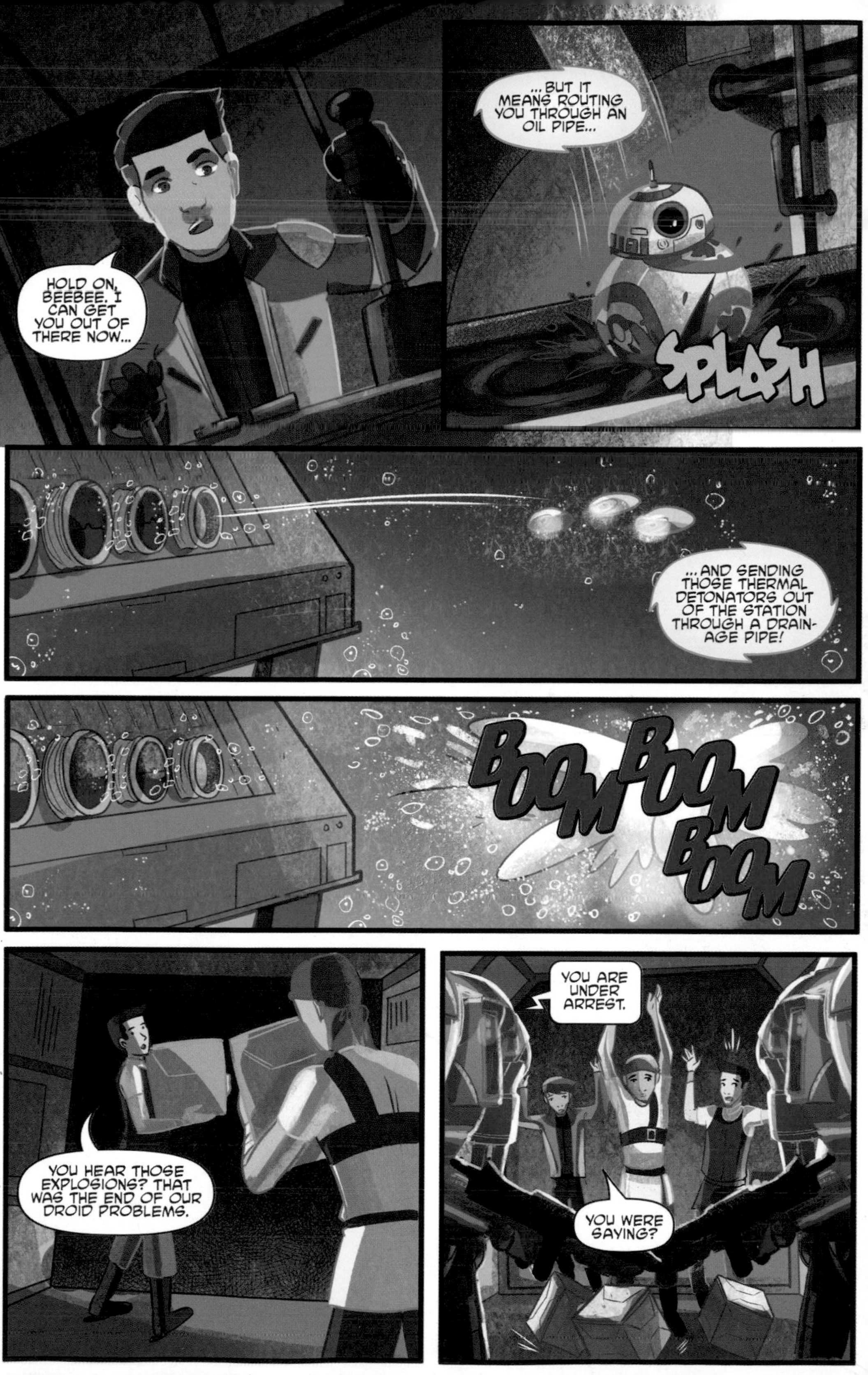
HOLD ON, BEEBEE. I CAN GET YOU OUT OF THERE NOW...
...BUT IT MEANS ROUTING YOU THROUGH AN OIL PIPE...
SPLASH
...AND SENDING THOSE THERMAL DETONATORS OUT OF THE STATION THROUGH A DRAIN-AGE PIPE!
BOOM BOOM BOOM
YOU HEAR THOSE EXPLOSIONS? THAT WAS THE END OF OUR DROID PROBLEMS.
YOU ARE UNDER ARREST.
YOU WERE SAYING?

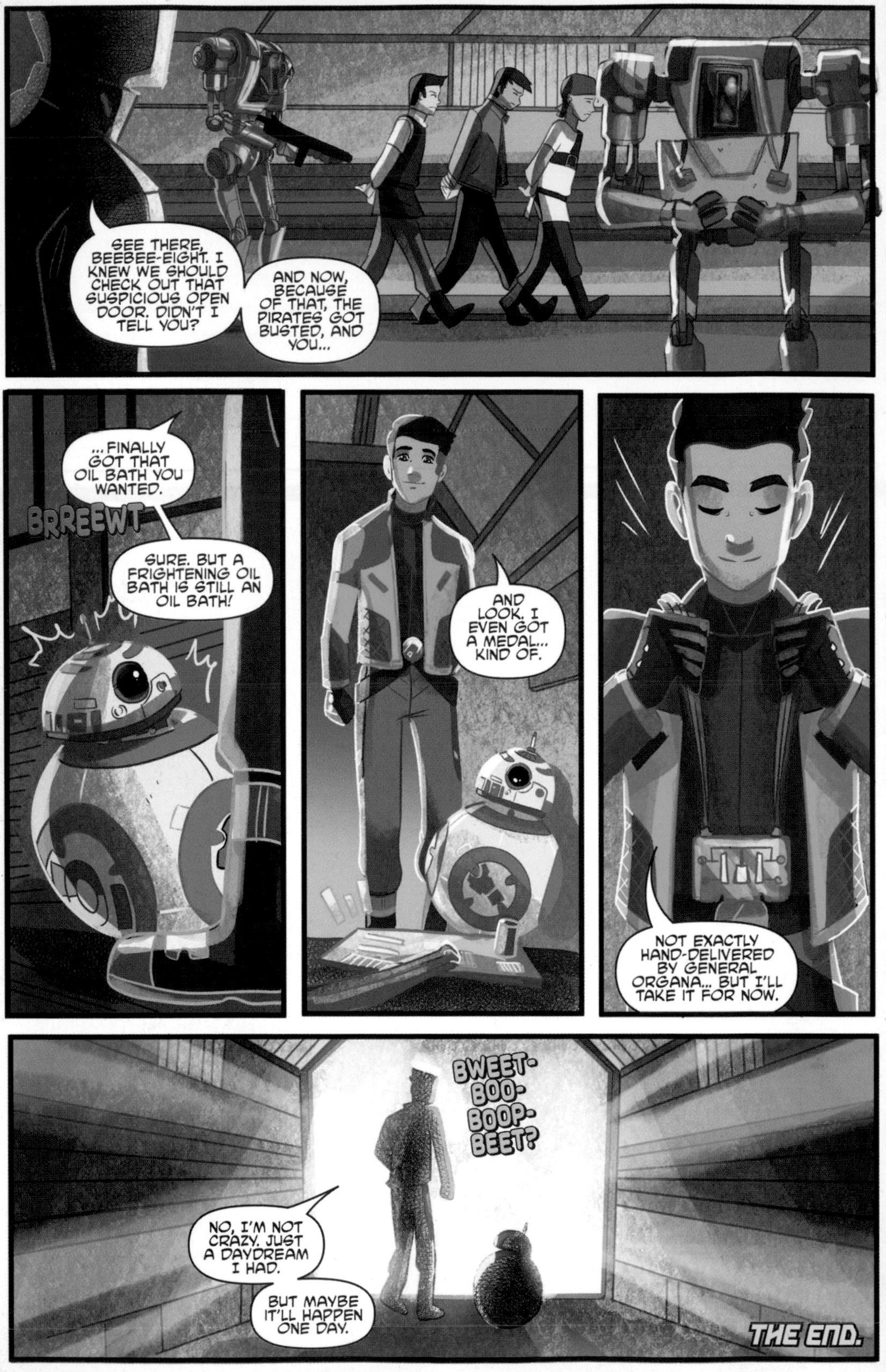
SEE THERE, BEEBEE-EIGHT. I KNEW WE SHOULD CHECK OUT THAT SUSPICIOUS OPEN DOOR. DIDN'T I TELL YOU?
AND NOW, BECAUSE OF THAT, THE PIRATES GOT BUSTED, AND YOU...
...FINALLY GOT THAT OIL BATH YOU WANTED.
BRREEWT
SURE. BUT A FRIGHTENING OIL BATH IS STILL AN OIL BATH!
AND LOOK. I EVEN GOT A MEDAL... KIND OF.
NOT EXACTLY HAND-DELIVERED BY GENERAL ORGANA... BUT I'LL TAKE IT FOR NOW.
BWEET-BOO-BOOP-BEET?
NO, I'M NOT CRAZY. JUST A DAYDREAM I HAD.
BUT MAYBE IT'LL HAPPEN ONE DAY.
THE END.

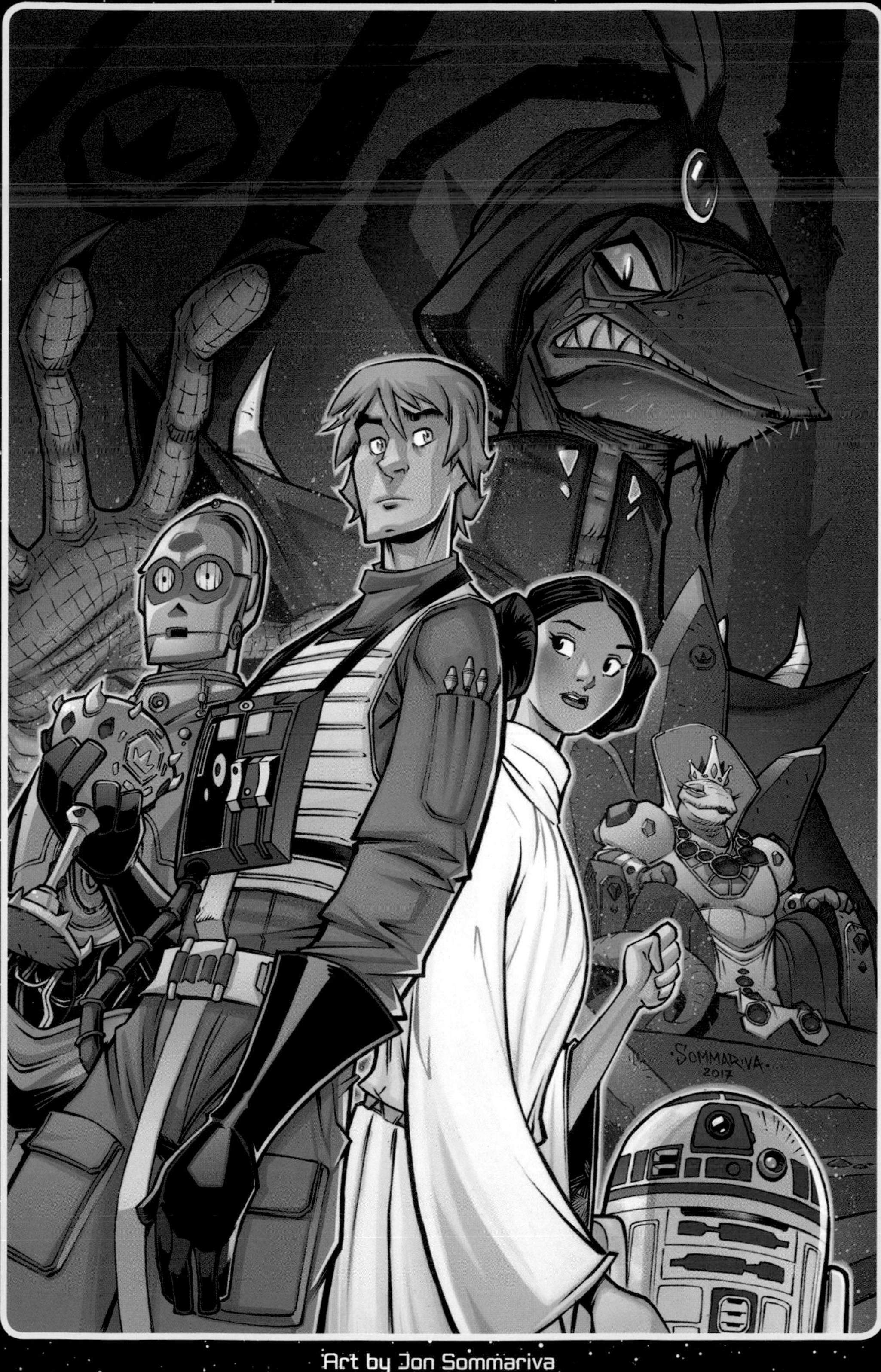
SOMMARIVA
2017

Art by Jon Sommariva

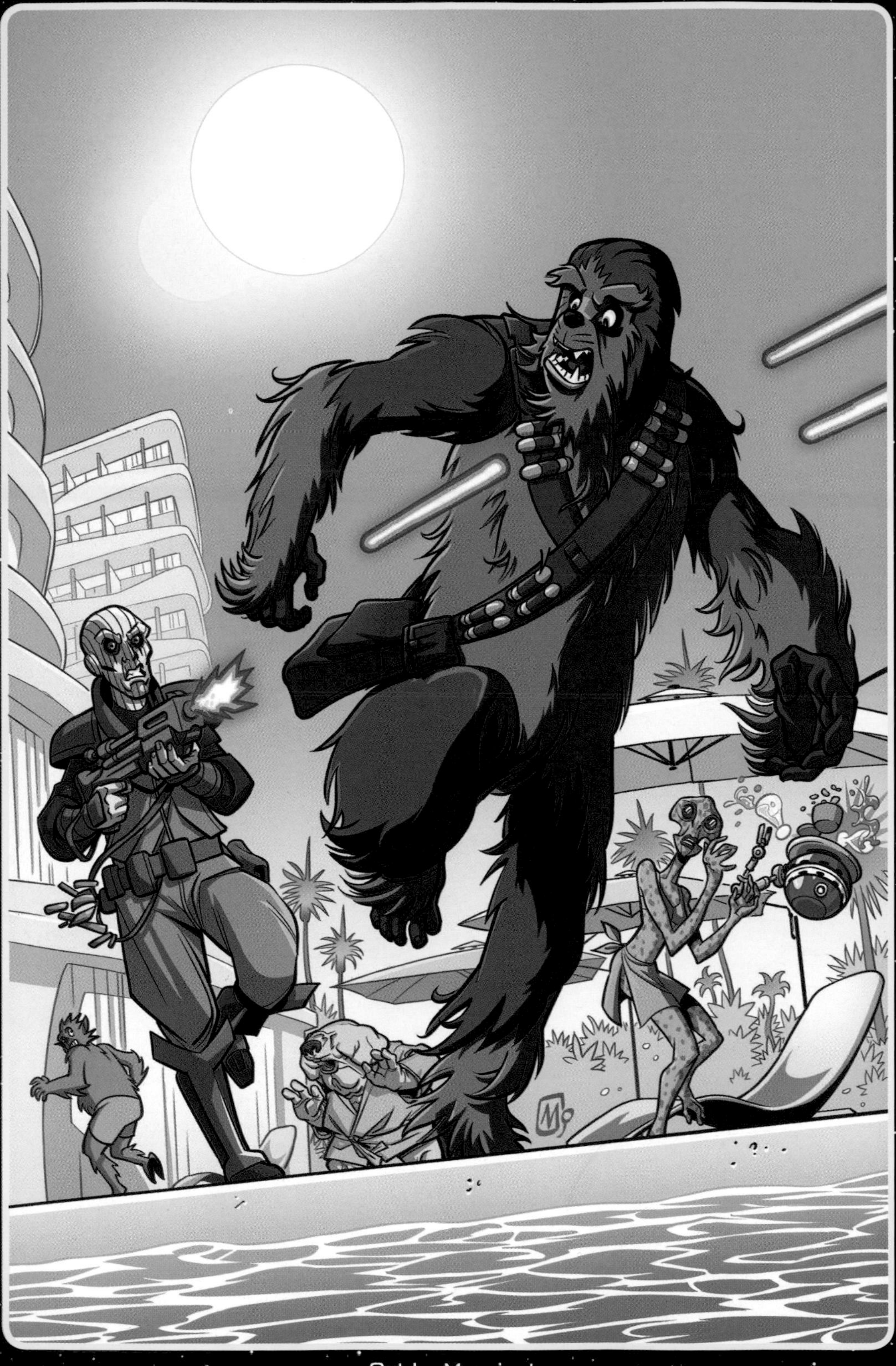

Art by Mauricet

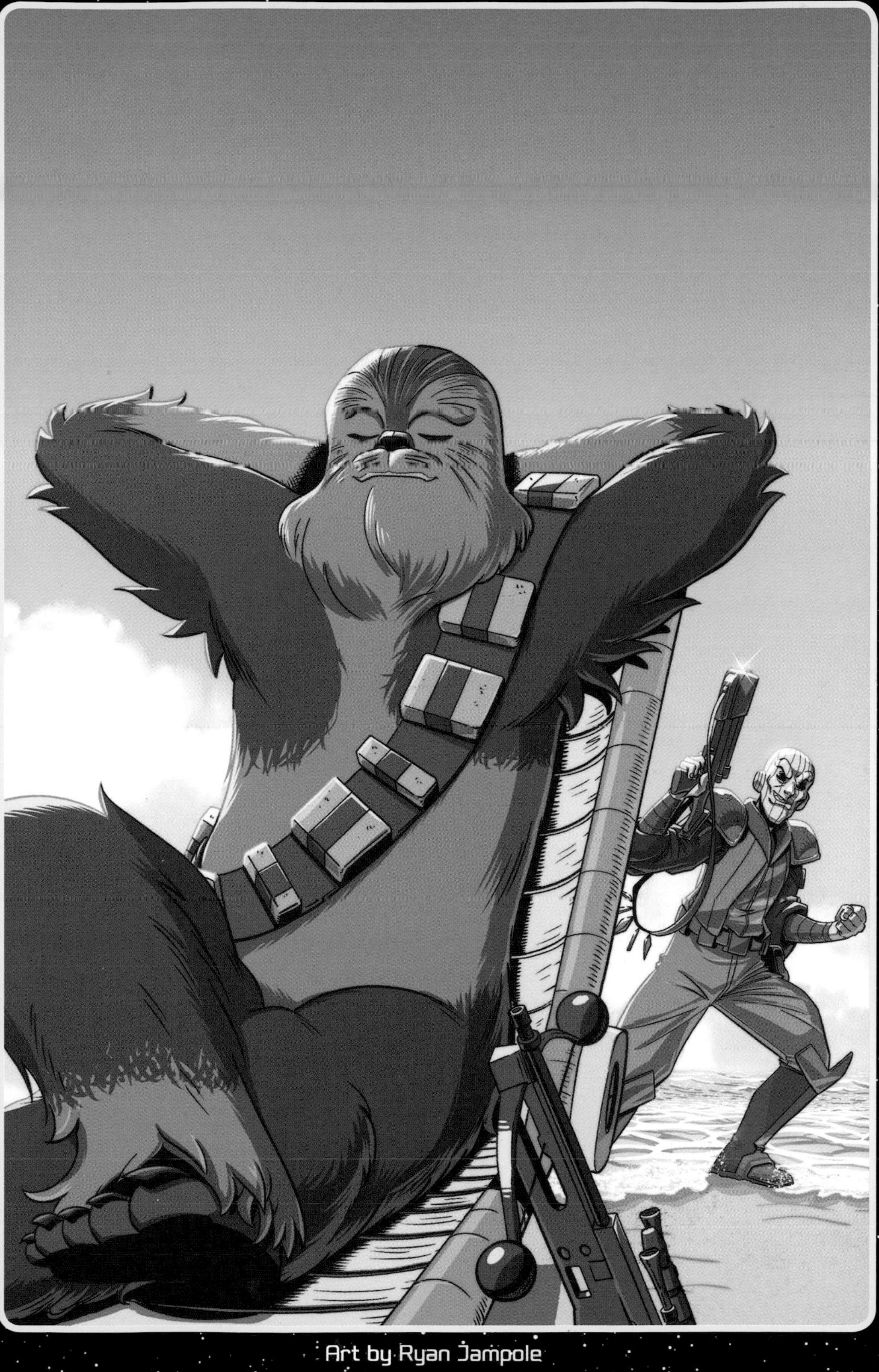

Art by Ryan Jampole

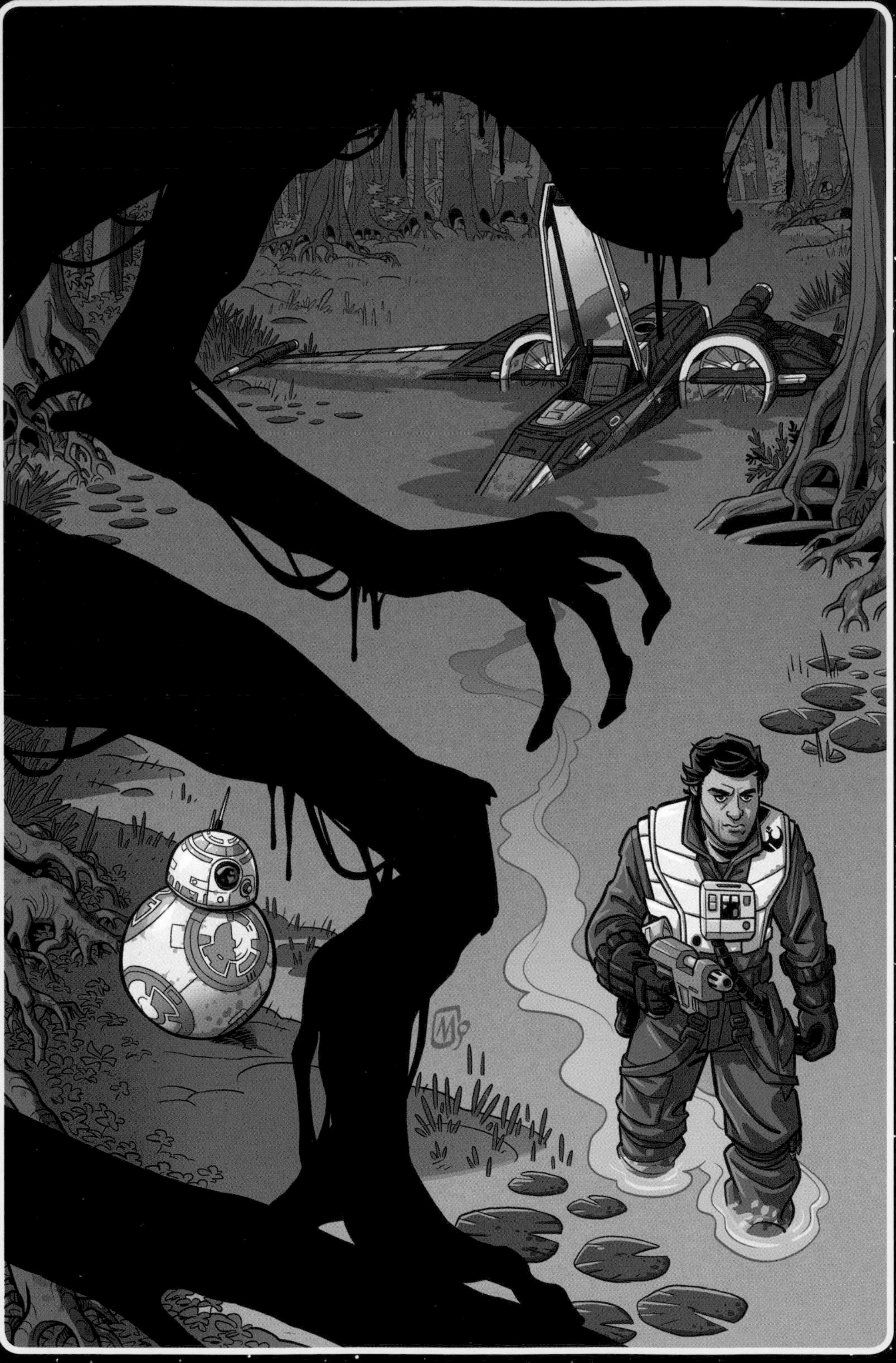

Art by Mauricet

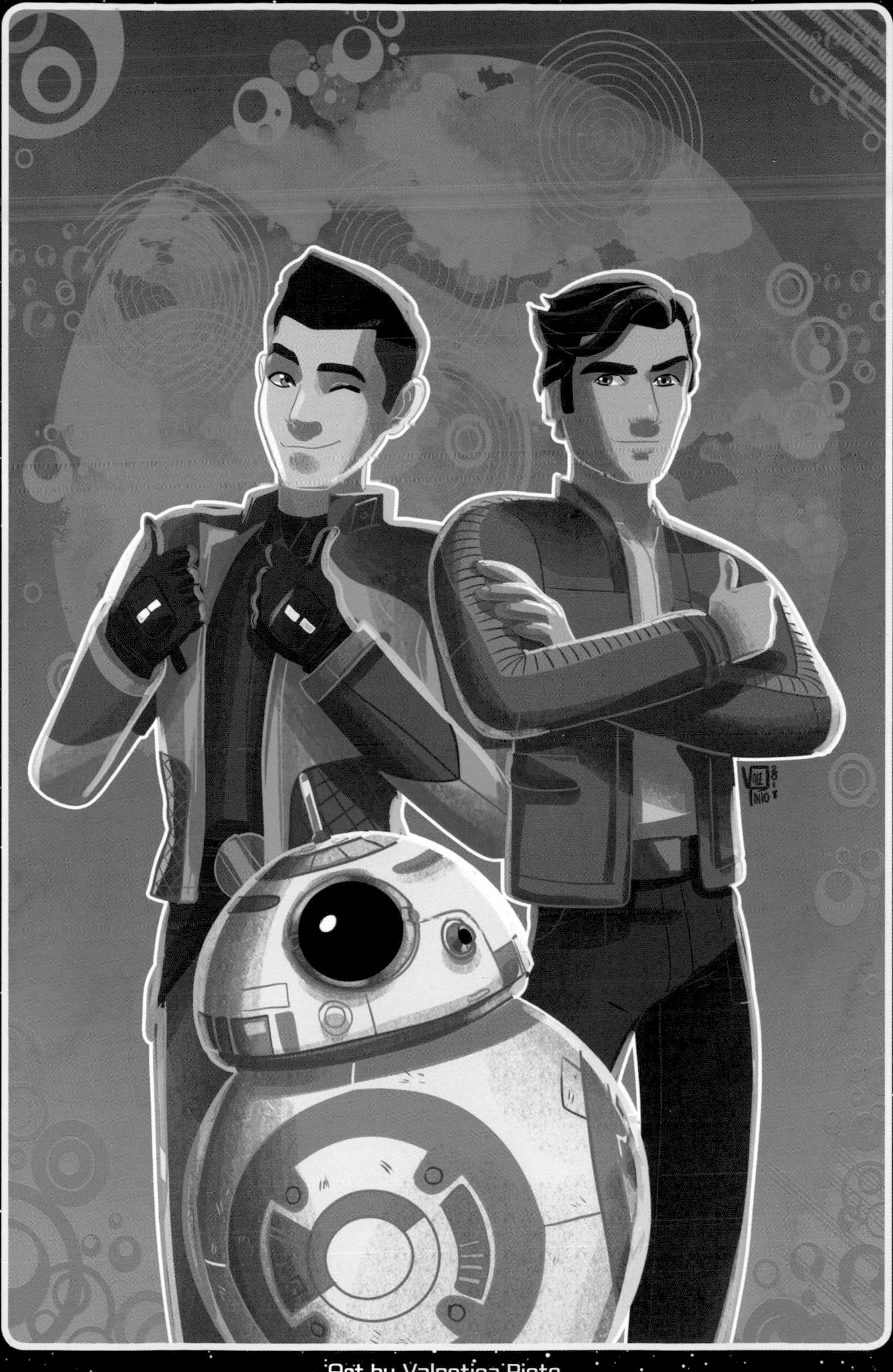

Art by Valentina Pinto

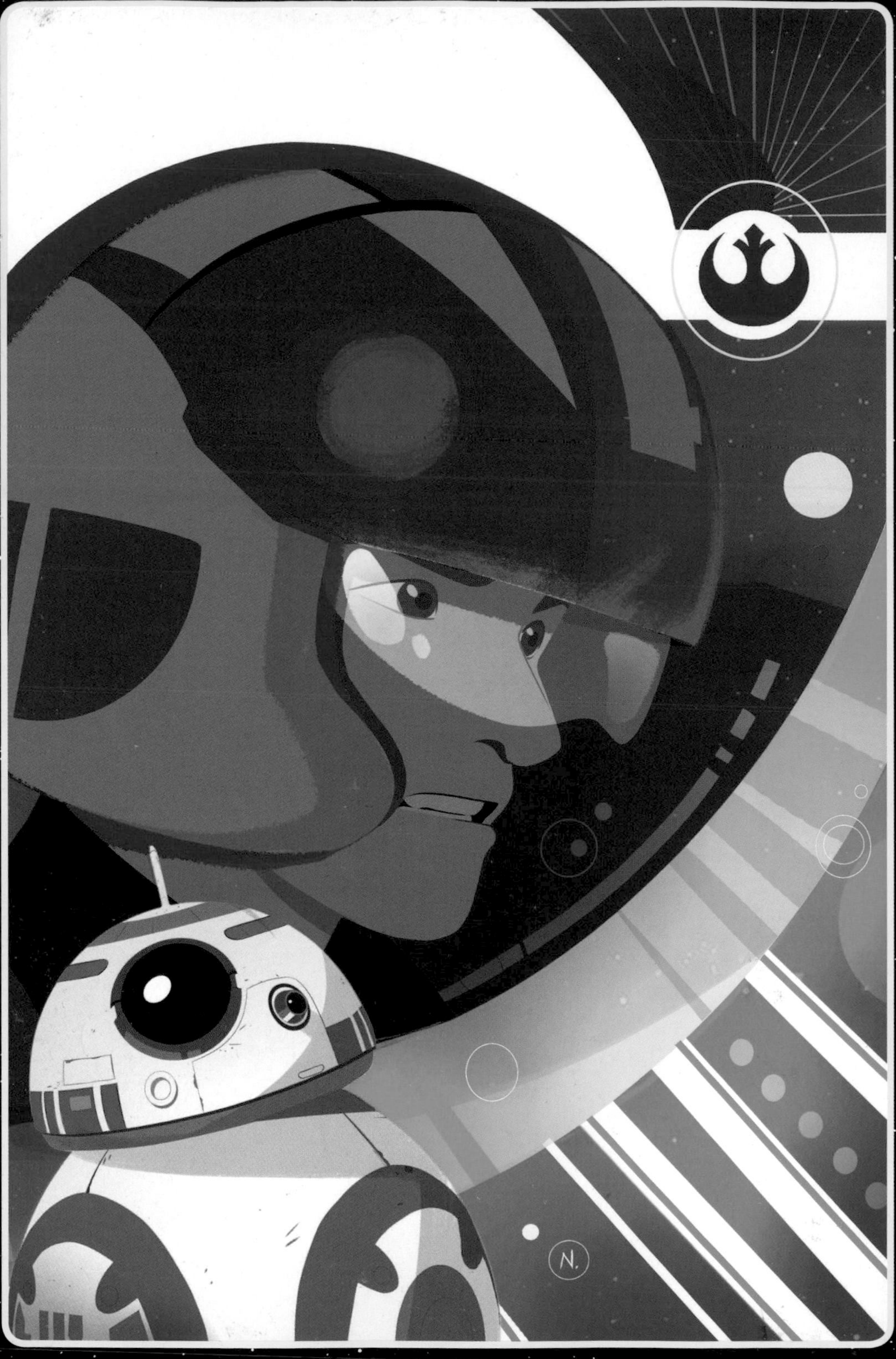
N.

Art by Nicoletta Baldari

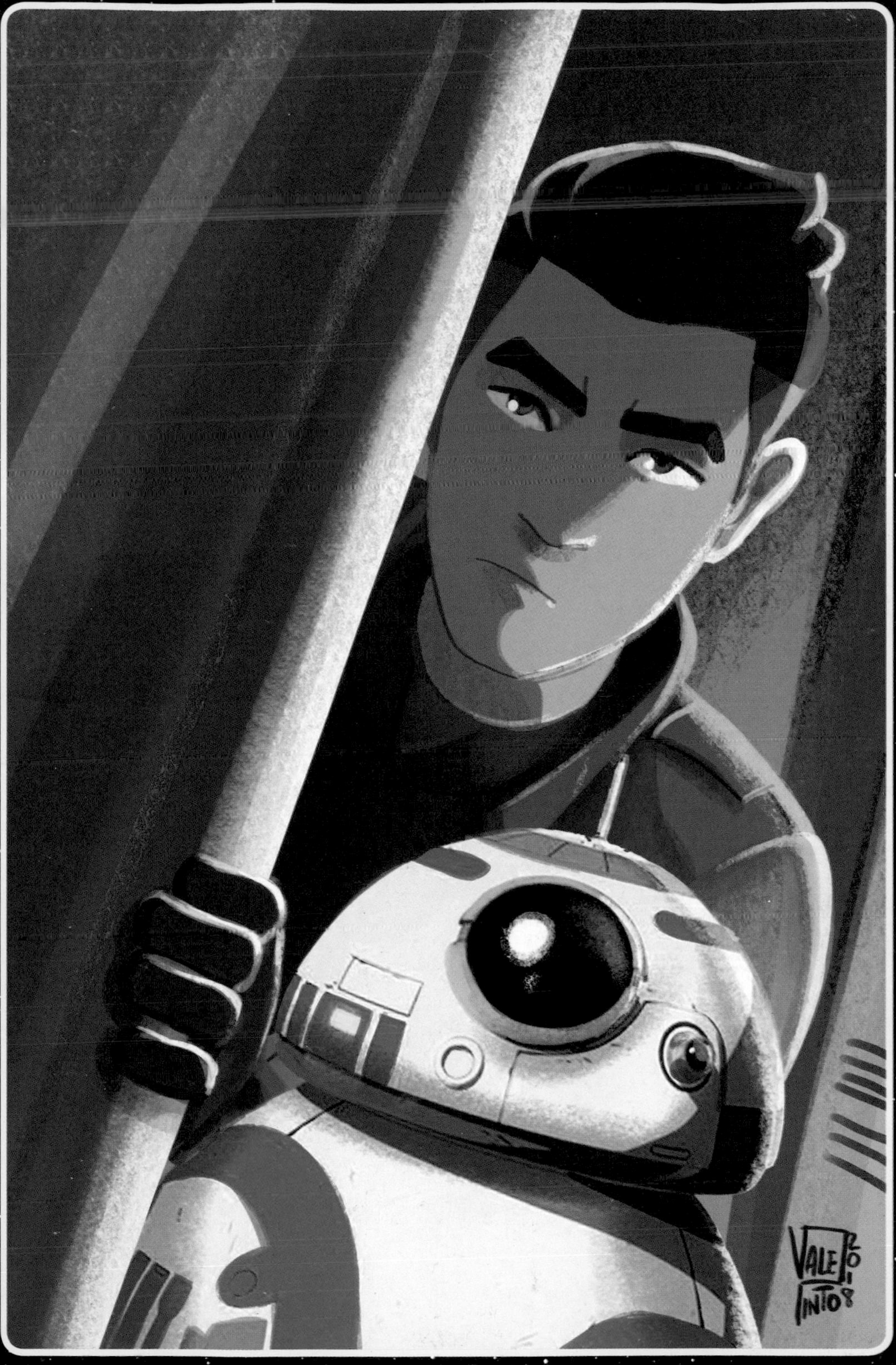
VALE PINTO 2018

Art by Valentina Pinto

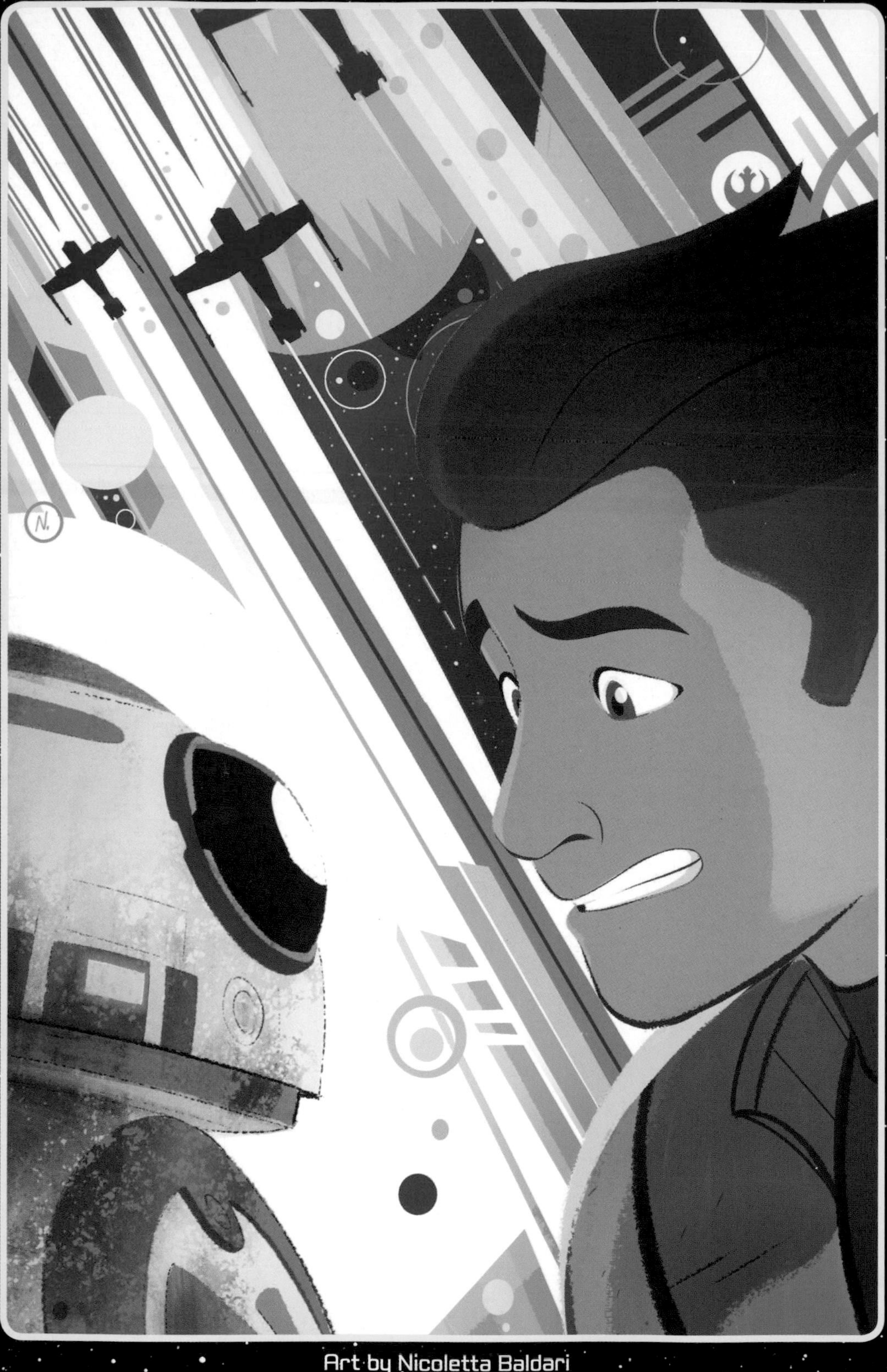
N.

Art by Nicoletta Baldari